D0936481

MURDER IN THE TEA LEAVES

MURDER IN THE TEA LEAVES

Tea Shop Mystery #27

LAURA CHILDS

BERKLEY PRIME CRIME
New York

BERKLEY PRIME CRIME
Published by Berkley
An imprint of Penguin Random House LLC
penguinrandomhouse.com

Copyright © 2024 by Gerry Schmitt & Associates, Inc.
Excerpt from *Peach Tea Smash* by Laura Childs copyright © 2024 by
Gerry Schmitt & Associates, Inc.

Library of Congress Cataloging-in-Publication Data

Names: Childs, Laura, author.
Title: Murder in the tea leaves / Laura Childs.
Description: New York: Berkley Prime Crime, 2024. | Series: Tea shop mystery; 27
Identifiers: LCCN 2023035700 (print) | LCCN 2023035701 (ebook) |
ISBN 9780593200988 (hardcover) | ISBN 9780593200995 (ebook)
Subjects: LCGFT: Cozy mysteries. | Novels.
Classification: LCC PS3603.H56 M87 2024 (print) | LCC PS3603.H56 (ebook) |
DDC 813/.6—dc23/eng/20230825
LC record available at https://lccn.loc.gov/2023035700
LC ebook record available at https://lccn.loc.gov/2023035701

Printed in the United States of America
1st Printing

This is a work of fiction. Names, characters, places, and incidents either are the product of
the author's imagination or are used fictitiously, and any resemblance to actual persons,
living or dead, business establishments, events, or locales is entirely coincidental.

PUBLISHER'S NOTE: The recipes contained in this book are to be followed exactly
as written. The publisher is not responsible for your specific health or allergy
needs that may require medical supervision. The publisher is not responsible
for any adverse reactions to the recipes contained in this book.

MURDER IN THE
TEA LEAVES

1

"*Quiet on the* set! Quiet on the set!"

As if someone had suddenly spun a dial and cut the volume, there was complete and utter silence in the darkened living room of the dilapidated Brittlebank Manor.

"Roll film, and . . . *action!*" shouted Josh Morro, the film's director.

Theodosia Browning watched, fascinated, as actors recited lines, cameras dollied in for close-ups, and producers, assistant directors, storyboard artists, set dressers, grips, writers, gaffers, production assistants, makeup artists, and costumers all stood by, ready to jump at the director's every command.

It was the first day of filming for *Dark Fortunes*, a Peregrine Pictures feature film. And the first time tea shop owner Theodosia had ever seen a full-fledged movie in the making. Of course, she wasn't actually *in* the movie. But this week was still extra special for Theodosia and Drayton Conneley, her dapper, sixty-something tea sommelier. They'd been tapped to handle the craft services table, an all-day munch fest for the cast and crew. It was proving to be a fun break from their normal roles as hosts at the Indigo Tea Shop on Charleston's famed Church Street, where they spent their days juggling morning cream tea, lunch, tea parties, afternoon tea, special events, and catering.

Catering. Yes, that's exactly why Theodosia and Drayton had loaded their craft services table with a bounty of tea sandwiches, lemon scones, brownie bites, banana muffins, cranberry tea bread, and handmade chocolate fudge. And of course tea, which was Drayton's specialty.

"This is exciting, yes?" Theodosia whispered to Drayton. The director had called a sudden halt to filming and now the crew milled about the darkened set like shadows flitting through a graveyard.

"Exciting but strange," Drayton said, touching a hand to his bow tie. "I had no idea so much work went into filming a single scene." He peered through the darkness to where the director was whispering to a cameraman. "And that director seems to be in a constant uproar."

Josh Morro, the director, was most certainly agitated. "Gimme some light, will you?" he barked. And lights immediately came up, revealing the shabby interior of a small, old-fashioned sitting room. "And we need something more dynamic here. A line or action that propels us into the heart of the story-line." Morro turned to Craig Cole, the scriptwriter, and raised his eyebrows in a questioning look.

"It's already in the script, babe," Cole shouted back at him. Cole was Hollywood hyper, rail thin with a pinched face and shock of bright red Woody Woodpecker hair.

"No, it's not. The script is dreck," Morro cried as he leaped from his chair, knocking it over backward in the process. He was tall and angular, dressed in jeans and a faded Def Leppard T-shirt.

Good-looking, handsome even, Morro had intense jade green eyes and wore a now-popular-again gunslinger mustache.

Cole's face contorted in anger. "Watch it, pal. I *wrote* that script." His lips barely touched his teeth as he spat out his words.

Morro shook his head tiredly. "Fess up, man. You plagiarized a Japanese film that won a Nippon Akademii-shou back in ninety-five."

Cole's face turned bright red to match his hair. "That might have been the seminal inspiration," he shot back, "but every line of dialogue is completely mine!"

The director stared thoughtfully at the small round table where a woman wearing a purple-and-gold tunic with matching turban sat across from Andrea Blair, the film's leading actress.

"She should read the tea leaves," Morro said slowly. "That's what we need. The fortune teller has to *read* the tea leaves before she delivers her line."

"Brilliant," Lewin Usher trilled. He was one of the film's investors and an executive producer, a hefty but slick-looking hedge fund manager in a three-piece Zegna suit with a Rolex the size of an alarm clock. He seemed positively giddy to be on set today.

Josh Morro pointed a finger at the fortune teller. "Fortune teller lady. What I want you to do is pour out the tea, then peer into Andrea's cup and actually *read* the tea leaves. Tell her, um, that her life is in terrible danger."

"That's not in the script," Cole called out.

"Well, it should be," Morro said. He stared earnestly at the fortune teller. "You got that?"

"No problem," said the fortune teller.

"Lights down, everyone quiet . . . and roll film," Morro instructed. He stood there, tense, arms crossed, watching his actors.

The fortune teller lifted the teapot and tilted it at a forty-five-degree angle. At which point the lid promptly fell off and clattered noisily to the floor while the tea bag tumbled out and landed in the teacup with a wet plop.

"No, no!" Morro shouted. "That's not going to work, you're doing it all wrong. Everybody, take five while we figure this out." He sighed deeply and gazed in the direction of Theodosia's craft services table as if there were an answer to be found there.

Turns out there was.

"Loose-leaf tea," Theodosia said. "You need to brew loose tea leaves in order to achieve the effect you want."

"Huh?" The director peered at Theodosia as if really seeing her for the first time. "You know something about tea?"

"She should," Drayton said, suddenly speaking up. "She owns a tea shop."

"Come over here, will you?" Morro said, waggling his fingers.

Theodosia slipped around the table and walked toward the director, aware that more than a few eyes were following her. She stepped over a tangle of wires and black cables that connected lights, cameras, and sound equipment to the main power source.

"So you're a tea expert?" Morro asked.

Theodosia lifted a shoulder. "Of sorts."

"Because you own a tea shop."

"The Indigo Tea Shop over on Church Street."

The director seemed to relax. "Truth be told, I've been known to imbibe a cup or two of tea myself. You might say Earl Grey was my gateway drug."

"Because of the bergamot," Theodosia said.

Josh Morro reached out, gently grabbed Theodosia's arm, and pulled her toward him. "Right."

"Hard to resist that rich flavor."

Morro's face lit up as if he'd been suddenly struck by a wonderful idea. "Since you seem to know what you're doing, we'll have *you* pour the tea and read the tea leaves!"

"What!" screeched the fortune teller, who suddenly saw her big scene going up in smoke.

"Oh no," Theodosia said, breaking away from him and holding up her hands. "I'm no expert when it comes to tasseography."

"You're referring to . . ."

"Reading tea leaves."

Morro gazed at her and smiled. "Oh yes, I think you're perfect. I definitely want *you* to read the tea leaves and be in the scene."

"I can't do that," Theodosia said.

Morro's brows puckered. "What's the problem?"

"I'm not an actress," Theodosia said. She glanced around quickly, looking for confirmation. Wasn't it glaringly apparent that she was only here to oversee the craft services table? Wasn't it? Come on, somebody please pitch in and give her some backup.

But Josh Morro had already made up his mind. He looked over to where Andrea Blair, the star of the movie, was now lounging in a folding chair as she scrolled through her phone messages. Her script lay on the floor next to her, unopened. "You're no actress?" Morro said. "Neither is she." Then he lifted a hand, snapped his fingers, and called out, "Sondra, we're going to need hair, makeup, and wardrobe for . . . what's your name?"

"Theodosia. Theodosia Browning. But I really can't . . ."

"Do it," Drayton urged from across the room. "It'll be fun."

"No, it won't," Theodosia said, shaking her head. "I'm not an actress, I don't even look like an actress."

"Actually, you do," Morro said. "You're young and pretty enough to look good in a close-up, but you also possess a seriousness and quiet maturity that will come across on-screen. A believability the audience can connect with." He appraised her from head to toe. "Good figure, ice-chip blue eyes that go nicely with that English rose complexion only a few women are naturally gifted with, and . . . well, I do love your tangle of auburn hair." He hesitated. "Though we'll have to tone it down some to fit under the turban."

Theodosia shook her head. "No," she said again. But even as her protest continued, Sondra and another production assistant rushed in, grabbed her, and pulled her down the hallway into a makeshift makeup and dressing room.

"This isn't going to work," Theodosia argued as they plunked her down in a pink plastic swivel chair and bombarded her with bright lights. The air was filled with the sweet scent of hair spray, styling gel, and a touch of Chanel No. 5.

"Of course it will work, honey," Brittany, the head makeup artist, told Theodosia. "All we need to do is line your eyes, pat on some makeup, and tone down that hair of yours." She ran a brush through Theodosia's locks and said to her assistant, "Tina, have you ever seen so much hair?"

Shaking her head, Tina snapped her gum and said, "Only on wigs."

"Really," Theodosia said, gripping the arms of her chair. "I can't go through with this."

"Honey, you gotta trust us," Brittany said. She was a bleached blond with over-plucked brows and a spray tan. A fake bake as Theodosia and her friends would say. "We're gonna do a first-class buff and puff that'll glam you up so good you'll look like a genuine Hollywood star."

"Good enough for a shot on TMZ," Tina echoed as she draped a plastic cape around Theodosia's shoulders.

"Oh dear," said Theodosia.

But ten minutes later, once Brittany had sponged on a light base coat, artfully powdered it down, then added some blusher to highlight her cheekbones, Theodosia started to feel a little better. And when Brittany gelled her brows and added eyeliner with a slight cat eye oomph at the outer corners, she peered in the mirror and liked what she saw.

"Not bad," Theodosia said.

"See? You're a natural," Brittany said.

Meanwhile, Tina had sussed out a cute tangle of curls to peek out from under her turban.

"You live here, honey?" Brittany asked as she carefully lined Theodosia's lips.

Theodosia nodded. "Born and bred in Charleston, South Carolina."

"Quite the place," Brittany said. "I've never seen so much historic architecture in my life. Then again, I'm from L.A., where anything before 1980 is considered ancient history."

"Some of our homes and churches date back to the Revolutionary War," Theodosia said. "There are churches that George Washington worshipped in, narrow alleys where duels were fought, and Fort Sumter, where the Civil War began."

"This house must be plenty historic, too," Tina said. "I mean, it sure is a spooky old place. Dark and drafty, practically falling down—it kind of gives me the creeps just being here. But I can understand why the location scouts chose this place. It's the perfect set for a scary movie."

"It does look the part," Theodosia agreed. Even she'd been slightly put off by the dingy walls, threadbare rugs, dried-out woodwork, and bare wires dangling from the ceiling where a grand chandelier had once hung.

"It feels as if nobody's lived here in years," Brittany added.

"That's because nobody has," Theodosia said. "This place is known as Brittlebank Manor and it's reputed to be haunted."

"No!" Brittany cried. "Seriously?"

"Charleston is full of ghosts," Theodosia said playfully. "We've got haunted houses, haunted hotels, a haunted dungeon, and even a haunted cemetery. Actually, two haunted cemeteries."

Tina gave an appreciative shiver. "This place, Brittlebank Manor, is there some kind of legend behind it?"

"I don't know all of it," Theodosia said. "But apparently a woman was kept locked in the attic and then got killed when an enormous bolt of lightning struck the building."

"Why on earth was she locked in the attic?" Brittany asked as she helped Theodosia into a long purple velvet coat emblazoned with silver stars.

"Not sure," Theodosia said as Tina situated a turban on her head and gave a final touch to the swirl of hair that peeked out. "I never did hear the whole story."

Back on set, Drayton had brewed a small pot of Darjeeling while lights and camera angles were being adjusted. And when Theodosia emerged from the makeup room, Helene Deveroux, one of the members of the Charleston Film Board, rushed up to greet her.

"Bless me to bits, Theodosia, I hardly recognized you!" Helene cried. "You're all glammed up like a bona fide actress!"

"It wasn't my idea," Theodosia explained, patting nervously at her turban. "But the director wants me in the movie. You know, for a more authentic tea leaves read."

"Can you do that?" Helene asked. She was forty-something and a tad theatrical with her mop of honey-blond hair, zaftig figure, and overly broad gestures. Today Helene wore a red silk jacket over tight black leather jeans.

"If I follow the director's lead, then sure I can," Theodosia said. "I mean, I guess so."

Helene grabbed Theodosia's arm and gave a conspiratorial wink. "Aren't you glad Delaine set you up with this gig?" Delaine Dish was a friend of Theodosia's and served on the Charleston Film Board along with Helene.

"I'll let you know once we shoot this scene."

Helene grinned. "Later, sweetie, right now I have to bounce." She shook a handful of papers. "Gotta deliver these papers to the City Film Office." And she was gone.

"Are you ready?" the director asked. He was suddenly in Theodosia's face, looking a little anxious.

"Hope so," she said.

Theodosia and Andrea did a couple of quick rehearsals together, with Theodosia feeling more confident as they went along.

"This is working," Josh Morro said. "Very believable. I think we're ready for a take. Now, Andrea, when Theodosia tips your teacup sideways and stares in to read the tea leaves, I want you to look apprehensive. Do you know what that is? Can you give me apprehensive?"

Andrea pulled her mouth into a pout and widened her eyes.

"That looks more like a case of indigestion," Morro said. "Try to work up some genuine emotion. Try to actually . . . act. And, Willy . . ." Morro turned to his cameraman. "I want you to dolly in slowly for an extreme close-up on that teacup." He glanced up to his left. "Lighting guys, let's throw up a scrim and add a blue key light to create a spooky vibe. Then, when Willy goes in for his ECU, amp up the key light and give me a medium-sized flicker, okay?"

"Okay, boss," called the lighting director.

"And somebody get me a chair," Morro said. There was a flurry of activity behind him as somebody set down a metal folding chair. Morro plopped down, crossed his legs, and said,

"Quiet on set. Lights all the way down." There was sudden silence as the lights dimmed and everyone held their breath. "And I want *aaaction.*"

At which point the lights came up slowly, revealing Theodosia and Andrea huddled at the tea table. Theodosia picked up the teapot, poured tea into a floral teacup, and waited as Andrea took a couple of sips. Then she reached over and took the teacup back. As Theodosia leaned forward to peer at the tea leaves, she was aware of the camera moving in close and of a strange, almost electrical, feel in the room. There was a weird rumble, then a profoundly loud SIZZLE, CRACK, POP, as if someone had suddenly thrown the master switch in Dr. Frankenstein's laboratory. The noise continued to build as electrical flashes lit up the room like a string of exploding Black Cat firecrackers and Theodosia smelled a whiff of phosphorus. To add to the mayhem, a horrible gagging sound rang out, then slowly morphed into a strangled scream.

This isn't in the script, Theodosia told herself as a screeching, wailing wall of sound rose up around her from the cast and crew. At which point she jumped to her feet and saw Josh Morro thrashing wildly on the floor. He'd flipped over backward in his metal folding chair and was writhing in agony. His eyes had popped open so wide the whites were enormous, like a couple of boiled eggs. And for some bizarre reason Morro's body seemed almost welded to his chair as his arms flailed crazily, pounding out a drumbeat against the sagging wooden floor, caught in the throes of what had to be a terrible seizure. Seconds later, his back arched spasmodically and his legs kicked and jerked, as if dancing to some unholy tune.

"Somebody help him!" Andrea cried, setting off an even louder cacophony of screams and shouts.

There was a terrible gurgling sound as white foam spewed

from Josh Morro's open mouth. Then, in one final convulsive act, Morro's head snapped back and banged against the floor with a deafening CRACK. Then his crumpled body seemed to run out of steam as he let out a slow expulsion of air that sounded like a vampire's dying hiss.

2

"Won't somebody help him?" Andrea screamed as tears streamed down her face.

Who said the girl can't act?! was the single thought that flitted through Theodosia's brain.

Unfortunately, half the crew seemed to be struck dumb as they gazed in horror at Morro's body while others turned away or buried their face in their hands.

The lights had come up full force now, revealing a barely twitching Josh Morro lying on the floor amidst a tangle of black cables.

Willy, the cameraman, knelt down and reached out a hand to touch Morro's shoulder just as someone shouted, "Stop! Don't do that!"

His arm frozen in midair, Willy glanced up to find Ted Juniper, the lighting director, waving at him.

"Don't touch him," Juniper warned. "He may still be hot."

"Hot? What are you talking about?" Willy shouted. He was

wild-eyed and rumpled, a fifty-something guy in khakis and a green military sweater.

"Just look," Juniper cried. "Look at his chair!"

Willy turned his gaze on the twisted metal chair that Morro seemed to be welded to. "Jeepers," he said, his voice raw with emotion. "There's *wires*."

Theodosia crept around the tea table to have a look for herself. Drayton came up behind her, shaken but curious. The lighting director was right. There was a tangle of black and copper wires wrapped around Morro's metal folding chair.

"Sweet Fanny Adams," Drayton cried. "I think the poor fellow's been electrocuted."

"That can't be," Juniper said. Despair colored his voice and he was practically in tears.

"Somebody call 911," a voice called out. "Does anybody have their phone handy?"

At least fifteen sets of nimble fingers hurriedly called 911.

Which brought . . .

Two uniformed officers from the Charleston Police Department, an ambulance with two EMTs, and the fire department's rescue squad.

The EMTs arrived first and went to work immediately. With barely a wasted motion, they dropped to their hands and knees, pulling equipment from their medical packs.

"Priority one," the first EMT, a serious-looking Black woman, said to the second EMT. Her nametag read L. SINGER, his read T. ELMORE.

Theodosia figured priority one had to be code for a big bad emergency.

Both EMTs worked feverishly on Morro, following the ABC protocol of checking airway, breathing, and circulation.

"I've got a faint pulse," Elmore said. "But it's . . ." He shook his head.

Singer dug in her med pack and pulled out a syringe and a small bottle. "Epinephrine," she said as she carefully filled her needle, then plunged it directly into Morro's heart.

Still, it didn't look good. Even though they worked frantically for another five minutes, Josh Morro wasn't responding to anything the EMTs were doing and his lips were starting to turn blue.

Elmore placed his stethoscope on Morro's heart.

"Anything?" Singer asked.

Elmore looked stricken. "I think we lost him."

"No!" Ted Juniper shouted, clearly distraught. A few others shuffled forward, horrified and disbelieving.

"Get back, everyone stand back." A gravelly voice suddenly boomed out an order in the small room.

"Tidwell," Theodosia murmured to herself.

Burt Tidwell, head of Charleston PD's Robbery and Homicide Division, stormed into the room. A big, bearish man, he was dressed in a saggy, oversized jacket that was a cross between brown and purple (burple?), baggy olive drab slacks, and black steel-toed cop shoes. He looked down at the two EMTs and said, "Anything?"

"He's gone," Singer said. "We even tried . . ."

Tidwell cut her off with a thrust of his hand. "What happened here?" he asked as his beady eyes roamed about the room.

Of course everyone tried to speak at once, which forced Tidwell to hold up a hand and yell, "Quiet!"

At which point everyone quieted down and watched as Tidwell circled a very dead Josh Morrow and studied the scene. Finally, Tidwell turned to the group and thundered, "Who gave him this chair?"

A sea of blank faces stared back at him. It would seem no one had handled the hot-wired chair.

"Come on," Tidwell urged. "Gaffers, was it one of you?" He turned his bulk slightly as sharp eyes scanned the room and several crew members tried to shrink into the shadows. "Lighting guys? Talk to me, people. Someone must have seen or done *something*."

Even with his hectoring tone, Theodosia knew that Tidwell was trying to encourage a witness to step forward, to reveal what they'd seen. But nobody moved a muscle. Nobody wanted to take responsibility for tangling up the metal chair in the wires.

Or was this not an accident? Theodosia wondered. She let that nasty thought percolate in her brain for a few moments. Could this have been intentional? Could it have been . . . murder?

She peered at the chair again. Copper wire had been wound around the legs, more wire around the seat and back. Suddenly, Theodosia didn't think this was random at all. In fact, it did look downright *intentional*. As if someone had really wanted to electrocute Morro. She gazed at Burt Tidwell and saw the same notion lurking in his dark, piercing eyes. Yes, he suspected murder as well.

With no one stepping forward to offer an eyewitness account, Tidwell froze the scene. And five minutes later, a half dozen more uniformed officers came pouring in along with two Crime Scene techs.

The officers herded the onlookers into small groups, took down their names and addresses, and fired questions at them. The Crime Scene team shot photos of the victim from different angles, then made a video of the entire scene. A kind of movie within a movie.

When it was Theodosia's turn to be questioned, Detective Tidwell stepped in to interrogate her himself.

"You are here, why?" he asked.

Theodosia was well acquainted with Tidwell. She'd bumped heads with him on several other occasions. And though he was often brusque and short-tempered, he was also clever, keenly analytical, and dedicated to his job. The investigators who worked under Tidwell—and that included Theodosia's current boyfriend—feared and respected him and would probably walk barefoot across hot coals if he asked them.

Tidwell cocked an eye at Theodosia and said, "Well?"

Theodosia hastily explained how she and Drayton had been tapped to handle the craft services table. That her friends Delaine and Helene, who both served on the Charleston Film Board, had arranged this catering gig for them.

Tidwell looked skeptical. "And you were doling out tea and cookies in *that* costume?"

"Well, no. It just so happened I was offered a very small role in the movie," Theodosia said. "To read the tea leaves and deliver a single line."

"And who offered you this monumental part?"

"Um, the now-deceased film director." Her answer sounded weird, even to her.

"So you saw what happened here? You were an eyewitness?"

"I don't think anybody really saw what went on," Theodosia said. "The set was completely dark, with everyone kind of moving around in the shadows."

"And then?" Tidwell urged.

"And then I heard a bunch of weird popping noises and lights started flashing like crazy."

"And that's when you saw Mr. Morro down on the floor . . ."

Theodosia nodded. "Kicking and jerking as if he'd completely lost control. It was awful . . . I'm sure he was in terrible pain. And people all around him started screaming their heads off."

"How many cast and crew members would you say were on set at the time?" Tidwell glanced around. "How many people were crammed into this rather dingy, depressing-looking parlor?"

"I suppose fifteen people. Maybe twenty," Theodosia said.

"And no one saw anything," Tidwell said in a low voice.

"Like I said. It was dark. And then all hell suddenly broke loose."

Tidwell looked thoughtful. "So perhaps . . ." He suddenly fell silent as two men from the medical examiner's office came in dragging a clattering metal gurney behind them. The men checked with the two officers who were guarding the deceased's body, then went about their business efficiently, almost routinely, as a multitude of nervous eyes suddenly focused on them. The ME guys rolled Morrow's body into a black vinyl bag, zipped it up, then placed the bag on their gurney.

And once again, though nobody gave the order, it was quiet on the set.

3

Theodosia was exhausted by the time she escaped Tidwell's feverish barrage of questions, dropped off Drayton at his house, and finally let herself in her own back door.

But Earl Grey didn't know about any of that. Her sweet dog was sitting at attention in the kitchen, ears pricked forward, eyes focused on the back door. And when that door opened, and Theodosia walked through, he catapulted himself into her arms. Sloppy dog kisses were administered as his tail thumped wildly. And Theodosia couldn't help but embrace him back. Clutch his warm, furry body close to hers and be thankful for her dog's unabashed love.

"Hey, sweetie," she crooned. "It's good to see you. Good to be home."

A cross between a dalmatian and a Labrador (a Dalbrador?), Earl Grey was her roommate, best friend, and jogging partner. He lived with Theodosia in her little cottage in Charleston's Historic District, on a street that was crowded with enormous Italianate, Georgian, Victorian, and Gothic mansions. Most displayed elaborate columns, pediments, and balustrades and were surrounded by touches of wrought iron.

Unlike these grand homes, Theodosia's home was cute and cozy. It was a classic Queen Anne–style cottage with an angled roofline made of overlapping shingles, stucco exterior, and wooden crossbeams. Ivy curled up the sides of the house and the second floor sported a sort of turret. The interior was just as intriguing, with pegged wood floors, brick fireplace, leaded windows, and chintz-covered furniture.

"You must be hungry," Theodosia said to Earl Grey as she buzzed about her kitchen. She filled his dishes with kibbles and fresh cold water, then set about fixing something for herself. A peek in the refrigerator revealed leftover minestrone soup and two cream scones. She warmed everything up, placed it on a silver tray, and carried it into her dining room. She was about to sit down when her mobile phone rang. She grabbed it, looked at the screen, and saw it was Pete Riley calling. Her sort-of boyfriend. Well, he actually *was* her boyfriend.

"Hey," she said.

"I just heard about Josh Morro," were Riley's first words. Not "How are you, sweetheart?" or "I sure do miss you."

"Oh, no, you did not," Theodosia said. How could Riley know about Josh Morro's murder *already*? Were there errant atmospheric strobes? Did a flock of evil fairies wing their way all the way up to Chicago, where he was calling from?

"Tidwell called me."

"That was totally unnecessary. Doesn't he know you're at a law enforcement conference? That you're one of the keynote speakers? That you've got to be spot-on tomorrow morning for your big presentation?"

"He knows."

"Then I think it was rude of him to disturb you. I'm guessing you've been practicing your talk, going over it a final time."

"I got it. I'm ready," Riley said.

"Still . . ." Theodosia closed her eyes and pictured him. Pete Riley was tall, fairly athletic, but with a boyish demeanor about him. He had an aristocratic nose, high cheekbones, and blue eyes a shade lighter than Theodosia's. He was also one of the up-and-coming detectives on Charleston's police force, one of Tidwell's formidable weapons. Theodosia, of course, simply thought of him as Riley, her Riley. And he called her Theo. It was as easy as that because it suited them.

"Truth be known," Riley said, "Tidwell called because he wanted me to relay a message to you."

"A message for me?" Theodosia pretended to be puzzled.

Riley chuckled. This wasn't his first rodeo. He could see right through her.

"Do you want to hear the actual message word for word or just the general gist of it?"

"Do I have a choice?"

"Not really," Riley said.

"Okay, maybe just float me the basic premise."

"Actually, I'm going to clean it up and condense it a bit. What Tidwell wanted was for me to warn you about getting involved in Josh Morro's murder."

"That was sweet of him," Theodosia said.

"Don't be snarky," Riley laughed.

"The thing is, Riley, this guy Morro was electrocuted right in front of my eyes. Sparks flew, wires glowed red, and an entire room full of people—all witnesses, I might add—gasped en masse. And then they all pretended to be clueless when it was quite apparent that someone *there* had murdered Morro. So I have to say I'm more than a little bit involved."

"Theo, you know exactly what Tidwell was referring to. He doesn't want you to get pulled into the investigation. Or, more to the point, he doesn't want you to *insert* yourself into the investigation."

"The thought had barely crossed my mind."

"There's that snarkiness again."

Theodosia exhaled loudly. "Riley, if you could have seen that poor man. I mean, it was pure tragedy, like something of out a B horror movie. Morro was writhing on the floor while megavolts of electricity zapped through him. It was like . . . well, like an execution by electric chair."

"That sounds a trifle dramatic."

"Because it *was* dramatic! And, besides, who knows how to rig up a chair like that? I mean, wires were wrapped around it like something you'd see in a torture chamber. I don't think that kind of know-how comes from reading old editions of *Popular Mechanics.*"

"Probably not. Which means it was someone who knows what they're doing."

"You mean a clever killer?" Theodosia said.

"I would say so, yes. So I second Tidwell's notion of leaving it well alone."

"I'll think about it."

"You're incorrigible."

"Probably."

"Okay, then, wish me luck and try to stay out of things, okay? And when I get back we'll go out for a fancy dinner. Maybe Husk or the Quinte."

"Mmn, raw oysters. Sounds like a plan," Theodosia said.

"Okay, sweetheart, sleep tight."

"You, too."

Theodosia turned off her phone, then nibbled at her dinner.

Halfway through her second scone, she turned her phone back on and googled the IMDb website. Then she looked up Josh Morro's filmography.

His film credits were impressive to say the least. Second unit director on two feature films, *Basil's Countdown* and *Three Crickets*. Then director on two more feature films, *Storm Cloud Horizon* and *Shadow Girls*. Plus, there was TV work in there as well.

Interesting. So who would want Josh Morro dead?

Theodosia thought about this as she tidied up her kitchen, then took Earl Grey out for a short walk. The evening air was still warm as they tromped down her back alley, headed over toward the Cooper River, and watched a cruise ship, lights glittering, pull into one of the mammoth docks.

Back home and upstairs in her bedroom, Theodosia wondered about all the people who'd been on set today—the witnesses. But there had to be one stone-cold killer among them, right? One person with a motive, a person who hated Josh Morro or needed to get rid of him permanently. She took a shower, read a few chapters from a new Susan Wittig Albert book, and thought about Morro's murder some more. Finally, she climbed into bed and drifted off to sleep—with images of darkened movie sets, threatening tea leaf fortunes, and red-hot sparking chairs spinning in her head.

4

Drayton faced Theodosia from behind the front counter of the Indigo Tea Shop. He was perfectly turned out this Tuesday morning in a Harris Tweed jacket, dove gray slacks, highly polished Church's shoes, and his trademark bow tie. Today his Drake's tie was a punchy canary yellow.

"We have to tell Haley about the murder yesterday," Drayton said in a low voice. Haley was their young cook, baker, and occupant (with her orange-and-brown cat, Teacake) of the upstairs apartment.

"Agreed," Theodosia responded. "But we've got to go easy. You know how sensitive she is."

"Who's sensitive?" Haley called out as she emerged from the kitchen, kitted out in her white chef's jacket and toque, and carrying a baking tray heaped with slices of lemon bread and orange-walnut scones. The aromas ranged somewhere between delightful and heavenly.

"Oops," Drayton said.

Haley studied him. "What were you talking about? What *are* you talking about?"

"There's been a bit of a tragedy," Drayton said in hushed tones.

"A death occurred on the movie set yesterday," Theodosia said.

"Oh that," Haley said. "Josh Morro." She shook back her curtain of long blond hair and wrinkled her pert nose. "Yeah, I already know about it." She set her tray of baked goods down on the counter nonchalantly.

"You do?" Drayton said. "How?"

"Who told you?" Theodosia asked.

"Your friend Delaine Dish stopped by the tea shop late yesterday afternoon. She'd just gotten word about the film director's death and was wondering if you and Drayton had made it back here yet. When I told her no, she got that weird look on her face—you know the look . . ."

Theodosia nodded. She knew it well. You could always tell when Delaine Dish was bursting with news, good or bad. She pursed her lips and assumed a kind of pickle face. Dill, not sweet. Still, as a member of the Charleston Film Board—and the one who'd set them up with their catering gig—Delaine had good reason to be worried about Morro's strange death.

Haley stepped closer and threw them a questioning look. "Yesterday. Was it very bad?"

"Hideous," Drayton said.

"It's always a tragedy when someone is killed," Theodosia said.

"Not just killed, murdered," Haley said, putting a special emphasis on the last word.

"Yes, and the police are on top of it," Theodosia said. "They're questioning everyone involved and I have high hopes they'll come up with a suspect or two very shortly."

Haley shifted from one foot to another. "What about you?" she asked. "You've earned a kind of reputation as Charleston's own Nancy Drew. Plus, you were right there in the mix. What do *you* think?"

When Theodosia hesitated, Drayton spoke up and said, "Theodosia thinks, as do I, that we should put yesterday's unfortunate circumstances on the back burner for the time being. We need to get cracking and make sure our tea shop is organized and ready to go. Since we weren't here yesterday, I'm sure there's been some serious disorganization."

"No way," Haley said. "Not in my kitchen and certainly not in the tea shop. In fact, we managed quite well. Miss Dimple was here to help serve and so was Beth Ann."

Miss Dimple was their bookkeeper-slash-part-time-server and Beth Ann was Haley's cousin from nearby Goose Creek who'd been tapped to work as a server this week.

"In fact, Beth Ann should be here any minute," Haley said.

"Great," Theodosia said, glancing about the tea shop she'd lovingly crafted. And even though she'd been gone for one whole entire day, the Indigo Tea Shop had seemingly withstood total collapse. In fact, the heart pine floors fairly gleamed, tables were carefully arranged, and Drayton's floor-to-ceiling shelves of tea tins looked decidedly organized.

"What's on the menu for morning tea?" Drayton asked.

"Oh," said Haley. "My lemon bread and orange-walnut scones and then some apple spice muffins and banana bread for later." She gave a mischievous grin. "With everything late-summer ripe for the picking from surrounding orchards it looks to be a fruit-filled week."

"Let us hope it's also fruitful," Drayton added.

"Hah, I see where you're going with that," Haley said, pointing a finger at him.

They all got to work then. Drayton selecting his teas for the day and lining up an armada of colorful teapots, Theodosia setting the tables and choosing a fun mix of antique floral teacups and saucers from makers that included Belleek, Haviland, and Pickard.

The Indigo Tea Shop, to put it bluntly, was Theodosia's pride and joy. She'd scrimped and saved for a down payment on the small English-style brick building with its high-pitched roof, leaded windows, hunter green awnings, and rounded-at-the-top door that looked like it belonged on a Hobbit house. Then she'd tackled the inside and imbued it with a slightly British, quasi-French charm. This included artfully swagged blue toile curtains, faded Oriental carpets on pegged floors, and a small wood-burning fireplace in one corner. Hanging overhead, a French chandelier imparted a warm, almost hazy glow (Drayton referred to it as Rembrandt lighting) and in the far corner antique highboys held retail items that included tea towels, tea cozies, tins of tea, Theodosia's proprietary T-Bath lotions and moisturizers, and jars of DuBose Bees Honey. A velvet celadon green curtain separated the café from the back half and brick walls were hung with antique prints and Theodosia's handmade grapevine wreaths that were decorated with miniature teacups.

Drayton had been the first to come on board as tea sommelier. And Haley, casually answering a want ad, had found her baking skills and her grandma's recipes—also known as receipts—in high demand.

The rest of the tea accoutrements had come about organically, with Theodosia sifting through flea markets, antique shops, and tag sales to find the perfect vintage teacups, teapots, goblets, and silverware.

After a half dozen years together, Theodosia, Drayton, and Haley had become a well-coordinated team that took pride in delighting visitors and neighbors with their baked-from-scratch scones and muffins, dazzling array of fine teas, extraordinary catering, and ever-popular special event teas. They'd also come to realize that family didn't always have to mean blood relatives.

"Here come the customers," Drayton sang out from behind the counter as the front door banged open and a foursome hustled inside. Theodosia quickly seated them, then returned to greet a young couple and then a group of six women. She was kept busy as she took orders, recommended teas, and ran food orders in to Haley and tea orders to Drayton. And all the while, neighboring shopkeepers dropped in for their de rigueur cuppas, while multiple groups of tourists found their way in, drawn by the charm of the shop. Thank goodness for Haley's cousin, Beth Ann, who showed up in the nick of time.

Hours flew by and just as Theodosia was thinking about lunchtime, the front door whapped open and a virtual stampede came coursing in. But these were not customers—or even regulars from down the block. It was—wait for it, folks—a TV crew.

Theodosia glanced at Drayton, who was doing his almighty best to ignore them and decided he wasn't going to be much help dealing with this.

"Theodosia," said a slick-looking man with carefully gelled hair. "You're Theodosia Browning, right?" He was thirty-something and a minor on-air personality at one of the TV stations, though she couldn't remember which one.

Theodosia sighed. "Guilty as charged."

"Ken Lotter from W-BAM. I'd love to do a quick one-on-one with you," he said. "You know, about the murder at Brittlebank Manor."

"W-BAM?" Theodosia raised a single brow.

"We used to be WOXT but upper management thought W-BAM sounded punchier."

"Ken, this is not a good time. As you can see, we're rather busy."

"This won't take but a minute." Ken motioned for his cameraman to roll videotape and his lighting guy to turn on his flood lamp. Then Ken held a microphone up to his mouth and said, "We're talking to Miss Theodosia Browning, the owner of the Indigo Tea Shop. Miss Browning, I understand you witnessed the murder of director Josh Morro yesterday."

Theodosia held up a hand. "Stop shooting, please."

Lotter motioned for his cameraman to lower his camera. Then said, "But you were a witness, yes?"

"No," Theodosia said. "I was there, but I'm afraid I didn't see what happened."

"You don't know who hot-wired that chair?" Lotter asked.

"How do you know it was hot-wired?"

Lotter grinned. "I have my sources."

"I'm afraid I can't answer your questions," Theodosia said. "You'll have to talk to Detective Tidwell. He's the one in charge of the investigation."

"We tried that," Lotter said. "He turned us down flat."

"Maybe you should try to interview the cast and crew, then."

"Not sure where they're hanging out," Lotter said.

The cameramen piped up and said, "I heard a rumor that the screenwriter is holed up at a nearby B and B."

"Do you know which one?" Theodosia asked.

"Something Featherbed," the cameraman said.

Theodosia winced. Her dear friend Angie Congdon owned the Featherbed House B and B. If that's where Craig Cole was staying, then Angie would no doubt have to contend with this same TV crew showing up on her doorstep.

Ken Lotter tried again. "We heard there was bad blood between Josh Morro and his leading lady."

"You're talking about Andrea Blair?"

Lotter nodded. "The rumor du jour is that she got an offer to star in some reality show—something superhot and heavy, but Morro wouldn't let her out of her contract."

This was news to Theodosia. "So you're thinking . . . what?"

"That Andrea might have had a hand in yesterday's debacle," Lotter said. "Care to comment on that?"

"Just between you and me, I'm not sure Andrea would know how to run a salad shooter," Theodosia said. "Let alone rig up a homemade electric chair."

"Hah, love your sense of humor," Lotter said. "Okay then, what can you tell us about the new director that's about to step in?"

"Not a thing," Theodosia said. Then, "That's what you've heard? There's a new director taking over?"

"Some guy named Adler," Lotter said. "I suppose with the actors, crew, and location all locked down, it shouldn't be surprising that the shoot is slated to keep going." He smiled a shark's smile. "Business as usual, don't ya know?" He pulled a business card out of his jacket pocket and handed it to Theodosia. "Call me if you hear something, okay? Or if you change your mind about talking to me."

Theodosia had barely hustled Ken Lotter and his crew out the door when Bill Glass came stomping in. Glass was the publisher of *Shooting Star*, a glossy weekly tabloid that specialized in chronicling all the goings-on of the rich and sleazy in Charleston.

"Glass," said Theodosia when she finally turned to acknowledge him. He was her nemesis in a strange sort of way. Always hunting for tidbits of juicy gossip, but being faux polite about it. She didn't trust him but didn't quite disdain him, either.

"Hey, long time no see," Glass called to Theodosia. Today he was dressed in a horrible orange shirt that was untucked from his khaki pants. He also wore a pair of scuffed boots that looked like they'd seen better days in World War II, a paisley scarf, and two cameras dangling around his neck. If asked to describe Glass, Theodosia would've said war correspondent meets country bumpkin.

"How can I help you, Mr. Glass?" Theodosia said, fighting to remain polite.

Which was Glass's cue to be not so polite.

"Why do I miss out on all the hot news events?" Glass snarled.

"I don't know, why do you?" Theodosia said. Usually, Glass was front and center for any kind of accident, scandal, or murder. He was rumored to have informants all over town.

"For one thing, my police scanner is on the blink and in the repair shop," Glass grumbled.

"If you're referring to what happened at Brittlebank Manor yesterday, I wouldn't exactly call it a hot news event," Theodosia told him. "It was more like stone-cold murder."

"Same thing," Glass said. "What can you tell me about it?"

"Absolutely nothing."

"But you were there. Doing your tea table thing."

"Craft services table," Theodosia said.

"Whatever. Just give me your take on the whole shebang so I can write it up."

"I wasn't an eyewitness. I just happened to catch the aftermath."

Glass grinned. "I heard it was pretty gruesome."

"If that's the kind of information you're after, you should go talk to the medical examiner," Theodosia said.

"Yeah, he's on my list." Glass turned and tapped his fingers on the counter. "Hey, Drayton. Tea guy," he called out. "You got anything chock-full of caffeine?" He thumped his chest. "Got a big day ahead of me. I want to keep my engine tuned up and running."

"I do believe I have a pot of Puerh tea brewing," Drayton said.

"And it's guaranteed to perk me up?" Glass asked.

Theodosia smiled. She knew that if Glass drank enough Puerh tea, it would work like rocket fuel. As far as caffeine went, Puerh was one of the highest-caffeinated teas, topping out at about 120 milligrams per cup versus coffee's 95.

"Oh my, yes," Drayton said with a satisfied smile. "I think this tea should do the trick nicely."

5

"We need to talk about lunch," Theodosia said to Haley. She was standing in their postage stamp–sized kitchen watching Haley spread honeyed chicken salad on two dozen slices of bread, add crisp lettuce, top it with another slice of bread, then expertly cut off the crusts and slice the sandwiches into quarters.

"Besides these tea sandwiches I've got corn chowder, white bean cassoulet, and a bacon and goat cheese Bibb lettuce salad," Haley said.

"You never fail to amaze me, Haley," Theodosia said. Haley managed to turn out baked goods as well as creative bistro-style luncheons day after day.

Haley grinned. "Sometimes I amaze myself."

There was a CLUNK at the swinging door and Beth Ann came in. She was five years younger than Haley, slim with dark hair, and a junior at Clemson, where she was majoring in marketing. But Beth Ann had taken this quarter off. "A gap quarter," she'd explained. "Instead of a gap year. To get some practical experience."

"I need two more cream scones and a container of strawberry jam," Beth Ann said.

"Coming right up," Haley said. "Hey, are you having fun out there?"

"You know, I am," Beth Ann said. "I never understood how a small business operated until I started filling in here."

"You mean lean and mean?" Theodosia asked. "Since we do tend to run things on a shoestring."

"It's more your coordination and the planning that intrigues me. How you develop concepts for your various event teas, market them, then make them actually happen. All while still managing your day-to-day work. I have to say it's pretty cool."

"So you're learning a few things," Theodosia said.

"Lots," Beth Ann enthused.

"What would you say if I asked you to handle the craft services table on set tomorrow? I'd help you arrange things, but then I have to hustle back here for our Poetry Tea."

Beth Ann looked thoughtful. "At Brittlebank Manor? Where that guy was killed?"

"Look at it this way," Haley said. "The probability of another murder occurring in the same place is off the charts. You've been pre-disastered."

Theodosia and Beth Ann both chuckled at Haley's remark. Because it was, in a strange way, absolutely true.

"Okay," Beth Ann said. "I'll give it a shot."

Back outside in the tea room, Theodosia was setting tables for their luncheon crowd when their octogenarian bookkeeper, Miss Dimple, came flying in.

"Bless me," she said, registering surprise at seeing Theodosia and Drayton. "Aren't the two of you supposed to be on set today?"

"The operative words are *supposed to be*," Theodosia said. "But with yesterday's murder . . ."

Miss Dimple's smile collapsed. "Oh, that's right. How awful. I read about it in this morning's *Post and Courier*. I think the word they used was *heinous*. Was it heinous?"

"It was indeed."

"So what's going to happen now? Will they call it quits with the movie?"

"Apparently it's not only Broadway where the show must go on," Theodosia said. "We were told that the assistant director would be doing location shoots around Charleston today. You know, footage to use for the opening, a few transition shots, and footage for when they roll credits. I think they call it B-roll."

"And then what?" Miss Dimple asked. She was a grandmotherly type with pink-tinged hair and apple cheeks. Old-school all the way, she often tossed out quaint phrases such as *whoops-a-daisy* and *tickety-boo*.

"And then, hopefully by tomorrow, Peregrine Pictures will have a replacement director," Theodosia said.

"It's that easy? You just call Hertz Rent-a-Director and ask for a new one?"

"Don't know. But what you just said—that sounds like a smart idea."

As Miss Dimple was leaving with a stack of invoices and the tea shop's checkbook, Delaine Dish came striding in wearing a fire-engine red skirt suit and black leather stilettos. She nodded brusquely at Miss Dimple, then looked around for Theodosia. When she finally spotted her with a stack of plates, Delaine said, in a near hysterical voice, "Theo, we have to get to the bottom of this!"

Theodosia glanced her way. "Excuse me?"

"I'm talking about the murder. Yesterday." Delaine's heart-shaped face was pulled into an unhappy frown and her size-two frame fairly shook with indignation.

"The police are already on it," Theodosia assured her, setting down the plates. "I'm positive they're doing their absolute best."

"You don't seem to understand," Delaine said, wringing her hands. "I'm kind of involved."

"Of course you are," Drayton piped in. "You're a member of the Charleston Film Board. I'm sure this is a terrible shock to you—to all the members."

Delaine half squeezed her eyes shut and drew in a breath. "I'm a teensy bit more involved than that."

Theodosia stared at Delaine. There was something brewing and it surely wasn't a pot of tea. "How teensy?" she asked.

Delaine gave an anguished look. "The thing is, Josh Morro and I . . . well, we were . . . you know . . ."

"No, I don't know," Theodosia said. "Come on, Delaine, spit it out. Give it to me straight. What's going on?"

Delaine stomped a foot. "If you must know, Morro and I were *seeing* each other."

Theodosia blinked. "You mean like dating?"

"Um . . . more like friends with benefits?"

"Is that a question or an answer?" Theodosia asked.

"Answer," Delaine whispered, hunching her shoulders up to her ears.

"Oh." Theodosia stared at Delaine, digesting what her friend had just told her. Then her face softened and she said, "I had no idea you two were close. Delaine, I'm so sorry."

Drayton, who was still listening in on the conversation, favored Delaine with an appropriately sober look and said, "You poor thing."

Theodosia nodded in agreement. "You must be heartsick."

Delaine grimaced. "Not exactly."

Drayton frowned. "You're not?"

"Why not?" Theodosia asked. She realized that she needed to sort through Delaine's answer, figure out why she was hemming and hawing so much. "Is there something you're not telling us?"

"Josh and I *were* dating," Delaine said. "During the scant few weeks he was here in Charleston for preproduction meetings. And even though he was wrapped up a lot of the time, we managed to steal a few nights together."

"So you're saying . . . you two were an item." *Well, why not?* Theodosia thought. *He was a fairly attractive man.*

But Delaine was squirming mightily, fidgeting with her diamond rings. "We were an item until we weren't."

"I'm having trouble following this," Drayton said.

"No kidding," Theodosia said.

Delaine heaved a huge sigh. "Last week Josh and I had a horrible fight."

"You broke up?" Theodosia said.

"You might say that," Delaine said. "But the really unfortunate thing is we did it in front of at least a hundred people."

"What!" Drayton cried.

"Where?" Theodosia asked.

"We were having dinner at Candlewicks. You know, that fancy new place over on Archdale Street? With the French chef that used to work at Tanadoor in New York?"

"Okay," Theodosia said. She made a twirling motion with her hand to encourage Delaine to stay on the subject and keep talking.

"Anyway," Delaine said, "I was sipping a glass of rather superlative Mumm champagne and thoroughly enjoying my escargot when—kaboom—out of nowhere, Josh suddenly told me we needed to take a time-out."

"That doesn't sound like an unreasonable request," Drayton said.

"Are you daft?!" Delaine screamed at the top of her lungs. "When a man asks for a time-out it means he never wants to see you again!"

"Is that true?" Drayton looked at Theodosia.

"Pretty much," Theodosia said.

Delaine's lower lip quivered. "Josh claimed I was too self-absorbed."

Neither Theodosia or Drayton were about to touch that statement with a ten-foot pole. They both knew it was the honest truth.

Delaine continued on. "He also said our relationship gobbled up too much of his precious time. That he never got a chance to enjoy his favorite sports anymore."

"Which were?" Theodosia asked.

Delaine sniffled and blotted her nose with a hanky. "Well, tennis and scuba diving. Though I don't see much excitement in whacking a little yellow ball around or hanging out with a bunch of ugly old fish. Not when he could be hanging out with *me*."

"So this breakup at Candlewicks was mostly verbal sparring?" Theodosia asked.

"If you can call screaming and shouting verbal sparring, then yes," Delaine said. "But Josh also tossed his plate at me."

"At your face?" Theodosia was horrified.

"No," Drayton breathed.

"He kind of chucked it sideways like he was throwing a Frisbee," Delaine said. "But his clams casino hit my plate just so . . ." She flexed a hand to indicate the angle. "And launched my garlic butter escargot all down the front of my new cocktail dress! That's when our argument really escalated."

Theodosia clapped a hand over her mouth. She was starting to get the picture. Delaine and Josh Morro had a very public argument and now Morro was dead.

"Excuse me," Theodosia said. "Are you telling us this because you're worried you're a suspect in his murder?"

"Wake up and smell the banana bread," Delaine shrilled. "I'm *already* a suspect! Two detectives came to my home last night, asking rude questions and battering away at me for hours."

"But you weren't even there when Josh Morro was killed," Theodosia said. "You weren't anywhere near Brittlebank Manor."

"The police seem to think I *could* have been!" Delaine said. "That I might have *snuck* in and rigged up that awful chair thing."

"I'm sure you have a legitimate alibi, don't you?" Drayton said. "You were busy at your boutique? At Cotton Duck?"

Delaine shook her head. "Yesterday, no, I took the entire day off. I've been so frazzled what with Josh blindsiding me like that. And then I needed quiet time to finalize details on my Frills and Frolic Fashion Show. So, yes, I pretty much took the day off."

"No one saw you at all yesterday?" Theodosia asked. "You didn't talk to anyone?"

"Not until I got word about Josh's murder. It was Helene Deveroux who called me and broke the news. You know Helene, she's a fellow board member. So then I hotfooted it over here and spoke to Haley."

"Sure," Theodosia said. "Helene stopped by the shoot yesterday for a minute or two because . . ."

"Can I *please* finish telling my story?" Delaine asked in a peevish tone.

Theodosia and Drayton both fell silent.

Delaine cleared her throat. "So, anyway, I came here looking for the two of you. But Haley said you weren't here, so I went on home. Then the *police* showed up on my doorstep, frightened my poor kitty cats to *death*, and proceeded to browbeat me for *hours*."

"Hours?" Theodosia said.

"That's what it *felt* like," Delaine said. "What with their impertinent questions and nasty innuendos. And once they finally left I was so scared and worried I didn't get a wink of sleep. I spent the entire night tossing and turning. Then, first thing this morning, well . . . after I had my nails done . . . I rushed over here to see you two." Tears welled up in Delaine's eyes, then dribbled down her face, streaking her mascara. "I thought I might need your help?" she said in a small, squeaky voice. Then she pulled a second lace hanky from her bag, wiped at her eyes, and said, "And now I see that I definitely do."

"Delaine, I don't know what to say," Theodosia said. "I'm sure you're not in serious trouble. I mean, the police tend to question anyone and everyone who was in recent contact with a murder victim."

"That's all I am. A recent contact?"

"That's not what I meant."

"Theo," Delaine pleaded. "You've got to help me. You were there when it happened, and you've got good contacts within the police department, so . . ."

"So you want me to try and intercede?"

"I knew you'd say yes!" Delaine cooed.

"Actually, I didn't say yes."

"But you will help me?"

"I'll do what I can," Theodosia said, wondering just how much influence she might have with Tidwell and company. Probably not a lot. But if she could run a quiet shadow investigation, then maybe she could come up with some answers. Maybe even an actual suspect.

"Stay for lunch, Delaine," Drayton urged. "Sit down and let me brew you a nice relaxing cup of chamomile tea."

Delaine shook her head and frowned. "No, I have to get to Cotton Duck. I need to keep busy or this problem—this *murder*—will keep rattling around in my head and drive me batty."

"Then let us fix you something to take with you," Theodosia said. "Tea, a tea sandwich, maybe a scone?"

"Are the scones carb-free?"

Theodosia gazed at her. "What do you think?"

"Maybe just some green tea, then. And a teensy-tiny sandwich."

6

Theodosia finished setting the tables for lunch, lit a dozen tea-light candles, then sidled up to the front counter where Drayton was brewing pots of gunpowder green and Lapsang souchong.

"What do you know about Brittlebank Manor?" she asked.

Drayton glanced up from a steeping, steaming teapot. "Not that much. Unlike so many of our historic homes, I wouldn't consider it to be architecturally unique, so it's not on any of the regular guided tours or historical walkabouts. Really, most people are interested only because of the legend."

"The legend about the woman who was kept prisoner in the attic," Theodosia said. Her heart did an extra thump inside her chest when she thought about it. Really, how horrible that a woman had been imprisoned in that old house. What had she done to deserve such a terrible fate?

"From what I've heard over the years, it was her husband who kept her prisoner up there in the attic," Drayton said. "Apparently, he claimed she was stark-raving mad."

"Or maybe she was just mad at him," Theodosia said. "Was the poor woman ever able to escape? Or did she die up there?"

"I don't really know. I mean, there's legend and then there's fact."

"Maybe I need some facts?"

"You think so?" Drayton placed the lid on a green ceramic teapot. "Do you really want to get involved in an old mystery that has nothing to do with yesterday's murder?"

"When you put it that way, maybe not." *Or maybe I do*, Theodosia thought to herself as the front door opened and the first of her luncheon customers came bouncing in.

She and Beth Ann got busy with lunch then, taking orders, grabbing pots of tea, chatting with their guests, pouring refills, and having a pretty good time of it. Haley's white bean cassoulet proved to be the hit of the day and was the first item they ran out of.

"Maybe I should have made a double order," Haley said in the kitchen later. She felt bad that some of their customers had missed out.

"Next time do that," Theodosia said. "Because I think a lot of folks will be coming back just to enjoy that one lovely dish."

Haley gave a thumbs-up. "Works for me."

As Beth Ann cashed out customers and cleared tables, Theodosia took a breather at the front counter.

"Here," Drayton said, pushing a cup of tea toward her. "Try this."

"What is it?"

Drayton smiled. "You tell me."

Theodosia took a sip, nodded, then said, "I taste hints of apple, peach, apricot, and . . . maybe strawberry?"

"A gold star for you. This is Peach Bellini tea from Plum Deluxe. Rooibos tea loaded with bits of fruit."

"Delicious," Theodosia said. Then, hearing the front door click open, she turned to find—surprise, surprise—Detective Burt Tidwell shuffling into her tea room.

She met him halfway.

"Detective, what brings you in today?"

Tidwell regarded her with hooded eyes. "I think you know."

"I couldn't possibly guess. But would you care to sit down and . . ."

Tidwell sat down heavily at the nearest table.

"As I was saying, would you care to sit down and have a cup of tea? And perhaps a scone?" Theodosia knew Tidwell had a particular weakness for scones.

"I could do that," Tidwell agreed.

Theodosia signaled for Drayton to brew a pot of tea, then hurried into the kitchen to place two cream scones on a small silver tray, then added a small dish of Devonshire cream and a dish of strawberry jam.

As she deposited the food on Tidwell's table, Drayton came over with a pot of tea.

"Japanese Sencha," he said. "But to get the full benefit of the lemongrass, it needs to steep another two minutes."

"Thank you," Theodosia said to Drayton as she sat down across from Tidwell. She smiled at him and said, "How on earth was Josh Morro electrocuted?"

Tidwell took his time answering. First he broke off a bite of scone (a large bite), slathered it with Devonshire cream and jam, then popped it in his mouth. Chewing thoughtfully, he said, "Obviously there was a huge array of cables and wires wrapped around his metal folding chair."

"You're saying this must have been preplanned," Theodosia said.

"The word is *premeditated*," Tidwell said. "Since we're referencing a homicide. And as far as the deadly chair goes, once we cleared the set we discovered that the wires—most all of them—were connected to a metal awl that had been jammed into a circuit breaker."

"And that alone was what killed Morro? It sounds awfully makeshift."

"Are you serious?" Tidwell's chair creaked noisily as he leaned forward. "There was enough juice running through that chair to turn every person inside Brittlebank Manor into crispy critters."

"I'm glad you're finding humor in this," Theodosia said.

"Actually, I'm not. I take this murder—any murder—very seriously."

Theodosia reached for the pot of tea and poured a stream of Sencha into Tidwell's teacup. "And Delaine Dish is a suspect?"

"That's correct."

"No," Theodosia said. "That's wrong."

Tidwell picked up his teacup, took a noisy sip, then set it back down in its saucer with a loud *clink*.

"The fact of the matter is, Miss Dish was *involved* with Mr. Morro," Tidwell said. "Romantically involved. Until that relationship ended abruptly, badly, and very publicly. In front of a number of horrified witnesses."

"Oh please."

"The woman is erratic."

"Of course she is. Delaine is erratic, eccentric, and has a personality that can set your teeth on edge. But that doesn't make her a killer."

"She also has no decent alibi for the time frame in which the film director was killed," Tidwell said.

"Ninety-nine-point-nine percent of Charleston's citizens probably don't have an alibi for that time frame, but it doesn't make them killers."

Tidwell held up an index finger. "But they weren't seen by several dozen witnesses screaming at Mr. Morro inside a fancy restaurant."

"You're using the old 'a woman scorned' argument."

"Exactly."

Theodosia sat back. "I think Delaine has thicker skin than that. She's gone through any number of breakups and survived just fine. Truth be known, she runs through men like a buzz saw. Besides, Delaine wasn't anywhere near Brittlebank Manor yesterday."

"You don't know that. The witnesses I interviewed all said it was pitch-dark inside that old place. That they were filming some kind of spooky movie."

"*Dark Fortunes,*" Theodosia murmured.

"That's it? That's the name of the film?"

"The working title anyway." Theodosia considered this. "No, I guess it's the actual title."

"Uh-huh." Tidwell was already working on his second scone.

"What do you know about the lighting guys? If anybody is adept at wiring it would be those folks," Theodosia said.

"We're looking hard at one of the men."

"Which one?"

In lieu of an answer Tidwell took a sip of tea.

"I see. You're not going to tell me. Hmm. Maybe I will have to do a little investigating on my own."

"No, you will not," Tidwell said.

"Excuse me," Theodosia said. "Have we met?"

Tidwell heaved a deep sigh, then said, "There's more here than meets the eye."

"Is that fact or mere suspicion?"

"Let me put it this way," Tidwell said. "People are pointing fingers at each other, there's an unhappy young actress, directors are playing musical chairs, and the film has a completion guaranty so even if it doesn't get made there's a payoff." He picked up the last of his scone and stared at her.

"Huh," Theodosia said. "Sounds like you've got your work cut out for you."

Tidwell scowled as crumbs dribbled down his shirt. "Unfortunately, yes."

Just as Theodosia was finishing up for the day, sweeping floors, putting all the teacups and plates back in the cupboard, Helene Deveroux came in. She'd always been a pretty woman, bouncy and vivacious. But this afternoon, wearing her emotions on her face, she looked tense and unsettled.

"I'm worried sick about Delaine," Helene said, rushing up to Theodosia and clutching her arm. "I dropped by Cotton Duck a while ago and found her sobbing into their new collection of hand-painted silk scarves."

Theodosia nodded. "Delaine stopped in here a little while ago."

"Was she upset?" Helene asked.

"Is the Pope Catholic?" Drayton asked from behind the counter.

"Got it," Helene said with a nod of her head. Helene was not only bubbly and smart; she was also a socialite of sorts, serving on the Opera Committee, Charleston Arts Council, and Charleston Film Board. She was widowed, well off, and tended to be a bit flamboyant—there were rumors that she'd done dinner theater in her younger days. Now, Helene and another lady ran a small shop over on Queen Street—what Theodosia had always figured was a hobby shop—that dealt in antiques and collectible ceramics.

"Helene, you were at Brittlebank Manor for a short time

yesterday. Did you see Delaine prowling around?" Theodosia asked.

"I certainly did not."

"The police are insisting that Delaine could have been there. But . . . I don't see how that's possible. Besides, she's not the murdering sort."

"Not one bit," Helene said. "Delaine tends to be a trifle touchy at times, but behind her hard-shell exterior she's actually very sweet. I mean, look at all the work she does with animals . . . rescue animals at that. Poor dogs and cats that have come from unbearable circumstances. She not only raises money to fund their rescue, she fosters some of them in her own home. Delaine's heart is clearly in the right place."

"I hear you," Theodosia said.

Helene nibbled her lower lip. "So it can't be Delaine."

"I never thought it was."

"Then who's really to blame?" Helene asked. She was clearly in agony for her friend.

"Let's think for a minute," Theodosia said as they both sat down. "You were involved in several of the movie's preproduction meetings, right?"

Helene nodded. "Some of them. Mostly because Peregrine Pictures needed the board's input regarding tax rebates and incentives from the City of Charleston—and I served as point person for all of that."

"And everything's been on the up-and-up? You haven't detected any political kickbacks or anything like that?"

"It's all been fairly straightforward. Peregrine Pictures submits copies of their production costs and then the city finance office cuts a tax rebate check." Helene paused. "So far it's been good for the city. Some local actors and crew got hired and the restaurants and hotels are faring well, too. It's also a point of pride that a genuine Hollywood movie is being filmed here. It will no doubt attract other filmmakers and production companies."

"I'm sure that's true. But as far as actual Hollywood types are concerned, you're fairly well acquainted with them? With the key players who were on set when Josh Morro was killed?"

Helene shrugged. "I guess. Some of them anyway. Like yesterday, when I popped in to get those signatures . . . well, you saw me . . . I had a lovely chat with that agent, Sidney Gorsk. Of course, then I had to toddle off to file the papers." She paused, looking suddenly nervous. "Thank goodness I left before Josh Morro was electrocuted. I would have hated to have that horrible image seared into my brain." She shook her head as if it were all too much for her. Then she swallowed hard and said, "But, to answer your question, I'm familiar with most of the cast and crew, yes."

Theodosia decided Helene might be a possible source of information.

"Okay, then," Theodosia said, "I have a rather odd question for you and I'd like you to give it your full consideration."

Helene nodded.

"Was there anyone, anyone at all, that you can think of who didn't get along with Josh Morro?"

Helene looked startled. "You mean who hated him enough to kill him?"

"Let's just keep it at 'didn't get along with' for now."

Helene leaned back in her chair and closed her eyes. She was quiet for so long that Theodosia worried she might have fallen asleep. Then Helene opened her eyes and said, "I can only think of two people who might have had a serious axe to grind."

"Okay, that's a start."

"The first one's Andrea Blair."

"The film's leading lady," Theodosia said.

"Rumor has it Andrea despised Josh Morro."

"Because he was tough on her?"

"I think Morro was tough on everybody. But the big rumor was that Morro wouldn't let Andrea out of her contract so she could star in some new reality show."

"I heard that," Theodosia said. "I wonder why Morro was being such a stickler about it?"

Helene shrugged. "Search me. I don't know the particulars."

"Who else?"

"Maybe . . . Craig Cole, the screenwriter? I know that he and Morro were constantly at odds."

"When I was there I overheard Morro refer to Cole's script as total dreck."

"There you go!" Helene said, lifting a hand with a grand flourish as if ready to conduct an orchestra.

"Anyone else?" Theodosia asked.

Helene frowned as if considering someone else. "Well, since Morro was electrocuted, I imagine the lighting guys or rigging people or whatever they're called might come under suspicion as well."

"I think you're right."

Helene reached out and touched Theodosia's hand. "Just because we've got a semi-disaster on our hands, you're not going to quit on us, are you? I've heard wonderful things—raves, actually—about your craft services table."

Theodosia shook her head. She'd been musing about the circumstances of Josh Morro's murder, about Delaine being a prime suspect, and about how maybe she could help figure out who the real killer was.

"Quit?" Theodosia shook her head. "Not on your life. In fact, I'm just getting started."

7

Drayton and Haley had already gone home for the day, leaving Theodosia sitting in her office. She was munching on a chicken salad sandwich that Haley had fixed for her, half-heartedly going through a few catalogs, trying to decide if she should order a few more tea cozies, trivets, straw hats, and other gift items.

But Theodosia was also musing about what Helene had said about Craig Cole. About how Cole and Morro hadn't gotten along. Yes, Craig Cole did strike her as a hothead. And the kind of guy who might go a little berserk if his creativity was challenged. She knew something else about Cole, too. She knew he was staying at the Featherbed House. And maybe, just maybe, if she went over there, she could have a quick conversation with him.

Theodosia looked at her watch. It was just five thirty. Maybe she could catch Cole before he dashed off for dinner.

The Featherbed House B and B was just a short stroll from the Indigo Tea Shop. It was an enormous old home constructed of brick and clapboard that had been added onto over the years—

an extra wing here, an annex there—and turned into a cozy but luxurious inn. Wicker furniture and lazy swings graced a wrap-around front porch; a second-floor balcony was the perfect sunning and stargazing spot. And looking up at the structure from the street, the architecturally ornate third floor offered a virtual wedding cake display of turrets, finials, and balustrades.

When Theodosia walked into the lobby, a young woman with long blond hair, wearing a kind of peasant blouse, was sitting at the reception desk.

"Good evening," Theodosia said as the girl looked up with a smile. "Is Angie around?" Angie Congdon was the owner as well as a good friend. "Tell her Theodosia would like a quick word with her."

The girl looked slightly amused. "Tea shop Theodosia?"

"That's me."

"Angie's in her office. Hang on a minute while I go grab her."

Theodosia looked around at the lobby as she waited. There were comfy, cushy sofas and armchairs slipcovered in red and yellow chintz, handwoven fabric rugs, and a redbrick fireplace. In keeping with its namesake, the Featherbed House was chock-ablock full of plush geese, ceramic geese, carved geese, and metal geese. Geese were even embroidered on sofa cushions and a few stood guard in the form of four-foot-high sculptures. A myriad of watercolor paintings of geese in flight hung on the walls.

When Angie came out she looked worried but adorable. Curly blond hair cascaded onto her shoulders and she wore the same kind of peasant blouse as the receptionist, except hers was paired with a long, filmy beige skirt and sleek buff-colored leather cowboy boots. An Annie Oakley innkeeper.

"Theodosia," Angie said, her eyes wide and blue. "I heard about what happened on the movie set yesterday. It must have been awful."

"It was awful," Theodosia said. "Which is kind of why I'm here."

A small line inserted itself between Angie's brows. "A TV crew already stopped by."

"Because Craig Cole, the screenwriter, is staying here?"

Angie nodded. "Cole is here. I hear the rest of the crew is staying at the Saracen Inn."

"Here's the thing. I was hoping Cole might be in so I can ask him a few questions."

"You mean pick his brain?" Angie asked. "To see if he has any ideas about the murder?" Angie was well aware of Theodosia's skill at ferreting out clues and suspects.

"Something like that, yes."

"Well, I'm pretty sure Craig Cole is here since I just saw him go up to his room ten minutes ago."

"And what room might that be?"

Angie chuckled. "He's staying in our Honeymoon Suite."

Theodosia blinked. "Seriously? And Cole is the sole occupant?"

"To my knowledge he is. I guess Mr. Cole just wanted to spread out in the nicest suite we have." Angie grinned. "A soaking tub roomy enough for two, heated towel rack, vintage furniture, cozy window seat, and featherbed duvet."

"Complete with a turndown and mints on his pillow?"

"We've recently switched to miniature pralines. Our guests find them more authentically Southern," Angie said.

"And you say Cole is up there now?"

"I'm fairly sure he is. Probably tippy-typing away on his computer, working on one of his scripts."

"Or maybe a script revision," Theodosia said. She rapped her knuckles against the antique wooden reception desk and said, "I do believe I'll pay Mr. Cole a visit."

"Third floor," Angie said. "Room at the end of the hall."

Theodosia climbed two flights of stairs and walked down a

short hallway where cushy cinnamon-colored carpet whispered softly under her feet. She hesitated, then knocked on a door where two brass cherubs hovered above the stenciled words HONEYMOON SUITE.

Cole opened the door immediately. "What?" He had his cell phone in hand, as if he'd just gotten off an important call. He wore faded denim jeans, was barefoot, and wore a T-shirt that said WE'LL FIX IT IN POSTPRODUCTION.

Theodosia didn't waste any time. "Mr. Cole, I'm Theodosia Browning . . . I'm not sure you remember me or not . . ."

"Not," said Craig Cole. He stared at her blankly, as if she were the chambermaid there to deliver fresh towels.

"My tea sommelier, Drayton, and I are handling the craft services table for your movie shoot. And then, just yesterday, Josh Morro asked me to step in and read the tea leaves?"

"Oh sure." Cole gave an indifferent shrug. "I guess maybe I do remember you."

"Are you busy?" Theodosia leaned forward and peered into the room. It was empty. "May I come in for a few minutes?"

"I suppose so. But . . . why?"

"I'd like to ask you a few questions."

"About?"

"Josh Morro's murder."

"And your concern is what?"

"Let's just say I'm an interested party."

"Well, for heaven's sake, then we simply *must* talk," Cole said in a facetious tone of voice. But he opened the door, stepped back, and waved Theodosia in.

Theodosia's first impression confirmed that it was indeed a bridal suite and that the decor was maybe even a little over the top. A four-poster bed decorated with frilly heart-shaped pillows dominated the room. A fire crackled merrily in a white brick fireplace and there was a hot tub, certainly large enough for two, in the corner. The rest of the decor was romantic and slightly Victorian—a wing chair, beveled mirror, wall sconces, and a few statues of chubby Cupids cavorting here and there. There was also an antique spinet desk where a laptop computer sat alongside a messy stack of papers.

"Sit, please," Cole said, indicating a small overstuffed chair while he plunked himself down on the edge of the bed. "Now tell me again what you want, what you wanted to ask me?"

"Can you think of anyone who hated Josh Morro enough to kill him?"

Cole didn't waste any time in answering. "Sure can."

"And that would be . . . ?"

"Andrea Blair. She didn't just hate Morro, she *despised* him," Cole said with relish.

"Because Cole was constantly needling her?"

"That and mostly because Andrea had gotten a major offer to host a reality show but was already locked into this movie contract."

"I heard a rumor about the reality show, but you're saying she was actually going to *host* it?" Theodosia was surprised. The girl seemed so young, so inexperienced.

"This news was spread all over the *Hollywood Reporter*." Cole hesitated. "You read the *Hollywood Reporter*, don't you?"

Theodosia shook her head.

"Oh, well, permit me to enlighten you. It was a reality show with the working title *Camp Glamp* and the producers were salivating to get Andrea. They thought she'd be the perfect host— young, beautiful, chatty as all get-out, and a total Gen Z airhead."

"I'd have thought Morro would have *wanted* Andrea to accept that reality show role. Then he could work around her, shoot all her parts first, and be mercifully rid of her."

"I'm sure he did want her gone. Probably burned sage and offered up prayers to the gods of filmmaking."

"Who are?"

"I don't know," Cole said. "Probably Alfred Hitchcock and Francis Ford Coppola." He leaned forward. "But here's the stickler. Lewin Usher, our big pooh-bah executive producer, didn't want to let Andrea out of her contract, either, just in case there were rewrites or the shooting schedule ran longer than anticipated."

"Okay," Theodosia said. "I can understand that as a sound business practice." She hesitated. "Can you think of anyone else who might have wanted Josh Morro dead?"

"You want my honest opinion?" Cole asked. He leaned over, opened the top drawer of the nightstand, and pulled out a baggie full of grass and some rolling papers.

"Absolutely I do," Theodosia said. She wondered if Cole was trying to put her on or if he was really going to roll himself a joint.

Turned out he rolled himself a joint, quickly and rather expertly. Then he sparked up, took a hit, and offered Theodosia a toke.

"No thanks," she said.

Cole blew out a steady stream of smoke, cleared his throat, and said, in a tight voice, "It could have been the new director that's stepping in, Joe Adler."

"I've never even heard that name before," Theodosia said.

"You'll get an earful when you're on set tomorrow. Adler is a legend in his own mind. He's been waiting *dog years* for a chance to direct a feature film. Rumor has it he just finished a documentary down in Savannah, something about the Landmark District. Then, late yesterday, he got the call about Josh Morro's murder and was asked to step in to direct *Dark Fortunes*. Adler didn't hesitate, even negotiated his contract to get back end on the movie. You know, profit participation." Cole took a second toke, held his breath until his face turned brick red, then blew out. "Adler's quite the character. Larger than life you might say."

"So you're saying that Adler might have arranged to have Josh Morro killed just so he could take over the directing job?" It sounded a little improbable, a little too scripted.

Cole looked at her sideways. "Didn't you ever see that old movie *All About Eve?* With Bette Davis and Anne Baxter?"

"I have, but that was just a clever script, mostly pure conjecture."

"Honey, you don't know anything about the movie industry, do you?"

"I guess not."

"Everyone in Hollywood is all air-kissy and take-a-lunchy. But when push comes to shove, money and power always win out. Industry people will stab you in the back, step over your dead body, and never give it a second thought."

"If Hollywood is so terrible, why do people want to work there? Why do you work there?"

"For the glamour, darling, don't you know?" Cole said with a condescending smile. "If we couldn't eat at the Ivy or cruise down Sunset and hit clubs like Avalon or Drai's we'd be just like the rest of you people."

"Us people?" Theodosia was both amused and insulted.

Cole waved an index finger in front of her. "Just wait until you meet Joe Adler. He's such a profoundly arrogant snake in the grass that you'll understand how he earned his nickname."

"And what is that?" Theodosia asked.

Cole favored her with a self-satisfied smirk. "We call him the Puff Adler."

8

It was still early when Theodosia got home. So, after feeding Earl Grey, she changed into running clothes, snapped on his leash, and headed out the door.

The night was warm and fairly humid with a myriad of stars sparkling in an indigo blue sky. Theodosia ran down her own back alley, going slow, kind of warming up. She continued at that pace for another three blocks, then broke into an all-out sprint when she hit Queen Street. They pounded along, blowing out the carbon, reveling in their pace. They breezed down Chalmers Street past the Pink House, the second-oldest residence in Charleston. It had started out as a tavern, then became a law office, housed a graphic arts firm, and was now an art gallery. They hooked a turn down Cumberland, then slowed when they came to Philadelphia Alley.

A three-hundred-year-old city, Charleston was famous for its picturesque alleys and hidden walkways. Some of them included Stoll's Alley, Longitude Lane, Price's Alley, and even St. Michael's Alley. But Philadelphia Alley was one of Theodosia's favorites. For one thing it had long ago been dubbed Dueler's Alley, the name lending a certain *frisson* of danger, since duels had actually been fought and blood spilled there. Now, Theodosia and Earl Grey walked down this secret passageway with its cobblestones, overgrown shrubbery, and hidden back doors to any number of homes. It was hard not to feel the great weight of history here, especially since the brick wall on Philadelphia Alley's western side flanked St. Philip's Church and graveyard, one of the oldest churches and cemeteries (that was definitely haunted!) in the City of Charleston.

Emerging onto Queen Street, with its antique shops, galleries, and restaurants, Theodosia turned for home. One block east and she was deep in a residential area again, where darkness and wrought-iron fences protected homes as if they were tiny principalities, and drifting fog lent an ethereal feel to the already atmospheric environs.

As Theodosia and Earl Grey walked down their own alley, closing in on home, Theodosia saw that someone had parked a car near her back gate. She glanced at the Granville Mansion and saw lights on. Probably the culprit. Robert Steele, the man who owned the mansion, was still in London, and he'd had a long string of short-term renters. Actually, they were probably well-heeled renters because that monstrosity of a place couldn't be cheap.

As she drew closer to the property, she saw that the garage door was up and a faint light was on. Then a shadow crept across the inside wall and disappeared before she could speak to . . . whoever.

No matter. Theodosia and Earl Grey disappeared into their own yard. They checked out the little fish pond with its newly installed bubbler and newly purchased fish, then went inside, both craving a late-night snack. While Earl Grey munched a chew bone, Theodosia had a fruit salad and a piece of Swiss cheese.

Then, with windows locked and doors double-checked, they went upstairs for the evening.

When Theodosia had first moved in, she'd designed a kind of bedroom / reading room / walk-in-closet suite. Laura Ashley wallpaper graced the walls and the matching bedspread covered her four-poster bed. The tower room held a comfy reading chair and footstool and a bookcase jammed with books. Her mother's antique vanity featured a round mirror and a half dozen drawers, and was strewn with Dior and Chanel perfume bottles, Le Labo moisturizer, an upside-down abalone shell that held necklaces and pearl earrings, and a leather-bound journal with her dad's Montblanc pen.

While Earl Grey settled in his overpriced L.L.Bean bed, Theodosia peeled off her running gear and went into the bathroom to take a nice hot shower.

The phone was ringing as she stepped out of the shower.

Has to be Riley.

Theodosia snatched her phone up and said, "How was your talk?" She'd been kidding Riley about delivering a TED Talk instead of a seminar on protocols for firearms recovery.

"Great, it went great," Riley said. "A willing audience and no hiccups with the AV equipment, which was a total blessing."

"When will you be home?"

Theodosia could detect a smile in his voice as Riley said, "Is tomorrow too soon?"

"Not soon enough," Theodosia told him.

"I've got an early flight so I'll probably hit town midmorning and head into work. Apparently, Tidwell's got a new assignment for me."

"Something interesting?"

"Nothing as exciting as working a murder case," Riley said.

Theodosia held her breath, wondering if he was going to say something about the Morro murder.

Instead, Riley said, "Listen, once I get back we need to sit down and plan our trip to Savannah."

"Agreed," Theodosia said.

"Did we settle on staying at Planters Inn?"

"Talked about it, but didn't make a reservation. I've been looking online and the River Street Inn looks good, too. It's right on the waterfront."

"Then let's stay there."

"Also there's this really cool Victorian in the Historic District, Roussell's Garden Bed and Breakfast."

"Sure, that's good, too," Riley said.

"Then there's the Hamilton-Turner Inn. It's expensive but it's four-star. Also more centrally located since I know you want to do some exploring."

"Seems to me you're the one who's all hot to visit Bonaventure Cemetery."

"Me?" Theodosia tried to sound innocent.

"Even though I know you've been there before."

"What can I say? Ever since I read *Midnight in the Garden of Good and Evil* I've been hooked." She paused. "So you'll be back tomorrow."

"For sure."

"Come for dinner tomorrow night? At my place?"

"I thought you'd never ask."

"Good. Great," Theodosia said. They talked for a few minutes more, then said goodbye and hung up. Theodosia yawned, turned off the lamp, snuggled down in her four-poster bed, and went to sleep with a smile on her face.

9

❧

Wednesday morning found Theodosia back on the set of *Dark Fortunes* along with the same crew and a brand-new director, Joe Adler. As she hurriedly arranged cranberry muffins, double-chocolate scones, coffee cake, and the rest of her goodies, she was aware that Adler seemed very businesslike, shouting out explicit orders to everyone in the crew. But in a good way, a kind of let's-rally-the-troops way. Adler also spoke with the actors and actresses individually, talked with Ted Juniper, the lighting director, and even bent his head down for a confab with script-writer Craig Cole, who looked a little sullen.

Theodosia watched the two of them interact and wondered—might Cole really have had an axe to grind with Josh Morro? Was he sick of having his script belittled in front of everyone? Better yet, how extensive was his knowledge when it came to wiring and electricity? Last night, when she'd talked to him, Cole had come across straightforward and slightly amusing. Or maybe that was because he'd been semi-stoned?

Just before they were about to begin shooting, while props

were still being moved around on the set, Adler came over and spoke to Theodosia. He was tall with a narrow, inquisitive face and hair pulled back in a man bun. He wore a cashmere sweater, purposely ripped jeans, and loafers without socks.

"I understand we're going to be neighbors," Adler said as he helped himself to a piece of cinnamon coffee cake.

"Excuse me?" Theodosia drew back. What did he mean by that? Neighbors?

Adler hastily explained. "I'm moving into the house right next to yours. You know, the Granville Mansion."

"How on earth . . ." It didn't happen often but Theodosia was suddenly at a loss for words. She thought about the shadow she'd seen last night. Must have been him. "So you've moved in already?"

"Mmn," Adler said, chewing. "I'm planning to do that tonight."

Theodosia expressed more surprise. "Not until then. Because I'm fairly sure I saw someone moving around in the garage last night."

Adler shrugged. "Must have been my real estate agent." He took another bite. "Say, this is really terrific coffee cake."

"Thank you," she said.

"The thing of it is," Adler continued, "Charleston is apparently in the throes of a housing boom. Or should I say a not-enough-housing boom. Rentals are full, short-term rentals are nonexistent. And a hotel . . . well, who in their right mind wants to live out of a suitcase?"

"Unthinkable," Theodosia said.

"Anyway, when I rented that big place my real estate agent told me I'd be living right next door to the tea shop lady who's also handling our craft services table. And here you are." Adler favored her with a bright smile. He popped the last of his coffee cake into his mouth and said, "Lovely to meet you, but now I'd better get to work. Show 'em who's boss."

Ten minutes later, Beth Ann came hurrying in to take over the craft services table from Theodosia. She was carrying a wicker basket filled with fresh-baked lemon poppy-seed scones.

"Oh," Beth Ann exclaimed. "You've got the table all set up."

"Don't sound so disappointed," Theodosia said with a smile. "Trust me, this food won't last long. Actors and crew members will be stopping by all day, keeping you ferociously busy. I think half of them have hollow legs."

"Thanks for the warning," Beth Ann said.

"Here," Theodosia said, pushing a plate of brownie bites aside to make room for the scones. "We'll wedge your scones in here."

While she was talking, Theodosia was slowly aware of a man watching her from across the room. He was tall, lanky, and dressed like a cowboy—or a reasonable facsimile anyway—wearing a denim shirt with pearl buttons, jeans, boots, and a battered cowboy hat.

"There's a man . . ." Theodosia began.

"Staring right at you," Beth Ann said. "From across the room. I noticed. And I have to say, he certainly looks interested. He's been kind of giving you the side-eye for the last couple of minutes."

But when Theodosia went over to talk to the man—perhaps they actually knew each other?—he'd somehow disappeared from the set and Joe Adler was shouting out last-minute instructions and calling for absolute quiet on the set.

Which was Theodosia's cue to duck out of the way and head down the hallway. Halfway between the set and the makeup room, she ran smack-dab into Andrea Blair. She'd just had her hair poufed and her makeup airbrushed, but still looked grumpy and unhappy, as if she'd woken up on the wrong side of the bed.

Today Andrea was costumed in a cream-colored floor-length gown that could've been a snappy nightgown or a casual ball gown, if there was such a thing.

"Andrea," Theodosia said. "Do you have a minute to talk?"

Andrea turned toward Theodosia and, with lids half lowered, said, "Excuse me, but I'm due on set. Also, my name is actually pronounced Ahn-dray-ah."

"Andrea," Theodosia said, pronouncing the name correctly. Then, because Andrea still wore the expression of a petulant teenager, asked, "Is something wrong?"

"This new director," Andrea said, jerking her nose in the air. "He's supposed to be a total jerk."

"Seems to me you didn't get along all that well with the previous director, either."

Andrea gave a nonchalant check of her manicure. "Whatever."

"How do you know you won't get along with Joe Adler if you've never worked with him?"

"I've heard all the rumors and none of them are favorable."

Theodosia figured this was as good a time as any to toss a few questions at Andrea. "Speaking of rumors . . . what kind of scuttlebutt have you been hearing on set? About what happened to Josh Morro? About who might have been responsible?"

Andrea raised a single eyebrow. "You really want my opinion? Because nobody else around here does."

"Of course I do," Theodosia said.

Now Andrea wore a coy expression. "The talk on set, or should I say, the nasty innuendos, point to Big Red."

"Excuse me?"

"You know, Craig Cole."

Interesting, Theodosia thought. Since last night Cole had pointed his finger directly at Andrea.

"Why do people think that Cole might have had a hand in Morro's murder?" Theodosia asked.

"Because Cole's a crazy doper who thinks he's God's gift to screenwriting," Andrea said. "But Morro always saw Cole for what he really is—a mediocre hack." She gave a wicked smile, really getting into her trash-talking now. "Morro always said that Cole would be stuck in limbo writing B-movie scripts or assigned to some obscure writer's pool where he'd have to crank out screen adaptations."

"But what do *you* think?" Theodosia said. "Truth be told, I'm very interested in hearing your candid opinion. More so than rumors and innuendos."

Andrea frowned, once again looking annoyed. "Everybody here thinks I'm just a dumb blonde, but I see things. I know what goes on around here."

"That sounds awfully cryptic," Theodosia said. "As if you have a few ideas that don't coincide with what everyone here thinks—or even what the police think."

"That's me," Andrea said. "An independent thinker."

"Care to share your ideas with me?"

Andrea stared at her. "Maybe," she said slowly. She glanced down the hallway to where Joe Adler was now standing, gesturing for her to hurry up and take her place on set. "But not right now," she whispered. "And certainly not here."

Theodosia stood there as Andrea hustled away, thinking about the dope angle. Cole *could* be a crazy doper. Or maybe even a drug dealer. What if Josh Morro had found out that Cole was involved in some kind of drug deal and Cole had killed Morro to shut him up? But where was the evidence? So far, Theodosia hadn't found anything that pointed in that direction. After all, smoking a single joint wasn't exactly a druggie crime spree.

She sighed, deciding she'd better hurry back to the Indigo Tea Shop so she could help set up for today's Poetry Tea. She'd just reached the back door when, out of the blue, her curiosity gene kicked in big-time and she was seized with a daring idea.

Should I?

Theodosia continued down the hallway, peering into rooms that were shabbily furnished and would probably serve as sets for additional scenes, until she came to what had to be the back stairs, probably the old servants' stairway. Putting a hand on the ancient banister, she looked around quickly, then started up.

Why am I doing this?

Theodosia didn't have a good, solid answer. Perhaps because she was curious? About the old house and about what had happened on the third floor? Or maybe snooping satisfied some kind of itch she had.

Okay, that could be it.

As Theodosia explored the second floor, she found it was just as dingy as the first floor and jam-packed with props and gear. Here were rooms with racks of costumes, extra klieg lights, and boxes of camera cables and cords.

Is there a spool of wire? Or a stack of metal folding chairs?

Nary a spool nor a chair jumped out at her, but that didn't mean they weren't there. But time was running short—somebody would surely come upstairs and catch her snooping—so she had a decision to make. Bail out or continue on up.

The decision was easy. Theodosia walked back to the stairs and continued up. Halfway there, the stairs took a sharp left turn and narrowed considerably. And they creaked. Old wood that had endured more than a century and a half of heat, cold, and industrial-strength humidity suddenly felt flimsy and unstable beneath her feet. Would it hold her? She shook her head to dispel any nasty thoughts and continued her climb to the third floor.

And that's when Theodosia started to get cold feet.

No, I'm not. Well, maybe a little.

Summoning her inner reserve, she reached a hand out to touch the old-fashioned glass doorknob attached to an ugly green door with peeling paint. She was ginning up the nerve to open the door that led to . . . what?

She hesitated.

Would she be stepping into the old servants' quarters with narrow rooms crowded with old metal-frame beds? Or the room where that poor woman had been held prisoner for so long?

Theodosia swallowed hard. And as her fingers closed around the doorknob, a sudden cool breeze wafted past her. It caressed her cheek, gently lifted her hair, and scared her to death. It was almost as if some unknown being had let out a long, deep sigh.

A warning?

Theodosia didn't believe in ghosts, didn't normally believe in haunted houses, either, but this was a little too eerie, a little too spooky even for her.

Deciding a full stop was in order, she turned and hurried back downstairs, anxious to be among the living, even if they did tend to grumble and argue among themselves.

Like Sidney Gorsk, Andrea's agent, whom she found sitting in a chair in the hair and makeup room. He was in the middle of a semi-rant about politics when his eyes suddenly landed on Theodosia. He stopped mid-sentence, looking slightly embarrassed at being caught shooting off his mouth while having his hair fluffed and his face moisturized.

"Hey there, Theodosia," Brittany, the head makeup artist, called out. "What brings you back to my lair? Did you score another part in our movie?"

Theodosia let loose a nervous chuckle. "The one I did with Andrea on Monday was enough for me. I think it might have been the swan song of my career."

"To Josh Morro's career, too," Brittany said under her breath.

"But you did a fine job," Gorsk put in, ignoring Brittany's remark and looking interested. "Andrea said you did good. *Enthusiastic* was her word for it."

"Kind of her to say," Theodosia said. "Considering the circumstances."

Gorsk bounced out of the chair and said, "Have a seat, Miss Browning. Your turn."

"Sure," Brittany put in. "Let me tame those brows again with a little gel."

"If it's not too much trouble," Theodosia said. Truth be told, she loved the idea of a quick touch-up.

"No trouble," Brittany said as Theodosia climbed into the chair, while Gorsk leaned in the doorway to watch.

"How's it going on set?" Theodosia asked Gorsk. "With the new director."

"I must say I'm pleased," Gorsk said, jingling the change in his pants pocket. "I don't believe they've missed a single step."

Except for Josh Morro getting killed, which shut down almost two days of shooting, Theodosia thought.

"I think that new director is kind of cute," Brittany said. "In an intense, bad boy kind of way."

"By the way, do either of you know who the guy in the cowboy shirt is?" Theodosia asked. "He seems to be new on set as well."

"That's Joe Adler's personal assistant," Gorsk said. "He's supposedly from New Orleans."

"A director needs a personal assistant?" Theodosia said as Brittany worked on her.

"It's an industry thing," Sidney Gorsk explained. "A kind of status symbol that tells people you're an important guy, that you've made it in showbiz."

"I heard that Adler and the cowboy are good friends that go way back," Brittany added.

"Interesting," Theodosia said. Then, nonchalantly, "Are the police still talking to the cast and crew? Asking questions?"

Brittany and Gorsk exchanged glances.

"What?" Theodosia said.

"An investigator stopped by first thing this morning to ask Craig Cole a few more questions," Brittany said.

"Is Cole a suspect?" Theodosia asked.

"I wouldn't be surprised," Gorsk said under his breath.

"There, all finished," Brittany announced, patting Theodosia's shoulder and handing her a small hand mirror.

"Wonderful. I love it," Theodosia said, gazing at her perfectly arched brows. "You're a genius."

"And it looks like I've got more customers," Brittany said as two more actors pushed their way into the room.

Theodosia followed Gorsk out into the hallway.

Gorsk gave her a meaningful look, lowered his voice, and said, "I think any concern about Craig Cole may be justified."

"Why do you say that?"

"Just the fact that Cole and Morro famously didn't get along. I also think Morro tried to block a deal that Cole was trying to get going with a new screenplay."

"What kind of deal?" Theodosia asked.

"Cole's written some potboiler called *Devious Women* and was pitching it to FOX as well as that new streaming service, Plum Tree. Plum Tree especially is desperate for content. But rumor tells me Morro tried to torpedo it."

"Why would he do that?"

"Spite?" Gorsk said. "Professional jealousy? Or maybe Morro was pitching something himself and Cole was in his way. There's no telling what goes on in the minds of these creative types. They all think they're natural-born geniuses."

"I'm beginning to see that."

"When the truth of the matter is they're all just bit players in an industry that doesn't much care about them in the long run," Gorsk said. "Hollywood eats 'em up then spits 'em out."

As they stepped back to let two crew members carry an unwieldy cardboard fireplace past them, Theodosia said, "What do you know about something called a completion guaranty?"

Gorsk stared at her. "Nothing. Why?"

"Just a random thought I had."

10

✿

"Hey," Haley cried out the minute Theodosia walked in the back door of the tea shop. "Riley just called."

"His plane landed?" She was pleasantly surprised.

"Uh-huh, and he asked me to pass on a special request."

"Which is?"

"He's asking—hoping, really—that you'll make lemon chicken for dinner tonight." Haley paused. "Want my recipe?"

"By all means."

"Actually, I have two recipes," Haley said. "You want the straightforward easy one or the tricky one with yogurt?"

"I think straightforward and easy will work just fine."

"Gotcha," Haley said.

"Is Miss Dimple here?"

Haley gave a quick nod as she added chopped onions and halibut fillets for her seafood casserole. "Out in the tea shop."

Miss Dimple was indeed out in the tea shop, pouring tea, running orders to Drayton and Haley, and doing a bang-up job.

"You're back," Drayton said as Theodosia approached the

front counter. He consulted his watch, an ancient Patek Philippe that ran a few minutes slow, and added, "With time to spare." He tapped his watch face. "I think."

"And I have news," Theodosia said.

"Do tell."

"A couple of things. First, I paid a visit to that screenwriter Craig Cole last night at the Featherbed House." Theodosia paused. "Where he was holed up in the Honeymoon Suite."

Drayton's brows rose. "Honeymooning all by his lonesome?"

"Apparently so. Anyway, I took it upon myself to ask him a few questions about the murder."

"And what did Mr. Cole have to say for himself? Or did he clam up?"

"Not at all. Cole pointed his finger directly at Andrea Blair."

"He thinks *she's* the killer? That mousy little actress?"

"Not so mousy. I had a short conversation with Andrea this morning and she's totally convinced that *Cole* was the killer. Her agent, Sidney Gorsk, seems to lean that way as well."

"Strange that Cole is accusing Andrea and vice versa."

"I'm guessing they dislike each other intensely," Theodosia said.

"Sounds that way." He paused. "But wasn't Andrea on set when the murder occurred?"

"Sure, but she could have had help. A coconspirator."

Drayton poured hot water over Assam tea leaves and placed the lid on his teapot so it could steep. "What do *you* think?"

"I don't think anything yet. I was only on set for forty minutes this morning, just long enough to set up our table, meet the new director, and ask a few questions."

"I'm amazed at how fast they replaced Josh Morro," Drayton said.

"I guess Joe Adler was waiting in the wings for his big chance."

"Does that strike you as strange?"

"A little bit. But I have to admit, Adler seems to know what he's doing. There was a little more snap-to on the set this morning."

"But you haven't seen him in action," Drayton said. "Haven't seen him actually direct a scene."

"No, I suppose that could prove to be another story. Then again, the movie really isn't our problem. So I think . . ."

The telephone rang, prompting Drayton to hold up a finger, then grab the receiver. Theodosia figured it was someone calling for a last-minute reservation—that often happened—but Drayton listened intently for a few moments, then suddenly lit up like a Christmas tree.

"Yes, yes, yes," he said, nodding his head in time to the beat. "That would work perfectly for us. In fact, it would be an honor. All right, we'll be ready. See you soon. Looking forward to it, actually!" Then he hung up, looking nervous but excited.

"What?" Theodosia asked. "You're acting as if you just won the lottery."

Drayton pulled himself up to his full height and gave her a cat-who-ate-the-canary smile. "Actually, we kind of did."

"What are you talking about?"

"That call was from *Tea Faire Magazine*." Drayton was practically breathless with excitement. "Willis Conklin, one of their feature writers, wants to come by and review our tea shop."

"Dear Lord, when?"

"Friday. For lunch."

"*This* Friday?" Theodosia cried. She was ready to hit the panic button. "No, that's our *Breakfast at Tiffany's* Tea! We can't possibly be ready!"

"We *have* to be ready," Drayton said. "I told Mr. Conklin he'd be most welcome. And, believe me, he's all atwitter to meet *you*."

"Gulp."

Drayton was fairly bursting with pride. "This is it, Theo, our big break. If Conklin loves us, then . . . well, his readers will, too. Just think, we'll be written up and our photos will be featured in *Tea Faire Magazine*."

"Exciting," she said with tempered enthusiasm.

But Drayton was still over the moon. "I'd say it's positively thrilling!"

"What? What?" Miss Dimple asked as she came over to grab a pot of English breakfast tea that was steeping.

"We have a writer from *Tea Faire Magazine* coming on Friday," Drayton said. "To take pictures and do an article on us."

"That's your *Breakfast at Tiffany's* Tea," Miss Dimple pointed out.

"Exactly," Drayton said. He spun around to peer at his floor-to-ceiling shelves of tea. "Oh my, this visit calls for a very special blend. I've got to entirely rethink my tea repertoire."

"Looks like Drayton's having a moment," Miss Dimple remarked.

"Looks like we're going to need your help on Friday," Theodosia said.

"No problem, you know I'm always happy to come in and help serve," Miss Dimple said. She struck a coquettish pose. "Since it's your *Breakfast at Tiffany's* Tea, shall I wear my black cocktail dress and pearls?"

"You know," Theodosia said, "that's a really terrific idea."

The two of them got busy then, setting up for their Poetry Tea. Theodosia had already selected their Wedgewood Wild Strawberry china, and while Miss Dimple pulled plates, cups, and saucers out of the highboy, Theodosia had printed out poems by Emily Dickinson, Robert Frost, and Walt Whitman onto pink, blue, and peach place mats and now those went on the tables. They were followed by the china as well as vases of shaggy white Gerber daisies. Theodosia added ceramic busts of Keats, Shakespeare, and Robert Burns that she'd borrowed from a friend who ran a museum-type store, then placed stacks of poetry books, borrowed from Lois at Antiquarian Books, on each table. At each place setting she arranged feathered pens and tiny gold notebooks as favors for her guests. Finally, dozens of small white candles were placed on the tables and lit, and overhead lights were turned way down.

Finished with their decorating, Theodosia and Miss Dimple stood back and gave their handiwork the once-over.

"Looks good," Theodosia said.

"Very romantic," Miss Dimple said. She reached out and picked up a book from the top of a stack. "Look at this," she said in hushed tones. "Emily Dickinson, one of my favorite poets."

At ten to twelve, their guests began to arrive. Brooke Carter Crocket, the owner of Hearts Desire Jewelry, and Susan Monday, owner of Lavender and Lace, came in. Then some of their regulars, which included Jill, Kristen, Allie, Linda, Jessica, and Joy, piled in. And Judi Cooper and two of her friends had driven all the way from Savannah.

Then Leigh Carroll, the entrepreneurial Black owner of the neighboring Cabbage Patch Gift Shop, showed up with her friends Tenesha and Kimberly.

"Girlfriend," Leigh said. "Your tea room is drop-dead gorgeous. What did you *do?*"

Theodosia grinned. "Turned down the lights?"

"Oh no, you did more than that. You always do. Say, when are we going to do a tea luncheon together?"

"Whenever you want, dear friend."

When everyone with a reservation was seated, when two late-comers without reservations arrived and were gently wedged in, Theodosia walked to the center of the room. This was the part she loved; this was also the part she feared, because you really never knew how a new tea event would be received. And job number one for her—for all of them—was to please and enchant their guests.

Turns out Theodosia didn't have a thing to worry about. She'd barely said, "Welcome to our first ever Poetry Tea," when she was met with warm smiles and a spatter of applause.

Heart thumping, palms tingling, she smiled back at her guests (never let them see you sweat!) and finished the welcoming words she'd prepared.

"This is an event tea we talked about at length, but never hosted before," Theodosia said. "Now we're fortunate to have all of you lovely people gathered here to celebrate some of the world's great poets. As such, we've also created a fairly inventive luncheon menu as an homage to all their wonderfully crafted words. As Robert Frost once said, 'Poetry is when an emotion has found its thought and the thought has found words.'"

Then, with all eyes still upon her, Theodosia said, "And now for a rundown of our menu, which really is a kind of tongue-in-cheek ode to some of our best and brightest poets." There was more applause and then she said, "First course today will be Oscar Wilde Berry Scones."

As laughter rang out followed by more applause, Theodosia continued. "Which will be followed by our Shakespeare Salad paired with T. S. Eliot Tea Bread."

Now she had her guests in the palm of her hand.

"Our hot entrée is William Blake Seafood Bake, a delicious casserole rife with halibut, scallops, shrimp, and white wine. And for dessert we'll be serving Elizabeth Barrett Brownies and Ezra Pound Cake."

"I love it," one woman cried out.

"So creative," another cried.

"But tell us about the tea," a third woman shouted.

"Drayton," Theodosia said, waving a hand and stepping aside. "That would be you."

Drayton, dressed in his pin-striped jacket and cream-colored slacks, stepped to the middle of the tea shop and posed like he was about to conduct an orchestra. "We'll be pouring two of our custom house-blended teas today," he said. "Our Lewis Carroll Chamomile and our Emily Dickinson Darjeeling."

That pretty much brought the house down and kicked the luncheon into high gear. Theodosia and Miss Dimple served the scones along with Devonshire cream and lemon curd, while Drayton made the rounds with a teapot in each hand. The salad was served and enjoyed by all, and when the entrée was ready, Theodosia, Haley, and Miss Dimple ferried it out in individual steaming ramekins.

A few of the guests requested special teas—one woman wanted a pot of Formosa oolong, another table asked for Russian Caravan—so that kept Drayton happy and hopping.

As dessert was being served, Theodosia and Drayton stepped to the center of the room again.

"I know you've all had time to peruse some of the poetry books stacked on your tables," Theodosia said. "Now Drayton and I would like to share a couple of our favorite quotes about tea." She ducked her head and said, "Drayton?"

Drayton looked around the tea room with a warm smile. "I think the American essayist Ralph Waldo Emerson was definitely on to something when he said 'Some people will tell you there is a great deal of poetry and fine sentiment in a chest of tea.'"

"And the English novelist Jane Austen summed it up brilliantly," Theodosia added, "when she said 'But indeed, I would rather have nothing but tea.'"

"And one more," Drayton said. "The novelist and critic Henry James was quoted as saying 'There are few hours in life more agreeable than the hour dedicated to the ceremony known as afternoon tea.'"

There was silence for a few moments, then applause broke out.

"I think they liked it," Theodosia whispered to Miss Dimple, who was also clapping with gusto. "Especially when Drayton speaks."

"He's got that rich orator's voice," Miss Dimple said, wiping a tear from her eye. "I think he could sell crushed ice to the devil himself."

"It's from all the work he does at the Heritage Society," Theodosia said. "Drayton's not just a board member, he very often conducts lectures and seminars."

But the tea didn't end there. Even though two or three people took off after the dessert course, most remained to linger and talk over a final cup of tea. And shop.

Because it was no coincidence that Theodosia had recently stocked the Indigo Tea Shop with all sorts of goodies. There were tea cozies, jars of honey, tins of tea, honey sticks, cups and saucers, Yixing teapots, tea caddies, mugs, and sets of small celadon cups. Theodosia's own line of T-Bath products was available, including Chamomile Mist, Sweet Tea Feet Treat, and Honey Jasmine Scrub.

Theodosia was inundated with questions as she cashed people out and wrapped purchases in their trademark indigo blue tissue paper. She'd just gift wrapped a small red glazed teapot and popped it into a blue bag when Drayton nudged her in the ribs and said, "Who invited that fellow? Have we interjected some sort of Western theme that I don't know about?"

Startled, Theodosia looked up to see the cowboy staring at her, a curious expression on his face.

11

Theodosia hurried over to greet the cowboy. "Excuse me, is there a problem?" she asked. She was suddenly worried that Beth Ann had run out of food or had made a misstep and was in some sort of trouble.

"Kinda dark in here," was the cowboy's laconic reply.

"Moody," responded Theodosia. "Now if you'd please tell me what . . ."

"You were at Brittlebank Manor this morning," the cowboy said, interrupting her. He hitched his thumbs in his belt and gave Theodosia an inquisitive look.

"That's right," she said. The cowboy wasn't acting as if something terrible had happened. So maybe this was supposed to be a friendly visit? But why? For what purpose?

"My name's Quaid Barthel and I'm a personal assistant for Mr. Adler, the director?"

"Yes, yes."

"The thing is, Mr. Adler is absolutely crazy about your cinnamon coffee cake." Quaid dipped his head as if he were slightly embarrassed now. "So he sent me over here to pick up another pan."

Theodosia let out a breath. Not a problem per se, just a director with a sweet tooth.

"I'm sorry, but we don't have any more coffee cake. This morning I brought two pans of it for the craft services table, so that was pretty much it. That's all we baked." Theodosia made a kind of helpless gesture with her hands. "And right now, as you can probably see, I've got my hands full."

Quaid Barthel leaned around Theodosia to inspect the tea room. "Looks like a full house. You having some kind of tea party?"

"An event tea. A Poetry Tea."

"Huh. Never heard of such a thing. I guess women like a fancy tea?"

"For the most part, yes they do."

When Quaid made no move to leave, Theodosia reached up, put a hand on his shoulder, and tried to spin him in the direction of the front door. He was your basic large, immovable object, but she was finally able to get him headed in the right direction. Which was back out the door.

"Tell Mr. Adler that we'll be sure to bring an extra pan of cinnamon coffee cake tomorrow morning, okay? One reserved just for him."

Quaid turned and touched his hand to his cowboy hat in a kind of salute. "Will do."

Theodosia hurried back to the counter, where lots more customers had lined up. More teacups and tea tins were hurriedly wrapped while Drayton gave explicit directions on steeping times.

One guest, Cordelia Sadler, who chaired the Friends of the Opera Society, wiggled a finger at Theodosia.

"Yes?" Theodosia said, leaning forward.

"Have you ever catered a Mad Hatter Tea?" Cordelia asked. Known to her friends as Cricket, she was petite with a frizzle of dark brown hair, and was dressed in a peach-colored tweed jacket and matching skirt. Both wrists clanked with real-deal fourteen-karat-gold bracelets.

"Not yet."

"Would you like to?" Cricket asked with a twinkle in her eye.

"What exactly did you have in mind?" Theodosia asked, more than a little intrigued.

"The Friends of the Opera plan to host a black-tie charity ball, a fundraiser for the Opera Society, and we'd like to do something a little out of the ordinary. Our initial thoughts were of a Mad Hatter Tea, but a truly elegant affair held outdoors, in the evening, by candlelight, with actors dressed up as the Red Queen, the Mad Hatter, and, of course, the White Rabbit."

"I not only adore your idea," Theodosia said, "but please believe me when I say I desperately want to work with you on this."

"Come to our planning meeting next week?" Cricket asked.

"Count on it!"

Twenty minutes later, the Poetry Tea was all over except for the cleanup.

"The thing to do now is move," Drayton said as the lights were turned back up to full power and they surveyed the detritus in the tea room. Candles had guttered down in their holders; dirty dishes and crumpled napkins were strewn across tables. "Let's leave this to chance and see if we can find a pristine new location."

"Nonsense," Miss Dimple said. "We can have this place picked up and set right in a heartbeat."

"Maybe one of yours but certainly not mine," Drayton said.

But Miss Dimple was as good as her word. She stacked the dirty plates, teacups, and saucers in blue plastic tubs, carried them into the kitchen, then came back for more.

"She's an Energizer Bunny," Drayton remarked as he collected his teapots.

"She's priceless," Theodosia said, as she pitched in to help Miss Dimple clear the tables.

Which was a good thing because five minutes later, Helene Deveroux walked in with Lewin Usher, the executive producer, on her arm.

"Is it too late for tea?" Helene asked as she looked around the tea shop expectantly. She was dressed in distressed blue jeans that had probably been hand-slashed by a famous designer and a form-fitting jean jacket covered in seed pearls.

"You just missed the tail end of our Poetry Tea by about forty-five minutes," Drayton said.

"A what?" Usher said. Today he wore a seersucker suit with a pink shirt and tie that perfectly matched his face.

His inquisitive look told Theodosia that he was interested, so she quickly explained the workings to him.

"That sounds wonderful," Usher exclaimed. "Poetry and tea. How very creative and symbiotic."

"It's just one of many event teas that we host," Theodosia said.

"What are some of the others?" Helene asked.

"Oh, we've done Mystery Teas, Victorian Teas, Chocolate Teas, Lavender Teas, Glam Girl Teas, and Pretty in Pink Teas," Theodosia said. "You name it, we've probably done it or are planning to do it."

"This Friday we're hosting a *Breakfast at Tiffany's* Tea," Drayton put in.

"How about just regular afternoon tea?" Usher asked. His eyes flicked over to the glass pie saver that sat on the counter. It was stacked with scones.

"That we can manage," Drayton called from behind the counter. "Can I interest the two of you in a pot of orchid plum tea? I just now brewed it fresh."

"And scones?" Theodosia added.

"Sounds right," Usher said.

"You have your choice of wild berry scones or butterscotch scones," Theodosia said.

"Wild berry," Helene and Usher chimed in together.

"Please have a seat and I'll be right back," Theodosia promised. She went into the kitchen, plated the scones, grabbed small containers of Devonshire cream and raspberry jam, and headed back out. When she returned, Drayton was pouring their tea.

"Here you go," Theodosia said as she set the scones in front of them. "Enjoy." Then, because she was curious as to whether they'd learned anything more about the murder, said, "Have there been any new developments in the Josh Morro case?"

"We've not heard a thing," Helene said.

"The police are playing it pretty close to the vest," Usher said. "Detective Tidwell has been interviewing everyone in the cast and crew, giving them the third degree, but not yet sharing any conclusions with us."

"Are there conclusions?" Drayton asked. He was listening in on the conversation as well.

"Not yet, though we do have our own suspicions," Helene said.

"Is that so?" Theodosia said. Maybe she could learn something more here. Helene and Lewin Usher were probably much closer to this case than she was.

"I hate to say this, but we've had our eye on Ted Juniper, the lighting guy," Usher said.

"Why would a lighting guy want to kill his director?" Theodosia asked. She remembered Juniper as being almost inconsolable after Morro's death.

Usher squinted at her. "You haven't heard the story, have you?"

"Apparently not," Theodosia said.

Lewin cleared his throat. "Back in L.A., Ted Juniper was involved in a hit-and-run accident. On the 101 Freeway just outside Studio City. The driver of the other car was killed."

"And how does this involve Morro?" Theodosia asked.

"Morro lent money to Juniper so he could hire a really good defense lawyer. You see, Juniper was driving under the influence when the accident occurred," Usher said.

"And the case was settled?" Theodosia asked.

"Sure, but it still cost a small fortune," Usher said.

"If I read this right, I'm guessing that Ted Juniper still hadn't repaid the money that Josh Morro loaned him," Theodosia said as she slowly put the pieces together.

"That's exactly right," Usher said. "And now, with Morro dead, Juniper probably doesn't feel the need for any reimbursement. Not even to Morro's estate."

"Is there an estate?" Drayton asked.

"I don't know. I assume there is," Usher said.

"So Juniper had motive," Theodosia said. She mulled this information over for a few moments, then asked, "Does Juniper still drink?"

Usher bobbed his head. "Like a fish."

"Oh no," Drayton said. He gazed at Theodosia, and as their eyes met, she detected a fair amount of concern.

"I guess desperate people do desperate things," Helene said.

"People have been known to hold up convenience stores for

twenty bucks," Usher added. "And these days, with crime on the rise . . . well, you never know what can happen."

Helene stared at Usher with rapt attention. "You really never know," she echoed. Then she took a quick sip of tea and said, "But let's not worry about that sordid business right now. Because this scone is utterly delicious and this tea is . . . what did you call it, Drayton?"

"This is orchid plum tea," Drayton said.

"It's really excellent," Usher said.

"Anyway, the movie's back on track?" Theodosia asked. The few facts she'd learned about Ted Juniper were enlightening, enough so that she decided to speak to Juniper herself.

"The movie's going gangbusters," Usher said, a note of pride in his voice. "I was on set for a while today and it was remarkably calm and well organized. We're lucky we were able to get Joe Adler to step in so quickly."

"From bumpy seas to smooth sailing," Helene said. "Which will no doubt please my fellow members of the Charleston Film Board, who've been more than a little jumpy these last couple of days. Anyway, thanks to Lewin here the film is moving full speed ahead." She flashed a quick smile at him. "We make a good team. In fact, we . . ."

"See eye to eye on almost everything," Usher said. "I can't thank Helene enough for all the hard work she's done in getting our Hollywood people the appropriate paperwork. Especially since she's busy running a thriving antique business as well."

"I'll have to stop by and see your shop some time," Theodosia said.

"Absolutely," Helene said. "Or visit our website. We do a nice online business as well."

"So you have clients from outside the Charleston area?" Drayton asked.

"We do," Helene said. "Though most are from around here. In fact, I'm planning to run an ad in *Charleston Today* magazine." She reached into her oversized bag and pulled out a color print-out. "Here, Theodosia, you were involved in advertising, what do you think?"

Helene handed the glossy print ad to Theodosia. It featured a nice photo of the interior of her shop, the Sea Witch.

"Sea Witch," Theodosia said. "Cute name."

"Thank you," Helene said. "We've only been around for six months or so, but, like I said, business has been good."

"She's too modest," Usher said. "It's been booming."

Theodosia continued to study the ad, which showed a jam-packed display of antique lamps, brass portholes, carnival glass, old bells, oil-burning lanterns, wooden propellers, antique porcelain, and a display of British and Dutch coins. "It looks great," she said as she passed the ad to Drayton. "You're showcasing a lot of tasty objects. I can see where collectors would be intrigued."

"Very nice," Drayton agreed.

"Oh, I almost forgot," Helene said. "We've arranged a memorial service for Josh Morro."

"It's slated for Friday evening at the Lady Goodwood Inn," Usher said. "So mark it on your calendars. Afterward, we'll serve wine and cheese. It'll be a tasteful soiree."

"Almost like a cocktail party," Helene said.

"I knew Helene had a shop," Drayton said after they'd left. "But I always assumed the Sea Witch was a hobby business. Something to fill the gaps in her time since her husband's passing."

"Why a hobby business? Why do you say that?" Theodosia felt that Helene's ad had looked fairly professional, as if she were indeed running a successful antiquities business.

"Because Helene probably has more than enough money to live comfortably for the rest of her life," Drayton said. "Her husband owned a major company with a huge fleet of trucks. Also, Helene's a social butterfly with a reputation for collecting board memberships like trinkets on a charm bracelet. As you well know, she serves on the Children's Arts Council, the Library Board, and now she's on the Charleston Film Board."

"That's interesting, because Delaine does almost the same thing," Theodosia said.

"Maybe it's a case of women taking over the world," Drayton said.

"Which may not be a bad thing." Theodosia picked up a tin of tea from the counter and turned it over. A tippy Yunnan tea from the Yunnan Province in China. She set it down and said, "Remind me to remind Haley to bake extra coffee cake tomorrow."

"I'll run into the kitchen and tell her myself," Drayton said. "By the sound of clanking pots and pans, Haley's putting everything right and Miss Dimple's almost finished with the dishes."

"Thanks," Theodosia said. She followed Drayton back down the hallway, then headed into her office. She sorted through the wreckage of boxes, bundles of magazines, tea paraphernalia, and stacks of sweetgrass baskets until she finally found the carton she was looking for.

Theodosia was busily restocking her depleted highboy with a new array of fruit jams and lemon curd when a woman suddenly came flying into her shop. The woman wore a green-striped Gucci sweater, tight leather jeans, and evil-looking black stilettos that looked like they were molded out of heavy-duty rubber. Around her neck she wore a silver cross and a bright blue evil eye amulet. Strands of brown prayer beads adorned both wrists.

The woman skidded to a stop when she spotted Theodosia.

"Well, was it Adler?" the woman demanded. She had a perfectly oval face, reddish-blond hair worn in trend-setting choppy layers, and curious green eyes that could have been enhanced by tinted contacts.

"Was what Adler?" Theodosia asked. "And who exactly are you?"

"My name is Carlotta Brandt—you can call me Carly. And I am . . . at least I *was* . . . Josh Morro's fiancée."

12

Hello, Delaine, *was* the thought that immediately streaked through Theodosia's brain. *Didn't realize you were being played, did you?*

"And you're here . . . why?" Theodosia asked.

"I called and talked to that Delaine person," Carly said. "The one who's on the Charleston Film Board?"

Theodosia gave an inward wince. "Uh-huh." She wondered if Carly knew about Delaine and Josh.

"This Delaine whoever-she-is said that you were on set when Josh was killed." Carly took a step closer. "Were you?"

"I was there," Theodosia said. "But I'm afraid I didn't see all that much. It was dark and things got terribly confusing very fast." Clearly, Carly wasn't aware of Delaine's brief fling with Josh Morro. Which was probably a good thing.

"And now there's a brand-new director," Carly said. Bright pink blotches bloomed high on her cheeks, conveying how angry and upset she was.

"Joe Adler," Theodosia said. She was pretty sure where this

was going and didn't have to wait long before Carly dropped the hammer.

"That jerk Adler wanted to direct Josh's movie so bad he could taste it," Carly snorted. "And now look what's happened. Adler got his way! He murdered my poor Josh and will probably get away with it." Tears leaked from the corners of her eyes.

"You don't know that," Theodosia said. In her mind there were several viable suspects. Maybe even some she hadn't considered yet.

Carly flattened a palm against her chest. "I'm just *so* upset."

"Have you talked to the police?"

Carly shook her head.

"You need to. For one thing, you may have background information concerning Josh that could help them. And I'm pretty sure they'd be willing to bring you up to speed on the investigation. There's a Detective Tidwell who's in charge of the case."

"Tidwell, you say. Okay, I will for sure go talk to him."

"I'm very sorry for your loss," Theodosia said. "I didn't really know Josh Morro. I only met him the morning of the shoot. But, um, a good friend of mine couldn't say enough wonderful things about him." It was a semi-white lie, but Theodosia hoped her words could help mitigate some of Carly's sadness and unhappiness.

"That's kind of you to say," Carly said.

"Oh, hello," Drayton said as he walked into the tea room. "I didn't realize we had a guest."

"This is Carly Brandt," Theodosia said. "Josh Morro's fiance."

Instead of doing a double take, Drayton's face showed immediate concern. "You have my deepest sympathies, Miss Brandt. I'm truly sorry for your loss."

"Thank you," Carly said.

"I was just suggesting that Carly have a talk with Detective Tidwell," Theodosia said. "That he might fill her in on any progress they've made in finding the killer."

"Indeed yes," Drayton said.

"Okay. Well, thanks," Carly said, sounding more than a little dispirited. "That sounds like something I'd better do." She looked a little lost for a few moments, then said, "Okay."

"You had a leading role in *Beverly Blues*, didn't you?" Theodosia said as she trailed Carly to the door.

Carly turned and shrugged. "I was a soap star, big deal. Now most of the soaps have been canceled due to lack of interest and I'm back where I started, auditioning for jobs again. Only now I'm five years older and eight pounds heavier."

"TV . . . the movie industry . . . must be a very tough business," Theodosia said.

Carly nodded. "I'm up for a part in something called *Finders Creepers*, which is supposed to be a limited series on the Hallmark Movies and Mysteries channel."

"I can't believe you won't get it."

Carly gave a rueful smile. "I can."

"Did you get a load of her jewelry?" Drayton asked once Carly had left. "Her crucifix, prayer beads, and evil eye amulet? It looks like she's on some random spiritual quest. As if she's trying to cover all the bases."

"On the other hand," Theodosia said, "she is a Hollywood actress."

"Point taken."

"You know," Theodosia said, "I'm still mildly curious about Brittlebank Manor. The legends, the woman who was held prisoner, the fact that a murder was committed there."

"And we don't even know if Morro's murder was the first murder," Drayton said. "There could have been others."

"Do you think a place like that could, um . . ."

"You think Brittlebank Manor might be haunted?" Drayton asked.

"Not in the sense of actual ghosts and goblins. But I wonder if a place can hold on to a kind of psychic memory or energy? Of bad things that happened there?"

"If you're so curious, maybe you should head over to the Heritage Society and do a little research in their library," Drayton said.

Theodosia smiled. "I just might do that."

The Heritage Society, a venerable granite building set smack-dab in the middle of the Historic District, was one of Theodosia's absolute favorite places. And not just because Drayton served on its board of directors. For Theodosia, the place stirred up feelings of history and romance. With its high ceilings and castle-like interior, the Heritage Society offered period rooms furnished with English and French furniture, priceless silver, and faded (but still marvelous) oil paintings. There were also amazing collections of historical paintings, books, objects, drawings, antique linens, important documents, and even antique weapons and firearms.

And then, of course, there was the library. Theodosia was on her way there now, hurrying down a hallway where antique tapestries dampened sounds, where a photo display titled CAROLINA GOLD, THE RICE BOOM YEARS had been hung on the walls. But when she opened the door to the library to peek in, to make sure there weren't any study groups using it, she had a pleasant surprise. Timothy Neville, the Heritage Society's octogenarian executive director, was standing at one of the tables looking over a scatter of papers.

"Timothy!" Theodosia exclaimed.

"Miss Browning." Timothy gave a respectful nod as a wry smile crinkled his face and stretched his skin taut over his cheekbones. Timothy was small, wiry, and impeccably dressed. His suits and vests were always hand-tailored and his shoes were British-made, probably at some marvelous Knightsbridge workshop that had been around for two hundred years.

"I'm not intruding, am I?" Theodosia asked. She looked around the library, with its floor-to-ceiling bookcases filled with leather-bound books, leather and hobnail chairs, and massive oak tables holding brass lamps with emerald green shades. Something light and classical was playing over the sound system. Maybe Debussy?

"You're not intruding at all," Timothy said. "I was nosing about, amusing myself with a few old maps of the Dill wildlife refuge on James Island. We have an archaeological project going on there that seeks to uncover a few more Civil War earthworks. But I digress. What brings you here? Some type of research project of your own?"

"As a matter of fact, yes," Theodosia said. "I was hoping to find some information on Brittlebank Manor."

"Brittlebank?" Timothy looked suddenly interested. "Are you by any chance working with those movie people?"

"I'm handling their craft services table. You know, the food and snacks. But the thing is, Drayton and I were both on set when that poor director got electrocuted."

Timothy cocked an eye at her. "I read about that. The newspaper said it was murder. That the police are investigating."

"It was and they are," Theodosia said. "But I've heard that the place has a strange history."

Timothy rocked back on his heels. "I've heard that as well."

Theodosia looked around at the packed bookshelves. "So I thought I'd try to unearth a little more information."

"I'm afraid you may have come to the wrong place," Timothy chuckled. "You might be better off asking one of those chaps who lead Charleston's nightly ghost tours."

"So you've heard those stories, too? That Brittlebank Manor is reputed to be haunted?"

"No more than any other old building in Charleston." Now a serious grin stretched across Timothy's face. "At last count there were supposedly over one hundred haunted buildings in Charleston."

"And two cemeteries," Theodosia said. "Let's not forget the cemeteries."

"Have you ever heard of the color haunt blue?" Timothy asked.

Theodosia shook her head.

"It's a special blue tint that people painted on the underside of their porches. To ward off ghosts and haunts."

"Do you think they still do that?"

"Probably," Timothy said. "You know how folks are when it comes to lore and legends. All of that gets passed down through the generations." He smiled at her. "And then gets embroidered a bit. Including stories about your Brittlebank Manor."

"There was a woman who was supposedly imprisoned in the attic. Do you . . . do you know anything about her? Who she was, why she was there?"

"Goodness," Timothy said. "I've heard bits and pieces of that legend, but that all took place before the turn of the century. Not this past century, the one before it. But here, let us take a look in our files. See if we can tease out a few threads of information."

Timothy Neville turned out to be a first-class researcher. After going through the card catalog, he was able to find a few books about Charleston's history that contained references to Brittlebank Manor and to the woman, Audra Baker.

"So she did exist," Theodosia said.

Timothy ran a finger down a paragraph he found in an old copy of a book called *Charleston High Society.* "Yes, in fact it says here that Miss Baker was married to Carson Brittlebank, a local shipbuilder. She was his second wife it would appear."

"And she was the woman who was imprisoned in the attic?"

Timothy continued reading. "It looks like . . . yes. She was the one."

"Was there a reason?"

"If there was it's not mentioned here." Timothy handed the open book to Theodosia so she could see for herself. "I can't imagine any good reason at all to hold someone prisoner."

Theodosia scanned the pages. "No, there's only just a few sentences about it. Strange it was even mentioned here."

"Things were strange a hundred and fifty years ago."

"Then it mentions that the home was uninhabited for a decade until it served as a convent," Theodosia said. "That was back in the nineteen thirties." She looked up. "It doesn't say what happened after that. Is there anything else that might shed a little light on Brittlebank Manor? Maps or old documents?"

"Let's check our historic document file," Timothy said. He went to an old wooden filing cabinet, pulled out a drawer, shook his head, then tried the drawer below it. His fingers flicked across several dozen files. "These are all plat maps for the Historic District. So maybe . . . this," he said, pulling one out.

Theodosia crowded next to Timothy as he placed the file on a nearby desk and hastily went through it.

"Okay, here's something," Timothy said.

"What have you got?"

Timothy carefully unfolded several sheets of paper, all crinkly and yellowed with age. "They're not plat maps, but would you believe—floor plans for some of the earlier, more spectacular homes."

"Is Brittlebank Manor there?"

"Let's see." Timothy's fingers scrabbled through the sheets of paper. "Um, yes."

"Really?" Theodosia was intrigued by their find.

Timothy slid the plans closer to Theodosia so she could see them.

"These look like original architect's renderings," she said.

"Looks as if we might have lucked out. Or you did anyway."

"Sure," Theodosia said, moving a finger across the plan for Brittlebank. "Here's the first floor, second floor, and, oh my gosh, the attic."

Timothy bent forward to look. "Yes indeed. It certainly is a large structure. Pity it fell into such disrepair."

"I'm not sure I'm reading these plans right, but it looks as if there's some kind of passageway," Theodosia said. "Or I should say a staircase from the second floor to the attic."

"Almost all these grand old Charleston homes have secret passageways," Timothy said. "My place on Archdale has two of them."

"I did not know that," Theodosia said. Timothy lived in baronial splendor in an enormous Italianate home that he shared with his Siamese cat, Chairman Meow.

"So maybe the woman wasn't a prisoner at all," Timothy said. "Perhaps she traveled freely between the second floor and third-floor attic. She could have had a room up there that functioned as a study or library, a place to get away from the chore of being the lady of the manor."

"Maybe." But Theodosia wasn't all that convinced. "May I make a copy of these plans?" She glanced at her watch, saw that time was starting to slip away from her.

"Certainly," Timothy said. "In fact, I'll do it for you."

Theodosia spun down Church Street, hung a fast right, and came out on East Bay Street where Harris Teeter was located. She lucked into a parking spot and raced into the crowded market. Grabbing a shopping cart, which Charlestonians preferred to call buggies, she circled the perimeter of the store, buying a frying chicken, lemons, sweet onions, a pound of butter, and bunches of fresh thyme and parsley. At the last minute she threw in a bunch of purple grapes, bouquets of roses and snapdragons, and a bag of pistachios. Then she drove a few blocks to the Charleston City Market, where she bought a vanilla pound cake (Riley's go-to dessert) from Fergie's Favorite bakeshop.

She hurried home, greeting Earl Grey and unloading all her groceries onto her kitchen counter. She arranged her red roses and purple snapdragons in a crystal vase, carried them into the dining room, and placed them in the center of her dining room table. Deciding she needed a centerpiece that looked a little more elegant, a little more of an ode to nature, Theodosia placed sprigs of eucalyptus, a few chunky pine cones, and three small white candles around her flowers. She bookcased that with grapes plopped into a wicker basket and a small green plant in a terra-cotta vase with overgrown moss. Opening her Sheraton buffet, she pulled out beige linen place mats with napkins to match, white plates, crystal wineglasses, and the good silverware.

Her table set and arranged, Theodosia hastened back to her kitchen to hopefully make serious magic.

13

"You're right on time," Theodosia said as she answered Riley's knock at the back door. "But why'd you come around to the back?" Earl Grey was already standing there, looking out through the screen and wagging his tail.

"Because all the enticing aromas emanate from right back here," Riley said. He stepped inside, put his arms around Theodosia, and gave her a kiss. "And this is where the cook is," he added, giving her another kiss. "See, sweetheart? Absence really does make the heart grow fonder."

"Rrwwr." Earl Grey was watching them carefully.

"Yes, I missed you as well," Riley said, giving Earl Grey a muzzle rub and an ear tug. Then he gave an appreciative sniff in the direction of the stove. "Wow, everything really does smell fantastic. Dare I ask what you're serving this evening?"

"Exactly what you requested," Theodosia said. "But you knew that, right?"

"More like hoped and prayed."

"Well, you got your wish." She picked up a bottle of white

wine and a silver corkscrew and handed them to Riley. "Here, go make yourself useful. Wineglasses are already on the table."

Riley studied the wine label. "Sauvignon blanc from Stonestreet Aurora Point? I've never had this before."

"I think you'll be pleasantly surprised."

Theodosia tinkered away in the kitchen, tasting, adding a little extra seasoning as needed. When everything was ready, she plated their servings of lemon chicken, added sides of locally grown Carolina rice that she'd steamed, and spooned the amber sauce from the pan over everything. She placed the plates on a large silver tray and carried it all into the dining room.

Riley had finished filling their wineglasses and looked hungry enough to wolf down a carburetor. "Oh wow," he said. "That chicken looks heavenly."

"Hope so."

"And your table is so enchanting," he said as Theodosia put his plate down in front of him. "Are all these lovely flowers and fancy things just for my benefit?"

Theodosia glanced at the candles, grapes, and flowers she'd so carefully arranged. "It's for you, yes, but also a little bit for me. I do this all the time at the tea shop, but I don't have that many opportunities to create a nice tablescape at home."

"That's what this is called? A tablescape?"

"It's what decorating magazines call it anyway," Theodosia said as she sat down across from him.

They smiled warmly at each other in the candlelight and clinked their wineglasses together in a toast.

"Here's to you," Theodosia said.

"To us," Riley said.

They both took a sip of wine.

"You like?" Theodosia asked, eyeing him carefully. When

they'd first met, Riley had been a mostly beer-and-lager type of guy. She'd been working to slowly change that.

"It's light, dry, but with a lively acidity. Saucy, you might say."

"You sound like a wine magazine."

"Aw, I knew you left that copy of *Wine Spectator* lying open on the coffee table for a good reason," Riley said. Which caused them both to chuckle and dig into their lemon chicken.

"I hate to say this myself," Theodosia said. "But yum."

"Ditto for me. How on earth did you get this chicken so juicy and bursting with flavor?"

"Secret's in the sauce," Theodosia said.

After Riley's fourth compliment and, count 'em, second helping (and a few tidbits slipped to Earl Grey), he looked across the table at Theodosia and said, "Tell me what you know so far about the Morro murder."

Theodosia set her fork down. "Not much. Do you think you'll get pulled into it?"

"Probably not. But I've picked up bits and pieces of scuttlebutt around the office and know that a lot of people have been questioned, but none of the investigators seem to have formed a solid conclusion as to who the guilty party might be."

"But you know about the actress, Andrea Blair, who hated Josh Morro?"

"Heard about her."

"And the screenwriter, Craig Cole?"

"I understand he's at the top of Tidwell's list."

Theodosia raised a single eyebrow. "Not Delaine Dish?"

"No. It's for sure Cole that he's focusing on now."

"Good. Cole's at the top of my list, too." Theodosia paused and took a sip of wine. It tasted mellow and slightly fruity. "Then there's Ted Juniper . . ."

Riley ticked a finger at her. "The lighting guy with the drunk driving charge."

"Right. And Joe Adler, the pinch-hitting director."

"Don't know much about him," Riley said.

"Adler was able to step in rather quickly," Theodosia said. "Almost as if he'd been waiting for this golden opportunity to be dropped in his lap."

"Maybe the producers simply cut a fast deal with him. They realized they were in a creative bind, so they offered Adler a pile of money to finish the job," Riley said as he poured two more fingers of wine into their glasses.

"What do you know about a cowboy-type guy named Quaid Barthel?"

Riley's hand jerked suddenly and a few drops of wine flew from his glass onto his place mat.

"Oh, you *do* know something about him," Theodosia said.

"I didn't say that."

"You didn't have to." Theodosia paused. "So. What's the story on this Quaid guy?"

"Nothing much, nothing concrete anyway. Quaid Barthel is what investigators like to call a person of interest."

Theodosia peered over her wineglass at him. "In other words, a suspect."

"Not necessarily."

"Then why is Cowboy Quaid a so-called person of interest?"

"Mainly because he's Joe Adler's hired henchman."

The word *henchman* sounded ominous to Theodosia. "Why is he a henchman and why is he of interest?"

"For one thing, our boy Quaid has a record," Riley said.

"No kidding. Here in Charleston or back in New Orleans?"

"You realize I shouldn't be telling you any of this."

"You've spilled the beans halfway out of the can, you may as well upend it completely."

"Well . . . maybe just a little."

"Good," Theodosia said. "So where does Quaid have a record?"

"New Orleans. He was popped for armed robbery."

"No kidding. What'd he do? Rob a bank?"

"Nothing that spectacular," Riley said. "Quaid was caught trying to recover a shotgun he owned from an old girlfriend's house."

"Hmm," Theodosia said. "So the girlfriend was attempting to separate a good old boy from his favorite shotgun? That wasn't very nice of her. I hope Quaid didn't have to do jail time for what seems like a perfectly justified act." She smiled. "At least it is in the South."

"You can't be serious."

"You're not from here, so you've gotta trust me on this."

As candles flickered and the evening wore on, Theodosia and Riley talked, cleared away the dinner dishes, and talked some more. For dessert Theodosia served the pound cake she'd bought topped with lemon curd and chopped, toasted pistachios.

And just as they were about to settle in for the night, Riley's phone rang.

"Really?" Theodosia said as he sheepishly pulled it from his pocket and answered it.

Even Earl Grey crawled out from under the table, looking a little annoyed.

Riley listened intently, then glanced over at Theodosia. "Now?" he said. "The thing is, I'm sort of . . . Yeah, okay, got it. I'll see you in ten. Or . . . make that fifteen."

Theodosia knew a work call when she heard one. Even if the conversation was one-sided.

"You have to leave? You just got back." She was keenly disappointed.

"Apologies, but duty calls."

"You mean Tidwell calls."

"Well, it was Glen Humphries, his assistant. But listen, I owe you big-time. Not just for this superb dinner, but for all the sweet things you do. How about I take you out to dinner this Saturday night? I'll make a reservation at High Cotton."

"Fancy," she said. High Cotton was one of the trendiest, foodiest restaurants in all of Charleston.

"Only the best," he said.

"You're sure you have to leave?"

"I'm afraid so."

But when Theodosia walked Riley to the door and snuggled up against him, it was a good several minutes before he actually left.

Theodosia cleared the dessert plates from the table and walked into the kitchen. Looked at the clock on the wall. Nine fifteen. Still early enough to take Earl Grey out for a run. She hurriedly cleaned up the detritus from her cooking, put the dirty dishes in the dishwasher, then ran upstairs to change. She put on a black hoodie, gray jogging pants, and her New Balance running shoes and snapped a leash on Earl Grey, who started to dance in anticipation. Then they went out the back door, through the gate, and headed down the alley. Running past the Granville Mansion next door, Theodosia looked up to see if Joe Adler had moved in yet. But the place looked completely dark. Nobody home.

Was Joe Adler out sampling Charleston's nightlife? Sipping a cabernet at Bin 152? Or eating charbroiled oysters at Leon's Oyster Shop? Maybe. Probably. On the other hand, she could have sworn she saw a pair of curtains move in one of the upstairs bedrooms.

Down the block they ran, and into the heart of Charleston's Historic District. Here were large homes built by Charleston's founding fathers, homes that had withstood wars, hurricanes, good fortune and bad. Homes that had entertained presidents, foreign dignitaries, old-name families, and newcomers as well.

Theodosia loved this part of town. It was gorgeous, charming, and still communicated a sort of Southern gravitas. Down every street, old-fashioned wrought-iron lamps with glass globes glowed like rosary beads. Historic brass markers announced the lineage of many of the homes. And if you ducked down the many tangles of narrow alleys and hidden walkways, you'd discover lush gardens overgrown with palm trees, magnolia, and jessamine, often accented with statuary, reflecting ponds, and pattering fountains.

Theodosia could hear the mournful toot of a tugboat over on Charleston Harbor a few blocks away. A gentle mist had begun to steal in, rendering everything in soft focus and creating a kind of dreamworld.

They'd run a good twelve blocks or so when Theodosia realized they'd just passed the Saracen Inn, where most of the cast and crew were staying. Which immediately brought her thoughts back to Andrea. The girl had seemed edgy and nervous this morning when she'd spoken to her. Or, Theodosia wondered, had she completely misread Andrea's emotions—had she actually been fearful? Did Andrea know something but was afraid to tell the police? Had she been that little mouse in the corner who'd seen what happened to Josh Morrow? Andrea had been sitting at the tea table across from Theodosia that dreadful morning, and she'd been facing the camera . . . as well as Josh Morro.

Maybe if I approached Andrea a little more carefully, I could get her to open up?

Theodosia gave a tug on Earl Grey's leash, turned, and headed back to the Saracen Inn. She'd once catered a tea here, so she knew the owners, as well as most of the managers. In fact . . .

Across a small lobby furnished with cocoa-colored leather sofas and Indian dhurrie rugs, she spotted Robert Jefferson Kay, the night manager. Known as Bobby Kay to all of his friends.

"Hey, Bobby Kay," Theodosia sang out in greeting. "How've you been?"

Bobby Kay was a tall, thin, redheaded guy with a mask of freckles over almost translucent skin. He'd started as a bellhop at the Saracen Inn and had worked his way up to general manager.

"Not too bad, Theo," Kay said. "I hear you're working with the movie people we've got staying here."

"Mostly handling their craft services table."

When Kay gave her a questioning look, she added, "You know, snacks and stuff. Munchies for the cast and crew."

"Ah, got it. Sounds like fun." Then, realizing what he'd just said, he colored slightly and added, "Except for the murder."

"That was . . . unfortunate," Theodosia said.

"But I hear things are back on track with a new director?"

"Seem to be." Theodosia paused. "I stopped by to have a word with Andrea Blair, one of the actresses. Do you know if she's in?"

"Should be," Kay said. He turned to his young assistant and said, "Jason, what room is Andrea Blair staying in?"

Jason hit a few keys and peered at his computer screen. "She's in room 401."

"Fourth floor," Kay said. "What we call our Tower Suites. There are only two rooms up there but both are over-the-top charming. That's if you don't mind climbing all those stairs."

"Good exercise," Theodosia said. "Okay to take the dog?"

"Dogs aren't generally allowed," said Kay. "But who's looking? Besides, I'm off in five minutes."

"Thanks a bunch," Theodosia said. She crossed the lobby and began her climb with Earl Grey in tow. Like many of the B and Bs in Charleston, the Saracen Inn had once been a private home. And even though it was now a commercial venture, it retained much of the charm from its former glory days. Old photos of previous owners and watercolor sketches of surrounding homes and pocket parks hung in the stairwell. Each landing had a small desk with a Tiffany-style lamp, chair, and writing materials. Oriental carpets led down the hallways.

Unfortunately, the overhead lighting was relatively dim. Theodosia didn't know if the lighting was always this dreary or if the lights had been purposefully turned down because it was almost ten o'clock.

She'd just hit the final staircase leading to the fourth floor when the lights flickered, the stairwell went completely dark for a few moments, then the lights flared back on again. But this time there was barely a faint glow.

Doggone. Hard to see where I'm going.

Up to now, all the stairs had been carpeted, but the stairs leading to the fourth floor were highly polished wood, which gave Earl Grey some trouble with his footing.

"Come on, boy. You can make it," Theodosia urged. She turned to check on her dog's progress and make another encouraging sound. But when she turned back, quick as a vampire in a shock-a-rama movie, a dark shadow rose up in front of her!

"What . . . ?" Theodosia gasped.

She was even more stunned when strong hands reached out and grabbed her around the neck and began to pinch her throat. Panicked, she tried to twist out of her attacker's grasp. But her right foot slipped and she went down hard on one knee, giving her attacker the upper hand.

Scared out of her mind, frantic beyond belief, Theodosia tried to scream. But all that came out of her mouth was a dry croak.

As his hands squeezed harder, Theodosia released Earl Grey's leash and fought blindly to strike out and push her assailant away. Even though it was too dark to see his face, she battered at his chest with all her might. But he continued grappling with her, pinching off her air supply as he bent her over backward. Theodosia tried her best to grab a gulp of air as she thrashed about, but the man—she assumed it was a man because of the brute strength—continued to increase the pressure against her windpipe.

Time seemed to stand still for Theodosia. Her vision began to narrow, first to a cone, then to a pinpoint, while bright sparks buzzed like angry hornets inside her head. She was distantly aware of Earl Grey's frantic barking and his toenails skittering and scrabbling hard against wood, fighting to find purchase. And then, just when Theodosia thought she couldn't hang on any longer, she felt Earl Grey's furry body streak past, hitting her hard, almost shoving her out of the way, as her dog made a flying leap at her assailant.

14

Theodosia was aware of frantic barking and loud cries as a wild melee broke out around her. There were thuds, bumps, snarls, and, most of all, a string of curses. Then, as if by magic, the man's hands slipped from her neck.

The death grip was gone and she could finally breathe!

But Theodosia's victory was short lived. In her oxygen-deprived state, she stumbled and lost her balance. Then, to her horror, began to topple over backward, knowing there was nothing behind her but thin air.

Theodosia flung her arms out to her sides as she fell, trying to grab a hand railing but missing by a mile. She skidded down a few steps, then spun around and ended up crashing down onto her right side. There was sharp pain upon impact and then she was helplessly, hopelessly sliding down a half dozen highly polished wooden steps. Bump, bump, bumping her way to the landing below as Earl Grey tumbled down after her. Seconds later, they both ended up in an ungainly sprawl.

"Earl Grey!" Theodosia cried. Her first fear was that her dog was badly injured. But Earl Grey immediately sprang to his feet, looked around, and shook himself, head to tail, doing a kind of doggy reset.

I just hope I can do the same.

Theodosia grabbed onto her dog's collar for support, pulled herself up gingerly, all the while trying to sort out exactly what had happened.

That's when a door at the top of the stairs opened with a loud BANG and a shaft of light filtered down. Theodosia looked up, fearing a second attack. But all she saw was Andrea Blair standing there in a long white robe, holding a brass candlestick over her head.

"What's going on?" Andrea shouted. "Who's there?"

"It's me, Theodosia," she said in a half croak. "Somebody just tried to choke me to death, then shoved me down the stairs!" She felt shaky and lightheaded as she tried to recover from her attack. Her heart was practically slamming out of her chest, while her knee throbbed and her ankle burned. Gingerly, she climbed the steps to the fourth floor as she fought to process what had just happened. Somebody—someone strong—had grabbed her by the throat—and what? Tried to *kill* her?

How does that compute?

"What'd you say?" Andrea's eyes were dark pools of uncertainty and she looked frightened to death.

Theodosia fought to explain. "It was dark—it's still dark—and then I saw a shadow." She reached up and touched her neck. "Somebody lunged out of the dark and started to choke me."

"What?" Andrea said again.

"They choked me and shoved me down the steps." Theodosia slid a hand down to her leg. "Made me bang my knee and twist my ankle." She gazed at Andrea. "Do you know who was lurking outside your room? Did you see who it was?"

Andrea didn't answer her question. Just stared at her, mouth open and the candlestick still wavering above her head. The girl wasn't just scared, she was shaking like a Chihuahua in a snowstorm.

"Were *you* the one who tried to pry open my door?" Andrea finally asked in quavering tones.

"Of course not," Theodosia snapped back. "Didn't you just hear what I said? I got shoved down the stairs before I even got to your floor. So I need to know, did *you* hear somebody outside your room? Creeping around?"

"I heard my door rattle and then a dog—" Andrea looked down at Earl Grey. "I guess it was *your* dog—started barking like mad."

"Do you have any idea why somebody would be lurking outside your room?"

"I wish you'd stop asking questions like that because you're scaring me to death!" Andrea shouted back.

"I don't mean to. I'm just trying to piece together what happened," Theodosia said in quieter tones. She was feeling slightly better. Breathing okay, the fright starting to wear off. Now she was mostly angry.

"How would I know who was prowling around?" Andrea cried, her tone sour and shrill. "My room's the only one that's occupied on this floor." She flapped a hand in the direction of her room. "It's, like, a garret, small and snug, but a little lonely, too."

"You're the only one on this floor?"

"I am now." Andrea pointed to the door across the hall from hers. "That's the room where Josh Morro was staying."

"So maybe someone was trying to break into Morro's room," Theodosia said.

Andrea lowered the candelabra. "I dunno. Maybe."

"Are his belongings still in there?" Theodosia wondered if that's what the intruder had been after. If she'd somehow interrupted him as he tried to pick the lock and ransack the room.

Andrea shrugged. "Maybe. I guess. Since it's none of my business I really don't want to know." She turned to go back into her room.

"Andrea, wait. You were about to tell me something this morning."

"I was?"

"Just before Adler called you onto the set."

"I don't remember. I don't . . . I don't want to talk about it. About anything," Andrea said as she slammed the door in Theodosia's face.

"Rude," Theodosia muttered as she picked up Earl Grey's leash. "Are all actresses that rude?" Earl Grey looked up at her and gave a commiserating look as they made their way downstairs.

Going down the last flight of steps, Theodosia ran into a huffing, puffing Sidney Gorsk.

"Were you just upstairs?" Theodosia asked the agent. "On the fourth floor?"

Gorsk looked startled. "No, why do you ask?"

"Because somebody slammed into me in the dark. Tried to choke me, then pushed me down the stairs."

"Are you sure?"

"Of course I'm sure. You see this bruise?" Theodosia slid up her pants leg. "It's going to be purple by tomorrow morning."

Gorsk peered at Theodosia's ankle. "Better put some ice on that."

"No kidding." Then, "You're out late."

"Just a business meeting."

Theodosia decided this might be a prime opportunity to

question Gorsk. "I know you represent Andrea Blair. Is she your only client right now?"

Gorsk tilted his head back and let loose a hearty laugh that sounded a little forced. "Goodness no. My talent management firm, Gorsk and Gadby Creative, represents dozens of actors and writers."

"Writers," Theodosia said. "Writers like Craig Cole?"

"A few screenwriters, yes. But mainly successful ones. Funny you should even mention that," Gorsk said. "I was meeting with a prospective client tonight."

"Talking to someone about a script?"

"Something like that," Gorsk said. "I'm always on the look-out for smart writing that holds promise." He looked down at Earl Grey and said, "Nice dog. He much of a guard dog?"

"He most certainly is," Theodosia said, thinking it was a strange question to ask.

"Well, good night," Gorsk said, brushing past her. "Have a nice evening."

Theodosia walked outside and hesitated on the front side-walk. The moon was a glowing orb, shuttling in and out of passing clouds as the breeze off the Atlantic picked up and cooled the evening. And tickling in the back of Theodosia's brain was the idea that Gorsk could have been the one who killed Josh Morro. If he represented Andrea's best interests, maybe he was the one who'd hot-wired that chair. Getting rid of Morro might have made Andrea deliriously happy. And as far as tonight went, Gorsk had been out *somewhere* and had been more than cavalier about her getting pushed down the stairs.

Interesting. Maybe even telling.

Could Gorsk have been the jerk who choked her and pushed her down the stairs? He'd been huffing and puffing like an old-fashioned steam engine when she ran into him. Had Gorsk delivered that final hard shove that sent her sprawling? Maybe Gorsk had found out through the grapevine that she was looking into things? Or maybe he'd deduced it from their conversation this morning?

Then, in the wild melee with Earl Grey, maybe Gorsk had escaped down the back stairs and come in through the lobby looking all innocent-like. But if it *had* been Gorsk, what would he have been doing up there? Wanting to talk to Andrea? Or was there another reason? Theodosia thought about this. Maybe Gorsk had been trying to get into Josh Morro's room and she'd interrupted him?

Josh Morrow's room. Had that been the real target? Not Andrea and certainly not her. And if someone had been trying to break into Morro's room, what had they been looking for?

There's only one way to find out.

Walking on dry grass with scant moonlight for their guide, Theodosia and Earl Grey cut through a stand of banana shrubs and circled around the Saracen Inn to the back door.

Jason, the sleepy desk clerk, was just coming out.

"Back again?" he said as he held the door open for her and her dog. "You must be working with the movie people, huh?"

Theodosia smiled as they slipped past him. "You might call it that. And it looks as if you've put in some long hours."

Jason nodded sleepily. "Been on since noon today. I'm the last one. Mr. Kay already skipped out. Hey, that's a nice dog. Is he in the movie, too?'"

"He's the star."

Jason did a fist pump. "Excellent."

Once inside, Theodosia and Earl Grey followed a dimly lit hallway to the front desk. She hunted around, opening drawers and looking for keys. She finally pulled the top off a ceramic cat dish and found a master key.

Perfect.

Then it was up the stairs again—the back stairs this time—to Josh Morro's room.

Theodosia had a bad moment when she slipped the key into the lock and it didn't immediately turn. But she jiggled it gently and, finally, the door swung open. She tiptoed in, Earl Grey behind her, then closed the door quietly and hit the light switch.

Two lamps winked on, giving the room a warm, pinkish glow. And just as Bobby Kay had said, these were small rooms but also quite charming. There was a queen-sized bed with a paisley coverlet, a small desk and dresser done in Shaker style, and a dormer that had a custom cushioned window seat. Original oil paintings—many depicting sailboats—hung on the walls. Overall, the room had a cozy, snug feel to it.

Theodosia headed for the closet and found that it was still packed with Josh Morro's clothes. Which suddenly dampened the coziness of the room and made it feel somewhat sad. Still, if her assailant had been trying to get into this room, what exactly had he expected to find? What had he been looking for?

That's for me to try and find out.

Theodosia hurriedly went through the clothing, checking pockets and poking in shoes. Nothing. She pulled a leather suitcase and large nylon tote bag off the shelf overhead, but found both of them empty.

The desk and dresser drawers were next. The desk was small, only one drawer, so all she found there were a lined yellow notepad with a few scribbles on it, a silver Waterman pen, and a phone charger. The dresser contained folded jeans, shirts, socks, and underwear. The bottom drawer held a pair of Teva walking sandals.

That left the top of the dresser, which was mostly a scatter of guy stuff. Pocket change, a set of car keys, a penknife, a large-face watch with a black rubber strap, two twenty-dollar bills in a money clip, and a business card for Delta Labs, which Theodosia knew was a local postproduction house. Probably, Morro had intended to have some of his film transferred to tape so he could take a look at it and maybe even do a rough edit.

So nothing of any interest. Nothing that had jumped out at her, anyway. Theodosia figured the police had already torn through Morro's rental car, and if something critical had been discovered, they'd be running with it.

Just as Theodosia and Earl Grey crept down the back stairs, what little overhead light there was suddenly winked out and the stairway was plunged into complete darkness.

Not again!

Theodosia halted, one foot in midair as her fingers clawed for the security of the railing. She had a few bad moments where she couldn't find it, and then, ah, there was solid wood.

She wondered if someone had turned out the lights on purpose—or if they were on a timer. In any case, she knew she'd better get out of there fast.

Feeling a tug on the leash, Theodosia allowed Earl Grey to lead her down the twisty staircase. Dogs have the ability to see in limited light, and after Earl Grey's heroic performance earlier, she trusted him completely.

They hit the first floor, put the key back, fumbled their way to the back door, and made it out okay. A little frightened but none the worse for wear.

But all the way home Theodosia continued to look back over her shoulder.

15

❧

Theodosia showed up at the movie set this Thursday morning armed with three pans of cinnamon coffee cake. Once she'd arranged all her goodies (and set aside a pan of coffee cake expressly for Joe Adler), she looked around for Sidney Gorsk. She spotted him over in a corner, jabbering away on his cell phone. Though Theodosia couldn't hear what Gorsk was saying, his head was bobbing like mad and he was smiling broadly. It looked as if he was delighted to get his way with something.

Sidney Gorsk. Could he have been the one last night . . . ?

Before Theodosia could even complete her thought, the cast and crew had descended upon her table, snatching up scones, grabbing pieces of banana bread, and fighting over corn muffins and chocolate-oatmeal cookies. Beth Ann arrived a few minutes later and hurriedly began pouring morning cups of tea.

"I can handle this if you want to take off," Beth Ann said to Theodosia. "I know you've got an event tea today."

"You're okay being here for the rest of the day?"

Beth Ann gave a thumbs-up. "I got this."

But Theodosia didn't leave quite yet. Instead, she wandered down the long hallway, past the makeup room, and found herself in a large parlor, where cameras and lights were being set up. Furniture was also being carried in—two high-back chairs, a round table, and a tufted velvet fainting couch—that all had a distinct Victorian look and feel. One of the prop guys broke away from arranging furniture to flirt with the script girl and explain how they were about to film one of the movie's few romantic scenes.

Craig Cole was also there, pencil and script in hand, half watching the action.

"Hey, tea lady," Cole said in a nasty, singsong tone of voice when he caught sight of Theodosia. "A little bird told me you're a natural-born crime solver. I guess I should have realized it was more than just a passing fancy when you dropped by to see me the other night." He moved a few steps in her direction. "And here I thought you were drawn in by my irresistible charm."

"I do find you charming," Theodosia said, lying through her teeth. "But I also find Josh Morro's murder morbid and absolutely fascinating—which is why I wanted to get your take on it." And then to further diffuse the situation, she said, "The way Morro was killed reminds me of one of those Agatha Christie locked-room mysteries."

Cole's face lit up and he cocked a finger at her. "Yes! A whole raft of onlookers and any one of them could be a vicious killer."

"Maybe you should write a modern-day screenplay based on that premise."

"That's not the worst idea I've heard," Cole said. "A familiar premise with a brand-new twist always goes over big in Hollywood. You know, like *E.T. the Extra-Terrestrial* was kind of an updated version of *The Wizard of Oz.*"

"The theme being that the main character will do anything and everything in their power to get back home."

"I'd have to say the 'want to go home' concept has to be one of the most powerful literary themes of all time," Cole said.

"It sure worked in Homer's *Odyssey*," Theodosia said. "Now all you have to do is rework that theme, add in a murder, and give it an updated spin."

Sidney Gorst wandered past them, still yacking on his phone. Cole's eyes followed Gorsk for a few moments, then he said, "I was just thinking. In an unpredictable twist of fate Sidney Gorsk ended up getting his way. Now that Joe Adler's on board, Gorsk managed to sweet-talk him into shooting all of Andrea's scenes first so she could leave the movie early and star in that reality show he set her up with."

"Do you still think Andrea could have killed Morro?"

Cole shrugged. "Doesn't matter what I think. The police don't seem to regard Andrea as a viable suspect."

"Well, if there's no concrete evidence . . ."

"Yeah," Cole said. "No evidence. Convenient, don't you think?" He tapped his pencil annoyingly against his script.

But Theodosia's attention was suddenly captured by Ted Juniper, who'd walked in and started adjusting a complicated arrangement of overhead lights.

"Whadya think?" Juniper asked one of his crew as he tinkered away. "This gonna do it? This gonna give Adler the moody look he asked for?"

"All we can do is try," the man said.

Theodosia turned back to Cole and said in a low voice, "Have the police been talking to Ted Juniper?"

"I know they've questioned him a couple of times." Cole narrowed his eyes, suddenly looking interested. "What's popping in that brain of yours? You think Juniper's the guy?"

"I don't know," Theodosia said. Still, she was curious about Juniper. And since he was staying at the Saracen Inn, maybe he'd been the one prowling the halls and stairways last night. Maybe there was more to Ted Juniper than met the eye. Maybe.

"No, no, no." Joe Adler came flying into the parlor, followed by a small, harried-looking woman who was dragging a long dress behind her. "I distinctly ordered the gown to be faded, to have an almost antique look."

"We've done that," the woman said, unfurling a long lace gown with a high collar and billowing sleeves.

Adler grabbed a handful of fabric and shook it in her face. "It looks *drab*, I'll give you that. But not antiqued. This dress has to look *authentic*!"

"I don't know what you want me to *do*," the woman said, nearly in tears. "We've tried everything."

"Keep trying!" Adler shouted.

"Tea dyeing," Theodosia said.

Adler spun on his heels. "What'd you say?"

"When you dip-dye fabric or lace in a large pot of tea you can usually achieve a warm, antiqued look," Theodosia said. "Because of all the tannins."

Adler squinted at his wardrobe lady. "How come you don't know about this?"

The wardrobe lady looked fearful. "Because I don't?"

Adler turned back to Theodosia. "You're the tea lady, aren't you? Did you bring my coffee cake?"

Theodosia couldn't help chuckling. "A double order."

"Cinnamon?"

"Yes." *My, we are the hotshot demanding director, aren't we?*

"And could you fix this dress? Can you do this fancy tea-dyeing technique you mentioned?"

"I could give it a shot," Theodosia said.

"Good," Adler said. "Call if there's a problem." Then he turned to the wardrobe lady and said, "Give her the dress. And pray that our tea lady comes through for you."

"Yes, sir," said the wardrobe lady, thrusting the dress into Theodosia's hands, happy to be rid of it.

Theodosia stuffed the dress into her bag, did a final check-in with Beth Ann, and hurried back to the Indigo Tea Shop. She found Miss Dimple taking orders, pouring tea, and serving morning scones and tea bread. Obviously, things worked like clockwork when left in Miss Dimple's capable hands.

Drayton was behind the counter, brewing tea and beaming at Miss Dimple's efficiency.

"I just hope I have that much energy when I reach her age," he said to Theodosia.

"I wish I had her energy now," Theodosia shot back.

"You're in a funny mood," Drayton said.

"I ran into a few problems last night."

"Trouble with Riley?"

"Nope, trouble at the Saracen Inn."

"What are you talking about?"

So Theodosia told Drayton all about stopping at the inn last night to talk to Andrea, getting shoved and almost strangled, Earl Grey coming to her rescue, and Andrea being scared out of her wits. She also told him about running into Sidney Gorsk, but conveniently left out the part about sneaking into Josh Morro's room and riffling through his belongings. Drayton, being a true Christian, wouldn't approve.

"What are you thinking now?" Drayton asked. "That Sidney Gorsk murdered Josh Morro?"

"Not sure," Theodosia said. "What I do know is that Gorsk is a skillful manipulator."

"Of course he is. He's an agent with instincts like a killer shark."

"It also turns out that Gorsk convinced Joe Adler to shoot all of Andrea's scenes first, so she can leave the movie early and star in a reality show."

"They can do that? Shoot her scenes first and it doesn't mess up the production?" Drayton asked.

"Sure. Movie scenes are rarely shot in sequential order. Sometimes the ending is shot first. Sometimes, as in the case of Andrea, there's a work-around and the scenes are bunched together."

"So how does this relate to Morro's murder?"

"What if Sidney Gorsk murdered Josh Morro knowing that Adler would step in?"

Drayton stared at her. "With Gorsk figuring that Adler would be easier to manipulate? To get Andrea out early?"

"Maybe. Or maybe Gorsk is Adler's agent as well. And Gorsk is making moves and countermoves that benefit all his clients."

"Does Gorsk represent Adler?"

"I have no idea."

"How would you go about finding out?"

"I suppose I could ask him," Theodosia said.

"That could tip him off."

"Okay, then, maybe call the SAG-AFTRA office in L.A.?" Theodosia was referring to the Screen Actors Guild and the American Federation of Television and Radio Artists, which had merged several years back.

"Are you going to tell Tidwell about your behind-the-scenes espionage?"

Theodosia shook her head. "Probably not. Because he'd just

smile tolerantly and tell me my suspicions are simply half-baked theories."

"Are they?"

Theodosia thought for a moment. "Maybe more like parboiled."

"Hah, funny."

"There's something else," Theodosia said. She pulled the lace gown out of her bag and showed it to Drayton. "What tea would I use to achieve a nice, golden, tea-dyed look?"

"Hmm." Drayton fingered the dress. "This is from the movie's wardrobe department, I assume?"

Theodosia nodded. "I volunteered to do a little extracurricular work for them."

"If it were up to me—and it looks as if it might be—I'd use a nice strong Keemun." Drayton turned to his shelf of teas, finger-walked across a half dozen tins, and pulled one out. "Here. This Mao Feng ought to do the trick."

Theodosia smiled. "Much obliged."

As soon as most of their morning guests had departed, Theodosia started decorating for today's Vintage Tea Party. She dug in her highboy and pulled out vintage lace tablecloths and as many pink and green teacups and saucer sets as she could find—in fact, the more mismatched they were the better. She wanted her tables to look like a wonderful calico quilt.

"So pretty," Miss Dimple said. "And I see you're mostly going with pastels."

"Pink and green and yellow do lend a lovely vintage effect. As does old silver flatware and pressed glass vases."

"Would the vases be for the bouquets of tea roses that got delivered a little while ago?"

"That's the plan," Theodosia said. "But let's just use four or five stems per vase because we want a scatter of arrangements across each table."

Once Miss Dimple had the tables set, Theodosia added a few more choice items. Lace parasols were hung from the ceiling, peacock feathers were stuck into tall silver vases, and a few old pocket watches (Drayton's contribution) and pairs of vintage lace gloves were placed on the tables. Favors for guests included small rose-colored sachets and fans wrapped with blue ribbons.

"How much ribbon do you have left?" Miss Dimple asked.

"Oodles. Why?"

"I thought it might be cute to hang ribbon streamers off the backs of chairs."

"Go for it," Theodosia said.

16

When it was twenty to twelve, when Theodosia figured she had a ten-minute window before her guests arrived, wouldn't you know it, Delaine Dish and her niece Bettina showed up early.

Delaine was buzzing like an angry hornet. Glancing about the tea shop and tossing her head nervously, she plucked at Theodosia's sleeve. Today Delaine wore a silver-gray knit dress with a wide silver-studded black leather belt that looked more like a corset. Maybe that's why Delaine was acting so hyper, maybe she was feeling uncomfortable and squished.

But, no, it was something else.

"We thought about not coming today," Delaine said, picking an invisible thread off Theodosia's shoulder. "Out of, you know, a grudging respect, a kind of mourning period for Josh Morro." Her shoulders rose then dipped. "But we already had our reservations, and Morro . . . well, let's just say our relationship didn't work out all that well."

"Whatever the reason I'm delighted you're here," Theodosia

said, trying to ease Delaine over to her table so she could still enjoy a few calming sips of tea.

But Delaine, never one to be rushed, crooked an index finger and said, "Bettina and I have big news. In fact, there's major cause for celebration." She beamed at Bettina and said, "Go ahead, dear, show Theodosia."

Bettina held up her left hand, where a marquise-shaped diamond shone on her ring finger.

"Bettina got engaged!" Delaine gushed. "Isn't that the most *fabulous* thing in the entire world!"

Theodosia, who didn't even know that Bettina had been dating someone, said, "It's absolutely wonderful. Congratulations are definitely in order. And, wow, is that ring ever a sparkler!"

"Three carats, certified at F in color and SI2 in clarity," said Delaine, as if she'd flown to Antwerp and picked it out herself. "You don't often see diamonds of that high a caliber."

"I should say so," Theodosia said. She hugged Bettina and said, "I'm delighted for you! You deserve every happiness in the world."

"Thank you," Bettina said. "As you can probably guess, I'm over the moon in love with Jamie. That's his name, Jamie Wilkes." She hitched up her shoulders in an expression of pure joy. "Don't you just love it?"

"Love's the easy part," Delaine said, suddenly interjecting a cautionary note. "It's planning the wedding that's a killer." She thought for a moment and rolled her eyes. "Then, of course, there's the actual marriage."

Theodosia just smiled. Delaine had been married twice and engaged . . . well, at this point everyone had pretty much lost count.

Five minutes later, Helene Deveroux arrived with Dorothy Roper, another member of the Charleston Film Board. As Theodosia greeted them, Delaine stood up and began waving wildly at Helene and Dorothy. So of course Theodosia seated the two newcomers at Delaine and Bettina's table.

More guests arrived and Theodosia and Miss Dimple greeted them warmly and led them to the various tables. Once the guests were seated, once Drayton had taken a head count, it was Theodosia's turn to take center stage.

"Welcome, dear guests," she said, "to the Indigo Tea Shop's Vintage Tea Party, where everything old is new again. As you might have noticed, our tablecloths are vintage lace, napkins are hand-embroidered linen, and our teacups and saucers, though mismatched, are all early incarnations from Shelley, Herend, and Minton.

"In keeping with our vintage theme, today's menu also hearkens backs to earlier times. You'll start your tea luncheon with old-fashioned maple scones and honey butter, followed by chicken salad and strawberry and cream cheese tea sandwiches."

There was a ripple of applause.

"But we're not done yet," Theodosia said. "Our entrée is lobster thermidor on buttermilk biscuits, our dessert is a delicious pineapple crisp, and our tea . . ." Theodosia paused and glanced over at Drayton. "Drayton, what *is* our tea today?"

Holding a calico-printed teapot aloft, Drayton strode across the tea room to join Theodosia.

"I've brewed two special Chinese legacy teas that are highly reminiscent of the teas our French and English ancestors enjoyed around the mid-eighteen hundreds. The first is a Hunan black needle tea and the second is a Fujian black plum tea. Both should be to your liking and be complementary to today's luncheon."

Theodosia and Miss Dimple ferried out scones and then tea sandwiches as Drayton kept busy pouring tea. Then, once the lobster thermidor was served, Theodosia was able to relax and stop by each table to greet her guests.

Mrs. Cornelia Eddie, also known as Miss Cornelia because she was a woman "of a certain age," reached out to grab Theodosia's hand.

"Dear, did I hear that your tea shop is planning a Fox and Hounds Tea?" Miss Cornelia asked.

"Probably in a month or two, though we haven't set an exact date yet," Theodosia said.

"That brings back memories." The old lady smiled. "In my younger days I used to do a bit of horseback riding."

"Don't let her kid you," her daughter said. "My mother used to trailer her horses up to Virginia to catch all the point-to-point races. And when I say catch, I mean she *rode* in them. Brought home a few blue ribbons, too."

"Then you for sure have to come to our tea," Theodosia laughed.

When Theodosia stopped at Delaine's table, Delaine was raving about Helene's shop, the Sea Witch.

"Theo," Delaine said, grabbing her wrist and pulling her close, "you absolutely *have* to visit Helene's shop. There's nothing like it in Charleston—she has all these amazing one-of-a-kind objects. It's truly a unique little jewel box of a shop."

"How do you go about sourcing your antiques?" Theodosia asked Helene.

"I get lucky," Helene said, which caused everyone at the table to laugh.

"No, really," Delaine prodded. "You must have some trade secrets."

"Would you believe I forage around, hitting area tag sales and asking a lot of nosy questions?" Helene said.

Theodosia nodded. That was basically how she'd furnished her tea shop.

"And if I'm lucky," Helene continued, "I get invited into a few farmsteads and old barns where I poke around for bits of treasure that have been stashed there for decades."

"I'm intrigued," Theodosia said. "Now I really do have to visit your shop."

"Stop by anytime!" Helene cried.

"I will, just not today," Theodosia said. She gestured at her filled-to-capacity tea room. "Too much going on."

Delaine narrowed her eyes. "Are you still digging in and asking questions about Josh Morro's murder? Snooping around?"

"On and off," Theodosia said.

"Good," Delaine said. "Because even though *I've* been discounted as a murder suspect—thank goodness for that!—I still want to see the killer, whoever he is, arrested and brought to justice."

"What if it's a she?" Helene asked.

Delaine gave her a sharp look. "Are you thinking about that actress, Carly Brandt? The one who showed up out of nowhere?"

"Thinking about her, that's all," Helene said. "I can't say I've heard any evidence against her. All she's been doing is trying to gather information about her dead fiancé."

"Carly could still be the guilty party," Delaine said in hushed tones. "She could have easily murdered Josh. Carly claims the two were engaged, but what if they really weren't? What if she *hated* him and this was her big chance?"

"I'm not sure Carly was even *in* Charleston when the murder took place," Theodosia said.

Delaine waved her hand in a dismissive gesture. "Pishposh, of course Carly could have been here. She could have flown in secretly, murdered Josh, then fled the murder scene. After the you-know-what hit the fan, she conveniently turned up two days later looking all distraught and innocent."

"I suppose there's a remote possibility that Carly was working in partnership with one of the crew members," Theodosia said.

Delaine pointed a finger at her. "That idea sounds cray-cray, but it's actually smart thinking, Theo. Carly Brandt could easily be a coconspirator. I wonder if the police have considered that angle?"

"My guess is they already have," Theodosia said.

Delaine made a lemon face. "Still, I'm going to call and give them a gentle nudge."

Theodosia sighed. "I'm sure that will be greatly appreciated."

17

‎❧

After such a busy morning, afternoon at the Indigo Tea Shop was almost relaxing. Miss Dimple puttered about, serving a scatter of guests while Theodosia hung out at the front counter with Drayton. She had a notebook open in front of her and was working on names for their new line of handmade artisan chocolates. So far she liked Church Street Chocolates, Celestial Chocolates, and Fleur Chocolates.

"Those are all good names," Drayton said. "But have you considered Dolce Chocolates?"

"Not bad," Theodosia said as she wrote it down. "It sounds both sweet and elegant."

Then Haley sauntered out with a pan full of lemon scones and said, "What are you two doing? Oh, working on our chocolate project?"

"Working on names, anyway," Theodosia said. "That's step one. I still haven't thought about actual product."

Haley placed the scones in the glass pie saver, then said, "The way I see it, maybe we could kick things off with three different chocolate products. You know, start small, kind of dip our toes in the water and test the market."

"Now you sound like an ad guy instead of a chef," Theodosia said.

"Maybe a few remnants of your old marketing career have rubbed off on me," Haley said.

"Do you really have ideas for three different chocolate products, Haley?" Drayton asked.

Haley bobbed her head. "Remember when I took that candies and confectionaries course at the Culinary Institute?"

"I do indeed," Drayton said. "After you started whipping up wonderful desserts like lime sugar madeleines and brown sugar meringues, I gained something like eight pounds."

"Hah," Haley said. "I had you frosting at the mouth."

Drayton had to chuckle at Haley's remark. "Indeed you did."

"More to the point," Haley said, "I learned lots of different techniques and recipes in that class. One of them being how to make caramel-pecan turtles. You know how much Southerners adore pecans, right? So that could be one of our candies. There are dozens of pecan farms around here, so it'd be a cinch to source ingredients."

"Turtles," Theodosia said. "What a great idea."

"Who doesn't love turtles?" Drayton said. He patted his midsection and said, "Oh my."

"Then maybe we could do a milk chocolate and sea salt bar," Haley said. "You know, just a straight-ahead chocolate bar."

"With a fun, artsy wrapper," Drayton said. "Maybe designed by one of our local artists." He was brewing three different pots of tea but listening carefully.

"And then maybe try our hand at a small line of truffles. For starters I was thinking chai truffles, cinnamon truffles, and amaretto truffles. Or we could do tea-infused flavors."

"All of which could be sold separately or gift boxed," Theodosia said. "I think those are all delightful ideas, Haley."

"You're quite the little chocolatier," Drayton said to Haley. Then he held up a finger. "But we still need to come up with a memorable name."

"We'll keep working away on names," Theodosia said. "Now that Haley's given us a preliminary game plan, maybe the name will come about organically."

"Or in a wild burst of creativity," Drayton said.

"Actually," Haley said, "I have a name."

"You do?" Theodosia said.

"Don't keep us in suspense," Drayton said. "What is it?"

Haley grinned. "Sweet Caroline."

Theodosia and Drayton exchanged glances. "We love it," they said together.

"Really?" Haley looked delighted.

"It's perfect," Theodosia said.

"Unless it's already taken," Drayton said.

Theodosia was more optimistic. "Of course we'll check out trademarks and such. But for now, I think we have a winner."

"Gee," Haley said, clearly pleased. Then, as she heard the front door snick open, she turned and muttered a quick, "Oh boy," and squirted toward the kitchen just as Bill Glass walked into the tea shop.

Today Bill Glass was dressed in a battered leather jacket, saggy blue jeans, and ratty loafers. In fact, his shoes were so old and beaten up that one of the soles actually flapped as he walked.

Theodosia shook her head. *Lord, give me strength.*

"Hiya," Glass said as he walked toward them. *Flap.* "How do?" *Flap.* Then he smiled his trademark cheesy smile and said, "I brought you guys a stack of papers so you can share 'em with your customers." He winked at Theodosia. "And I put a nice sensational story about Josh Morro's murder right on the front page."

"Do tell," Drayton muttered as Glass dumped his stack of *Shooting Star* tabloids onto the counter.

"Plus, I've got big news," Glass added.

Theodosia's ears perked up. "Something about the murder?"

Glass gave a conspiratorial nod. "My contact at CPD tells me Craig Cole is the number one suspect."

"Seriously?" Theodosia said. When she'd spoken with Cole that morning, he hadn't seemed to have a care in the world. If he was suspect numero uno, wouldn't he be mildly concerned? Or was he a total sociopath with ice in his veins?

"You look surprised. Who did you think it would be?" Glass asked. He reached a hand out, lifted the top off the cake saver, and helped himself to a scone.

"Not sure who's at the top of the list," Theodosia said. She was reluctant to share any information with Bill Glass for fear it would end up in next week's paper.

Glass took a bite of scone, chewed thoughtfully, and said, "Why do I not believe you, Miss Browning? Whenever you get involved in a nice juicy criminal case it seems as if you're always a half step ahead of the police."

"You flatter me, Mr. Glass," Theodosia said.

Glass gave her a serious look. "Not this time. I'll bet you've been whittling down your list. Care to whisper sweet nothings in my ear as to who you think the culprit really is?"

"Um, no," Theodosia said.

"Let me pour you a cup of tea," Drayton interjected.

"Hey, yeah," Glass said. "That'd be good."

Drayton poured a stream of amber tea into an indigo blue takeout cup, snapped on the lid, and shoved it across the counter. "Here you are. Tea to go."

"You guys are always trying to get rid of me." Glass sounded supremely wounded.

"Only because we're frightfully busy," Drayton said. He made a big production of looking at his watch and frowning. "What time is that group from the Dove Cote Inn supposed to arrive?"

"Two thirty," Theodosia said, picking up on his ruse.

"It's two fifteen now," Drayton said, looking harried.

"Time to hustle," Theodosia said. She put a hand on Bill Glass's shoulder, spun him around, and said, "Appreciate the papers, and thanks for stopping by. See you later, okay?" Ten seconds later, Glass was out the door and Theodosia was breathing a huge sigh of relief.

"Do you think Glass knew we were fibbing?" Drayton asked.

"Who cares? At least he's gone."

"You've become very skilled at ousting unwelcome guests."

"Do you think I offend them?" Theodosia asked.

"Actually," Drayton said, "you charm them."

When Riley called Theodosia's cell phone a few minutes later, she couldn't help herself. She had to ask.

"Is Craig Cole really your leading suspect?"

"Who's the idiot spreading that rumor?" Riley asked.

"Bill Glass."

Riley snorted. "That lousy hack."

"So Cole isn't under suspicion anymore?"

"I didn't say that."

"So he is? Is Ted Juniper still in the running as well?"

"Theodosia. Sweetheart. Leave it alone, okay?"

"I'm just . . . curious."

"No, you're prying. And, just for the record, I'm not working the Josh Morro case. I'm on something else."

"A murder?"

"No. And that's all I'm going to say, okay?"

"Okay."

"The reason I called is to thank you for the fabulous dinner last night," Riley said. "And to apologize for having to bounce out of there so early. I guarantee it won't happen again."

"You promise?"

"Cross my heart and pinky-swear," Riley said.

"Okay, apology accepted," Theodosia said as the tea shop line suddenly rang and Drayton answered it. Then he waggled the phone at Theodosia and mouthed, "Beth Ann."

"Gotta go," Theodosia said. "Talk to you later." She grabbed the other phone and said, "What's up, Beth Ann?"

"I just got word that today's shoot will be running late. Joe Adler wants to keep filming for another couple of hours so he can get this one scene finished and in the can. Anyway, they're asking for more food." Beth Ann paused and took a breath. "Can we do that?"

"Tell them yes. And I'll figure something out, okay?"

"Got it."

Theodosia looked at her watch. "I should be there in an hour or so."

"Okay, thanks," Beth Ann said. "And thank Haley for me, too. You guys are lifesavers."

"What's up?" Drayton asked once Theodosia hung up.

"The shoot is going to run late and they need more food."

"I wonder what Haley will have to say about that?"

"You can come with me while I ask her," Theodosia said.

Drayton held up both hands, palms out. "No thanks. I'm plenty busy here."

"Chicken."

Theodosia went into the kitchen and said, "Haley, please don't kill me, but we have a problem."

Haley looked up from where she was chopping apples and celery for tomorrow's tea sandwiches. "What? Somebody spilled the tea? Got a cleanup in aisle five?"

"A different kind of disaster. Beth Ann just called and the shoot at Brittlebank Manor is going to run late, so they're asking for more food."

Haley leaned against the butcher-block counter. "What kind of food?"

"I think if we took over a couple trays of tea sandwiches and a plate of scones we'd be okay."

Haley thought for a minute. "That we can manage."

"Really?"

"Sure, really." Haley tapped the side of her head with an index finger. "Good thing I've been planning ahead and have a few things prepped."

"How can I help?" Theodosia asked. But Haley had already grabbed a fresh loaf of sourdough bread and was throwing slices onto the counter as if she were dealing hands of five-card stud in Vegas.

"You can start buttering," Haley said.

So Theodosia buttered while Haley whipped up crocks of chicken pâté and cream cheese with olives and sliced a dozen or so tomatoes.

"Okay, once I spread my fillings on the bread, you slap on a tomato slice," Haley instructed. "Then top the sandwiches and get your magic little fingers out of the way so I can whack off the crusts."

"That's a technical culinary term? Whack off the crusts?"

Haley grinned. "It is in my kitchen."

"And you'll cut them into quarters?"

"Par for the course," said Haley.

"And we have scones?"

"Got a ton of lemon scones in the freezer. You run and grab the picnic baskets while I heat up the scones and finish them off with a dusting of powdered sugar."

They worked together for another forty-five minutes, wrapping, sorting, and packing everything up.

"You think we're good?" Haley asked.

"I think this will more than do the trick." Theodosia glanced at her watch and frowned. "Drat! I've really got to hustle—transport this food to Brittlebank Manor, arrange it, and probably stay for a while. I sure don't want Beth Ann to have to spend the entire day and night there."

"So what's the problem?"

"Oh, I promised the director I'd tea-dye a dress for him. It's a gown they're using in the movie."

"Jeez, if it'd help any I could probably do that," Haley said. "Teacake and I were just going to flake out tonight and watch a movie."

"You're not seeing Ben?" Ben was Haley's sometimes boyfriend.

"Not tonight, he's supposed to be studying."

"Then I guess it comes down to if you really have time?" Theodosia said.

"Is the gown here?"

"Hanging in my office. Along with a tin of black tea that Drayton said should do the trick."

"No problem. I'll put on a kettle and dye the dress right now. If all goes well it should be ready first thing tomorrow."

"Haley, you're a godsend."

18

The craft services table was practically depleted by the time Theodosia arrived at Brittlebank Manor.

"Thanks goodness you're here," Beth Ann said. "Even though we're basically down to crumbs I've still had to beat people off with a stick."

"Well, beat no more because Haley fixed us a bunch of tea sandwiches and scones," Theodosia said as she unpacked the baskets and began setting out the food. "How long do you think the shoot will go?" She had an idea buzzing inside her brain and wondered if she'd have time to pull it off.

"They were supposed to quit filming at four, but I'm hearing another two or three hours at least."

"This is the Victorian parlor scene?" Theodosia asked.

"They're setting up in that big room with the fancy chandelier and poufy curtains, so that must be it. A dramatic scene with lots of shouting back and forth. At least that's what it sounds like to me from listening to the actors rehearse their lines."

"Okay, you go ahead and take off for the day. I've got this." Theodosia was still processing her idea, wondering if she could muster up the courage to make it happen.

"Just to remind you, tomorrow's shoot is on location somewhere," Beth Ann said. "They're moving everybody out to the country, so we won't be needed."

"Ah, that's probably why they're working late tonight."

Theodosia was giving Beth Ann a goodbye wave just as Joe Adler walked up to the craft services table. He grabbed two sandwiches, stuffed one in his mouth, and said, "Did you do a tea-dye number on that gown yet?"

"Give me a break," Theodosia said. "I've been working all day."

"But you'll do it?"

"It'll get done one way or another," Theodosia promised.

"Here," Adler said, handing her a card. "Now you've got my cell number just in case."

"Thanks," Theodosia said. She picked up the tea urn from the table, found it was empty, and decided to brew a full pot.

Good thing she did. The shoot really did run late—the scene in the parlor consisted of horrific fighting and shouting, which seemed to drain the actors' spirits and energy—so the tea sandwiches and scones were very much appreciated.

When Adler finally yelled, "That's a wrap," the cast and most of the crew looked exhausted. They grabbed coats and bags, scurrying off like rats leaving a sinking ship, with just a skeleton crew staying behind to pack up.

Feeling tired yet accomplished—because, yes, it'd been a busy day for her, too—Theodosia packaged up the scant leftovers.

"Hey, Theo, you need any help?" Brittany, the head stylist, asked as she walked by, shrugging into a black leather jacket.

"Thanks, I got this," Theodosia said. *At least I think I do.*

Finally, when just a few muffled voices sounded from down the hall, Theodosia walked into the makeup room, poked around, and found a metal nail file. Gripping it firmly, she walked to the back stairway, making up her mind as she went. Then, slowly and stealthily, she climbed the stairs all the way up to the mysterious third floor. She knew that this might be her only chance to see, once and for all, what secrets might be contained in that attic room.

The third-floor landing still looked dusty and worn, the door leading into it still locked tight. No matter. Theodosia took the nail file she'd appropriated, inserted the pointy end into the doorjamb, and went to work. This wasn't her first rodeo and after some forty seconds of seesawing back and forth, the old lock clicked open.

The *click* of the lock synced with a jump in Theodosia's heart rate.

Scared? No, don't be, she told herself.

Drawing a deep breath, Theodosia pushed open the door and stepped inside.

Strangely, the third floor was all one large room. No row of small rooms where maids and butlers had once slept.

Maybe the help had slept in the basement?

She supposed it was possible. Or maybe the cooks and cleaners had gone home in the evening.

The room was pretty much empty, save for a myriad of dust bunnies, mouse droppings, and some piles of garbage. A musty smell permeated the entire place and old wallpaper peeled in long strips from the walls. There was no actual furniture except for a narrow iron bed frame hunkered over near a window.

Theodosia walked toward the bed frame and saw that it was completely rusted.

As she drew closer, she spotted a pair of leather handcuffs. The leather was old, dried, and cracked. But what made the cuffs really terrifying was that they were attached to a chain. With the chain bolted to the bed frame.

Dear Lord. This wasn't just some spooky legend, this was for real.

With a kind of morbid fascination, Theodosia poked a finger at one of the leather handcuffs. The cuff was old to the point of being brittle. In fact, anyone touching these handcuffs might cause them to crumble.

Still, she knew there was a time when these cuffs had been supple and strong. They'd been clamped around poor Audra Baker's wrists and had imprisoned her here for any number of years.

Theodosia shuddered. This was the stuff of nightmares. If she was ever going to write a script for a horror movie, here was the fodder for it, the absolute chill factor that would make the tiny hairs on the back of your neck stand straight up.

Was that why the film company had selected Brittlebank Manor? Because of its unsavory past? Its strange history? But no, probably a Hollywood location scout had looked at any number of old mansions in Charleston. Maybe this was the one that had been available. Or the cheapest to rent.

A feeling of sadness and isolation swept over Theodosia. She knew this attic was an awful place that could easily slither its way into her subconscious and haunt her dreams if she let it.

She vowed not to let that happen. Better to leave now, her curiosity satisfied, and go home to her cozy, safe cottage.

But when Theodosia tried to open the door to leave, she found that it was locked tight.

No!

Theodosia grasped the doorknob again and cranked hard,

turned it and twisted it with all her might. But the door still wouldn't budge.

Is it stuck? Or did someone lock me in?

Maybe this was supposed to be a joke. She poked her nail file into the doorjamb and jiggled it back and forth, but this time she wasn't able to work her magic.

Okay, whoever locked me in here, you've had your fun—now let me out!

Theodosia shouted at the top of her lungs, pounded hard on the door, and finally resorted to kicking it with all her might. The door didn't shatter, budge, or break. She was locked in the attic with nothing but the remains of a mystery—the bizarre tale of a woman's strange imprisonment.

And, of course, the sun was just about to set. Which meant that, in another fifteen minutes, the attic would be dark as a coal bin.

Theodosia spent the next sixty seconds in a blind panic. She shouted some more, paced the floor like a wild animal, and went back to the door and pounded on it. Nothing worked. Feeling as if her brain were about to explode, Theodosia forced herself to quiet her breathing and calm down. To relax, get a grip, and think this through.

That's when she remembered the secret passage she'd seen on the blueprints.

Okay, just where is this secret passageway?

Theodosia pressed herself up against the closest interior wall and began to explore. She pushed on all the walls, ran her fingers over any little seams and nubs she felt, and then along the baseboards. No magic escape way jumped out at her.

She reached into her pocket and pulled out her cell phone, used the light on it to scan the cracks, hoping they'd reveal some kind of gap.

Come on, Audra, I'm counting on you to show me the way.

Theodosia searched high and low, ran her fingers along more cracks, pushed on walls, but to no avail.

Now what?

Theodosia decided that when in doubt, call in the cavalry. So she made her call.

Drayton answered on the first ring. "Hello?"

"Drayton, I'm locked in!" Theodosia shouted.

"I'm sorry, you're locked out of your house?" He sounded relaxed. As if he'd just gotten home, kicked off his shoes, and fixed himself a gin rickey.

"No, I'm locked *in.*" Theodosia's voice quavered as she fought to stem the rising tide of panic.

"In?" Drayton was confused. "In where?"

"I'm locked in the attic at Brittlebank Manor."

"What on God's green earth are you doing there?" Drayton shouted.

"Investigating?"

"Is that a question or an answer?"

"Please don't try for humor at a time like this," Theodosia said. "This is a serious *situation.*" She walked over to where two dirt-covered triangle-shaped windows filtered in a small amount of fading light.

"What do you want me to do? Call the fire department? Wait, do they do attic rescues?"

"I'm thinking you should . . . Wait a minute." Theodosia cradled her cell phone in one hand, touched her other hand to one of the windows, and made a careful inspection. The window had a very large crack in it. Actually, it was a giant spiderweb-shaped crack, as if it had been smashed hard by someone's angry fist. "Hold the line a minute, Drayton. I have an idea. I think maybe I can bash out a window up here."

"Isn't that breaking and entering?" Drayton asked.

"Technically it would be breaking and exiting," Theodosia said. She glanced around and saw a three-foot-long hunk of wood, what might have once been a piece of banister, lying in one corner.

Drayton was still talking. "Breaking and exiting doesn't strike me as a legitimate . . ." he said as Theodosia set down her phone and picked up the wood. She hefted it over one shoulder, testing its weight. Then, clenching the wood in her hands, holding it like a baseball bat, she walked over to the window. She lined up her angle and swung with all her might, like Aaron Judge hitting a line drive in Yankee Stadium.

An earsplitting CRASH rent the air. It echoed through the entire attic, sent shards of glass flying, and frightened Drayton half to death.

19

"Theodosia!" Drayton's tinny-sounding voice echoed from the phone. "What happened? Theodosia? Are you quite okay?"

"I'm fine," Theodosia said, putting the phone back to her ear. "I'm just . . . well, I guess you could call it being resourceful. I broke out a window."

"You did not!"

"Now I'm about to climb out onto the roof."

"Don't," he warned. "You'll fall!"

Theodosia took the hunk of wood and poked it at the window ledge, clearing away all the broken glass. Then she hooked one leg through the window and stared down at a gentle slope of dark gray slate tiles.

"Actually, the roofline doesn't look all that steep."

"So what are you saying?" Drayton asked. "How on earth do you intend to get down from there?"

Theodosia studied the angle of the roof. "I figure if I creep down slowly, maybe I can . . ."

"What?" Drayton said. "Slide down?"

"No, that would probably be too dangerous. Probably just try to inch my way down a bit."

Theodosia climbed out onto the roof. Now that she was outside, feeling a breeze wash over her, looking at rounded treetops and dark sky with its faint glimmer of early stars, she felt better. As if she'd finally been set free.

"The slope of the roof is fairly gentle, maybe forty degrees at best," Theodosia said into her phone.

"Tricky," Drayton said. "What's it made of?"

"Looks like slate tiles."

"Tricky and slippery," Drayton said.

"I'm fairly sure I can ease my way down to . . . WHOOPS!"

Slick as grease through a goose, Theodosia's feet flew out from under her and she landed hard on her backside. Then she was hurtling down the roof, bumping over the tiles, practically out of control. Her high-pitched scream quavered as it was picked up and carried by the wind.

NOOOO!

Theodosia's phone flew out of her hand and tumbled down ahead of her, where it was stopped cold by the back-end peak of a dormer. Which also thankfully stopped her wildly caroming body.

BAM.

Theodosia hit hard and flopped up against the back of the dormer like a pancake hitting a plate. Shaking her head, feeling more than a little queasy, she tried to get her breathing under control as she checked for broken bones or bruised ribs. When she didn't find any, when she decided she was actually in one piece, she looked around and tried to get her bearings.

Yes, I'm still on the roof. But wow, what a crazy, unexpected ride.

When Theodosia was somewhat recovered, except for a slightly banged-up knee, she reached down and grabbed her phone.

"Are you still there?" Drayton was shouting. "Theo, talk to me! Please tell me you didn't fall three stories and break your fool neck."

"I'm still in one piece, Drayton. In fact, the crazy thing is I'm quite a bit lower than I was before." She glanced around. "I'm perched on some kind of ledge between the first and second floors."

"Glory be. Now what?" Drayton said. "I should call the fire department?"

"Wait one," Theodosia said. She glanced around and saw two large metal loops hooking over this portion of the roof. Barely ten feet from where she'd landed. A sudden burst of inspiration pinged inside her brain. She knew exactly what they were. And what she would do.

"No need for emergency vehicles," Theodosia said. "As luck would have it, I just spotted the remains of an old fire escape hanging off the back of the building. I think it's an old safety feature left over from when this place was a convent."

"It was a convent?"

"Only for a few years, back in the thirties."

"But the fire escape is still there? Talk to me, Theo, you've got me worried sick."

There were a few moments of silence as Theodosia clambered over to the edge of the roof, then she said, "The fire escape is rickety and rusted as all get-out, but I'm going to give it a shot and climb down."

"No!"

"Drayton, relax, I'm six steps down already." Theodosia's heart was in her throat as every step she took made a hollow-sounding *clunk*. Then, finally, she said, "Okay, I just hit a narrow metal grate that I guess is some kind of landing. It's a little tippy so I'll probably have to . . ." She studied the elaborate gear. "Yeah, I've got to jimmy this old gear so I can get the ladder to drop all the way down."

"Be careful," Drayton warned.

"I'm trying. But this doggone thing is stuck." There was the ungodly squeal of metal grinding against metal as Theodosia worked at the gears and the old fire escape protested mightily. "Maybe if I kick it."

Balancing carefully, holding on to both sides of the railing, Theodosia delivered a hard kick. There was a teeth-rattling CLANK and a long, drawn-out grinding noise. And then, suddenly, WHOOSH!

Nobody was more surprised than Theodosia as she hung on for dear life as the ladder she was standing on dropped like a shot. Her breath was ripped from her as she rode it down like a fireman sliding down a firehouse pole. And then . . .

BOOM!

The old ladder hit the ground with earth-shattering impact, sending up a puff of dust mingled with myriad rust chips.

Theodosia sneezed and then cried, "Drayton, I'm back on terra firma! No need to come and break me out."

"What about the broken window?"

She glanced up at the old house with trepidation. "I kind of don't care about that right now. Besides, I'm guessing the film company's insurance will cover it."

"And if it doesn't?"

Theodosia heaved a loud sigh. "They can bill me."

It was seven thirty by the time Theodosia got home. She still felt shaken and a teeny bit wired. So after feeding Earl Grey, and deciding her knee and ankle felt better, she changed into running gear and headed out for what she figured would be a twenty-minute slow jog.

But just as she was turning the corner onto Archdale Street, she saw Mrs. Robie, one of her neighbors, sitting on her porch in the twilight. The poor sweetheart, who had to be in her high eighties, had been robbed of most of her eyesight by macular degeneration.

"Hey, Mrs. Robie," Theodosia called out. "It's Theodosia."

"Evening, Theo," Mrs. Robie called back. "Do you by any chance have that lovely dog with you tonight?"

"You bet. We're both out for a jog."

"Come say hello before y'all go on your run, will you, honey?"

"Gladly," Theodosia said as she and Earl Grey headed up Mrs. Robie's flagstone walk, then climbed three steps onto her wraparound porch.

"Come here, sweet doggy," Mrs. Robie said. She was petite, with birdlike arms and legs and cottony white hair. Tonight she sat in a wicker chair with a pink blanket spread across her lap.

Dutifully, Earl Grey walked over and pressed his fine head into Mrs. Robie's waiting hands. She massaged his neck, gently tugged his ears, and rubbed his soft muzzle. Earl Grey let out a satisfied grunt.

"There's my boy, there's a good boy."

"He remembers you," Theodosia said.

Mrs. Robie laughed. "And I remember him. I'll never forget the time I was laid up in the hospital with my bad hip and you and Earl Grey came to visit. I never thought a hospital would let a dog in. Because of their silly rules, you know."

"Earl Grey is a certified therapy dog," Theodosia explained. "So he's allowed special access."

"I tossed a rubber ball right from my bed and he chased after it, the little rascal."

"He had a great time," Theodosia said.

"So did I," Mrs. Robie said. Then she patted Earl Grey's shoulder and said, "Have a nice run, Mr. Earl. Run like the wind."

*　*　*

They did run like the wind. Picking up speed as they cruised down Archdale, then over on South Battery as they ran past some of Charleston's grandest homes, ending up in White Point Garden. This was one of Theodosia's favorite parks. Located right on the tip of the peninsula, White Point Garden featured military statues and old cannons, stands of live oak and palmettos, and a wonderful classic gazebo that was often reserved for weddings.

Tonight, the wind was whipping in from the Atlantic at a good twenty knots, stirring up white caps on Charleston Harbor and tossing a few small craft around. Theodosia stood there and watched a large container ship come gliding in. Next to one of the small J/22 sailboats that flitted across the harbor, it looked like an enormous whale.

Theodosia ran past the gazebo toward the parking lot along the battery wall. A half dozen food trucks were congregated there and she realized she was feeling hungry. Famished, really, since she hadn't eaten a morsel of food since before noon. She looked at the food trucks and their various offerings—barbecued ribs, Creole chicken, tacos and gorditas, and one called Squeals on Wheels that featured brisket and pulled pork. Another truck had the word SMOOTHIES painted on its side in bouncy pink and blue letters. And underneath that, MADE WITH FROZEN YO-GURT. Perfect.

Theodosia walked Earl Grey over to the food truck's window and ordered a peanut butter and carob smoothie. Paid for it with the ten-dollar bill she'd stuck in her tennis shoe. Yes, a smoothie should do the trick. Stanch her hunger pangs and give her the kick she needed to run back home.

The smoothie proved to be cool, delicious, and so thick that

Theodosia had to use a spoon. Enjoying her treat immensely, she wandered over to one of the park's benches and sat down while Earl Grey collapsed in a heap at her feet. As she ate, she thought back over the day, almost chuckling at how bizarre it had been. Delivering a special-order coffee cake to Adler and then volunteering to tea-dye a dress for him, hosting their Vintage Tea, rushing more food over to Brittlebank Manor, and then getting locked in the attic only to escape via an alternative yet creative route.

And now she was sitting here, stars twinkling in a tuxedo black sky, breezes off the Atlantic stirring up ions in the air, waves slapping quietly against a nearby pier.

A decent ending to the day.

Deciding it was probably time to start for home, Theodosia stood up and gave a tug on the leash she'd casually looped over her arm. Earl Grey was ready, too. He clambered to his feet and walked along beside her as she finished her smoothie.

That's when another of the food trucks caught Theodosia's eye. It was the Rocco's Ribs truck, a white, squared-off van that must have been hastily painted with a kind of whitewash. But not painted over particularly well because on the back of the truck, in very faint letters, you could still make out the words DEVEROUX ELECTRIC.

Theodosia looked again, blinking hard as her brain registered what she was looking at. What was left of her smoothie dropped—SPLAT!—on the pavement. A nervous buzz spread slowly through her body.

Wait just a gol-darned minute. Deveroux Electric? Seriously?

20

As in Helene Deveroux? As in Helene's dead husband who'd no doubt been the owner of Deveroux Electric?

Is this something I need to investigate? Oh yes, I think it most definitely is. Because if Helene Deveroux was connected to Deveroux Electric, maybe she knew something about . . .

Theodosia shook her head to dispel that thought. No sense conjuring up bigger, crazier problems.

Yet she was fizzing with a knowledge that something was definitely wrong here. That something strange was going on. She looked down at her ruined smoothie and saw that Earl Grey was staring at it, too.

"C'mon," Theodosia said to him. "We gotta go." And with that, they cut across the park and down King Street, heading for Helene's shop, the Sea Witch.

And all the way Theodosia kept telling herself, *This is crazy, Helene's not going to be there. Her shop probably isn't open in the evening. But still . . .*

She spun down King Street anyway, passed Lanier & Love

Fine Bedding and Borchard's Jewelers, and came to a dead stop directly in front of Helene's shop. The Sea Witch was housed in a redbrick building with white trim and three tall, narrow front windows. Antique pots and ceramic statues were on display in one window; a few pieces of maritime art and some old lanterns and portholes were arranged in the other two.

Theodosia hadn't been sure what she would find here. But, heavens to Betsy, there was a light on inside! Heaving a sigh, Theodosia decided that maybe Helene was here after all, working late. And that she could clear up this mess right now. Helene would confess that she was a complete ditz when it came to electrical wiring and the two of them could have a good laugh over it.

After all, Helene couldn't have, wouldn't have . . .

Would she?

The image of sparks flying off Josh Morrow's writhing body lingered in Theodosia's head.

No, this has to be a weird coincidence. Although maybe Helene . . .

No. Theodosia's mind really didn't want to go there.

She peered in the small window on the front door of the Sea Witch, then knocked softly. There was no answer, no one moving about inside. But there was definitely a light on in back, as if somebody had stayed to work late. Maybe in a storeroom or office?

Touching the doorknob, not expecting it to turn, Theodosia found that the door was actually open a tick. She thought that was a little strange, but she squared her shoulders anyway and pushed her way in, wondering what she'd find.

Stepping across the threshold was like stepping into a jewelry store. There were rows and rows of low glass cases that contained antique ceramics, old Spanish coins, brass clocks, rare books, and old pistols. Shelves against the wall held an antique jeweled crown, ships' wheels, an old brass sextant, silver candlesticks, brass portholes, and lots more.

"Be careful," Theodosia whispered to Earl Grey. "Try not to bump or touch anything."

Now that she was inside she could hear faint music playing. The radio maybe, or one of those subscription music services that businesses often used. At any rate, she recognized a homogenized version of "Do You Know the Way to San Jose."

"Hello," Theodosia called out. "Anybody here?"

There was no answer.

"Helene?" Theodosia ventured again.

Still no answer.

Theodosia wondered if Helene or one of her staff had left in a hurry, maybe trying to catch the last FedEx pickup, and had forgotten to lock the front door. But that seemed awfully far-fetched. Who'd be so rushed and absent-minded to leave a shop like this unlocked, especially since it contained so many valuable items?

Moving quietly through the small maze of cases and displays, Theodosia and Earl Grey headed for the back of the shop, where a door stood half open. Helene's office, perhaps?

Maybe Helene was on the phone dealing with a client in another time zone.

But as Theodosia approached what had to be an office, she didn't hear anyone talking. Just the music, which had now switched to "The Girl from Ipanema."

"Helene," Theodosia called as she approached the office with some trepidation. "Helene, it's Theodosia. Are you in there?"

Again there was no answer, no sound, save the insistent ticking of two antique brass clocks that sat on a nearby counter. One clock was a split second slower, so the ticks sounded like echoes.

Theodosia pressed the flat of her hand against the office door and gave a gentle push. The door opened slowly and loudly, like the creak of a coffin lid. And revealed . . .

Helene's body lay crumpled on the office floor. Next to an overturned desk chair and surrounded by a sea of papers. A bright red pool of blood had soaked the carpet next to her head.

Oh, dear Lord what happened? And on the heels of that, *Is she dead?*

"Sit. Stay," Theodosia told Earl Grey. Once her dog complied, she took three steps in, mindful not to get too close and step in the spill of blood. She crouched down and carefully stretched a hand out to gently touch the side of Helene's neck. She prayed there was still a spark of life within her.

But no. There was nothing. No breath sounds, no warm throb of a pulse. Helene was tragically and catastrophically dead.

Theodosia retreated into the shop, where, with shaking hands, she pulled out her phone and dialed 911.

"I'm at the Sea Witch on King Street," Theodosia told the dispatcher when she came on the line. "And the owner appears to be dead. Shot, I think." Her words tumbled out thick and fast. "There must have been a break-in. Or robbery. Although I'm not sure anything's . . ." Theodosia wanted to be succinct and to the point, but knew she was tripping over her words. "We need help. The police, I guess. Maybe an ambulance?"

"Is anyone else there now?" the dispatcher asked.

Theodosia looked around the shop, suddenly fearful that she'd walked in and surprised Helene's killer. That he might still be lurking close by.

"I don't think so. At least I don't see anyone else."

"Go outside and wait on the sidewalk," the dispatcher instructed. "There's a car already on its way."

By the time Theodosia and Earl Grey threaded their way back through the shop and stepped outside, they could hear a siren screaming from a few blocks away. Then it grew louder and Earl Grey pushed his shoulder up against her hip. *Now* he was frightened.

"It's okay," she told her dog. "It's gonna be okay."

But when a cruiser pulled up, lights blazing and siren still blatting loudly, Theodosia knew it wasn't going to be okay.

The officers charged toward her, guns drawn but held at their sides. She gave them a quick rundown of what she'd found and they ran inside. They returned a few minutes later, looking grim, talking on their radios. And five minutes after that, a black Suburban bumped up to the curb, subtle red and blue lights flashing from above its front bumper. The rear door flew open and Detective Tidwell climbed out.

"You," he said upon spotting Theodosia. Tidwell was dressed in a baggy green jacket and dark brown slacks. His tie had been pulled down and his shirt looked halfway untucked.

"Me," she said back.

"What are you doing here?" Tidwell demanded.

"I stopped by to talk to Helene Deveroux, the owner of the shop."

"But I'm guessing you didn't talk to her?"

"I'm afraid she was dead when I arrived."

"Nobody else around?" Tidwell squinted up and down the dark street as if culprits might still be lurking.

"Not that I saw." Theodosia glanced at Earl Grey, who was watching her carefully. "Not that *we* saw."

The two officers huddled with Tidwell for a few minutes. Then Tidwell went in to look at the body. He came back out a few minutes later just as a shiny black van pulled to the curb.

"Crime Scene," Tidwell said to Theodosia. "You touch anything in there with your sticky little fingers?"

"Um, the front doorknob, then the door leading to the office." Theodosia thought for a moment. "And I touched two fingers against Helene's neck. I pretty much had to, you know, to see if she was still alive."

"And she was not," Tidwell said.

Theodosia shivered. "Unfortunately, no."

Two men from the Crime Scene unit, one tall, one short, laden with camera cases and other gear, hustled past them into the shop.

"You're doing video?" Tidwell asked.

"And stills," said the short one, patting his camera case.

"Good. Then I want every hair, smudge, and miniscule piece of dirt and particulate collected, bagged, and analyzed," Tidwell told them. "We need to get to the bottom of this ASAP."

"You got it," the tall one replied.

"And let me know when I can come in and take a closer look, will you?" Tidwell asked.

The short one nodded. "Will do, Chief."

Tidwell turned to Theodosia. "And we need to get a statement from you."

"Of course," she replied.

"So that will be . . . ah, here he is now."

A dark blue BMW pulled in behind the Crime Scene van and Pete Riley climbed out.

"Riley!" Theodosia cried. "What are you doing here?"

"I'm here because *you're* here," Riley said. He stopped a few feet from her, put his hands on his hips, and said, "But the real issue is, why are you involved with Helene Deveroux?"

"It's a long story," Theodosia responded.

"I've got time," Riley said. He walked into the small circle of light to join them. Three humans plus one canine. "What's going on, Theo? What on earth brought you *here?*"

"She's a magnet for trouble," Tidwell muttered.

Theodosia ignored Tidwell and touched a hand to her heart. It was still fluttering excitedly inside her chest as she explained: "Filming ran late at Brittlebank Manor tonight, so when I got home I decided to go for a run."

"Of course you did," Tidwell said.

"Anyway, after Earl Grey and I did a good two miles, I stopped at a food truck gathering," Theodosia said. "You know, where that little parking lot is, near the battery wall?"

"Yes, yes." Tidwell was impatient to hear her story.

"And I just so happened to see the words 'Deveroux Electric' kind of painted over on the back of one of the food trucks."

"What?" Riley said.

The two detectives exchanged skeptical glances, then Tidwell made a noise in the back of his throat as if he didn't quite believe her.

"Painted over, did I hear you correctly? On a *food truck*?" Riley said.

"Yes, a food truck," Theodosia said. She was starting to get irritated. They didn't seem to be taking her story seriously. "Rocco's Ribs, if you must know. Anyway, I started wondering about . . . I mean, Helene's husband owned an electrical repair company . . . so what are the chances?"

"You thought you'd made some sort of connection to the Josh Morro murder?" Tidwell said. "You thought Helene might have some knowledge of electrical engineering. Or wiring?"

"That's right. Which is why I decided to stop by her shop." Theodosia waved a hand in front of her face as if trying to clear the air so her words would get through. "Anyway, I saw a light on and thought Helene might be working late. Figured maybe I could ask her about it. I mean, was it simply a coincidence or was she somehow involved?"

"And then?" Riley said.

"Then I went in because the door was open, unlocked, I mean . . . and that's when I found Helene. Crumpled on the floor in her office." Theodosia drew a shaky breath as if to punctuate her sentence. "It looked to me as if . . . well, I think Helene's been shot."

"Shot where?" Riley asked.

"I'm not sure," Theodosia said.

"Ambulance," Tidwell said in a flat tone, as a white ambulance with the words UNIVERSITY MEDICAL CENTER painted on the side pulled up. "We'd better go in and have a look-see before they get antsy and want to haul her away."

"Right," Riley said.

They both turned and went inside, leaving Theodosia and Earl Grey standing on the sidewalk. Theodosia looked over to where one uniformed officer was stringing up black-and-yellow crime scene tape to cordon off the area, and the other officer had just started talking to the ambulance guys. Kind of yucking it up, like they knew each other. Then she looked down at Earl Grey, who'd been waiting patiently for something to happen. She shrugged, made up her mind, and led Earl Grey into the shop with her. Tidwell and Riley were already in the office, talking in low voices. The Crime Scene guys were also in there and had finished photographing the body and checking the area for trace evidence. Now all four of the men were studying Helene's body.

"Shot clean through the forehead," Riley said. He bent over Helene's crumpled body and studied it again, as if to confirm his words. Then he straightened back up.

"She looks surprised," Theodosia said.

They all turned to stare at Theodosia and her dog.

There was a long moment of silence and then Tidwell said, "You shouldn't be in here." Though he made no movement to throw her out.

"Surprised," Riley said. "What do you mean by that?"

"Helene looks as though she'd been sitting at her desk, talking to someone she knew. And then suddenly had the fright of her life—of her death, actually—when she realized what was happening," Theodosia said. "That something was going way off the rails. And then she . . ."

"And then she what?" Riley prompted.

"Got blown clean off her chair," Theodosia said.

"And shortly thereafter you walked in and found her," Tidwell said. "You shouldn't have been investigating." His tone was cold and accusatory. "You were warned not to get involved."

"Like I told you, I just stopped by to ask Helene a simple question," Theodosia said. "To clear up what I hoped might be some sort of coincidence or misunderstanding. I didn't know I'd stumble on her dead body. This . . ." She threw a hand out to indicate Helene's body. "This wasn't the outcome I was hoping for."

Tidwell gazed at her. "That's your excuse? You dropped by and found her like this?"

"Yes!" Theodosia said. "And badgering me isn't going to help things." She blinked hard, put a hand to her face, trying to keep her tears at bay, and half turned away from them. That's when her eyes fell on the large wooden bookcase that was positioned against the back wall of the office. It was stuffed with oversized art books on porcelains, antique furniture, Greek vases, Renaissance art, and nautical antiques.

But there was more.

A shock of recognition suddenly jolted Theodosia and she let out an audible gasp. Because leaning up against the end of the bookcase were two metal folding chairs!

Theodosia was so stunned she could only point.

Riley picked up on her astonishment first. "What?"

"Folding chairs," Theodosia rasped. "They . . . they look identical to the one that killed Josh Morro!"

"Good heavens," Tidwell said. He turned to his Crime Scene guys. "Did you test those chairs?"

"Why?" the tall one asked.

"Because a chair nearly identical to one of these was used in a murder this past Monday. The Josh Morro case."

"We didn't work that," the short Crime Scene guy said.

"Now that you know there's a possible connection, do you think you could get back to work?" Tidwell sounded testy and upset. He turned and stared at Theodosia. "Now out. Everyone else, get out."

Backing out of the office, Theodosia murmured, "That nails it," to Riley, who was following close behind her.

"Not quite," Riley said.

"No?"

"That nails it pending forensic testing."

"Look," Theodosia said as they zigzagged through the shop. "You and I both know that Helene's death—her murder—has to be connected to Josh Morro's murder."

"Does it really?" Tidwell said. They turned to find him huffing along behind them.

"Helene *had* to be involved," Theodosia said. "Somehow, someway. I mean, two people murdered, both involved in the production of the same feature film? What are the odds?"

"Not very good," Riley mumbled under his breath.

"Excuse me?" Tidwell glared at him.

Riley backpedaled. "I said I think we should call in the EMTs and have her body transported to the ME's office as soon as possible."

21

While Tidwell lingered inside, Theodosia and Riley stepped outside the Sea Witch only to find the two uniformed officers engaged in a heated argument with someone who'd apparently just arrived on scene. Even in the low light, she could see there was minor pushing and shoving going on.

One of the officers noticed Riley and said, "Detective Riley, this guy just showed up out of the blue. Said he was supposed to pick something up from a woman named Deveroux?"

"Quaid?" Theodosia cried. She recognized Adler's assistant immediately. "What are you doing here?"

"You know this guy?" Riley asked her.

"Sure. Well, sort of," Theodosia said. "Quaid is a personal assistant for Joe Adler, the film director."

"A director needs a personal assistant?" Riley said under his breath.

"It's a Hollywood thing," Theodosia told him.

"These guys," Quaid said, trying to shrug off the two uniformed officers, "tell me there's been a murder here. What happened? Who was killed?"

"Helene Deveroux was killed here tonight," Theodosia said.

"The Film Board lady? It can't be." Quaid looked pale and shaken. "That's who I was coming to see."

"What's going on?" Tidwell suddenly demanded.

Quaid was beginning to look genuinely frightened. "Someone from the Charleston Film Board left me a voice mail and said it was urgent I pick something up from Mrs. Deveroux," he said. "And now . . . you guys are telling me she's been murdered?"

"Pick up what?" Riley asked. He sounded skeptical.

Quaid grimaced. "They didn't say."

"Who was it that called?" Tidwell asked as he signaled to the two officers to let Quaid go.

Quaid straightened up, drew a deep breath, and said, "The caller identified himself as Harlan Jasper."

Tidwell gazed at Theodosia. "Is there someone named Harlan Jasper on the Charleston Film Board?"

"Let me check." Theodosia pulled up the Film Board's website on her phone and scrolled to the Board of Directors section. "Yes."

Tidwell looked at Riley. "Get the number and call him."

Riley walked off a few feet to make his call, while Quaid said, "You people have to believe me, I don't know anything about what happened here tonight." He was sweating now and his eyes were bugged out. "I've never even *met* Mrs. Deveroux."

"Too late now," Tidwell said as Riley rejoined the group. He glanced at Riley and said, "Well?"

"Mr. Jasper didn't know what I was talking about."

"And you believed him?" Tidwell asked.

Riley nodded. "I'd have to say . . . yes."

"Someone sent Quaid here on purpose," Theodosia said suddenly. "To serve as a patsy, a decoy, a suspect, whatever."

"I think Theodosia might be right," Riley said.

Tidwell scuffed the toe of his loafer against the sidewalk. "Maybe," he said. "Possibly." Then to Quaid, "You still have that voice mail on your phone?"

"Sure," Quaid said.

Tidwell reached out a big paw. "Hand it over. I'll see if our techs can trace the call."

Quaid gave Tidwell his phone. "When will I get it back?"

"When we're done with it," Tidwell said. Then he frowned and gazed across the street, where a banged-up SUV had just pulled in. "Hell's bells," he said. "Look what the cat dragged in."

Bill Glass came chugging across the street. He had two cameras slung around his neck and was busy thumbing his iPhone.

Earl Grey strained at his leash and growled.

"This just came across my police scanner!" Glass shouted. He was wearing the same pair of shoes because Theodosia could hear one of the soles slapping against the pavement. "There's been another murder?" When nobody answered, he said, "It must be the Deveroux lady. Which means this has to be directly related to the film director guy, right?"

Tidwell stepped in front of everyone to block Bill Glass's approach. "Go away," he said in a curt tone of voice. "No press, no comment."

"Come on," Glass wheedled. "You guys gotta give me something."

Bill Glass peeked around Tidwell's bulk, saw Theodosia standing there, and said, "This is about the film director, isn't it? And now there's been a second murder?"

"I can neither confirm nor deny," Tidwell said.

"No problem," Glass said with an excited yelp. "The look on Miss Browning's face says it all!"

"Look?" snarled Tidwell.

"Yeah, she looks like she's just seen a ghost." Bill Glass's head spun left, then right. "No other press here yet. Hot-cha. Looks like I'm the first. So when's the press conference? Later tonight? First thing tomorrow? When are we gonna get all the dirty details?"

Tidwell just lowered his head and glowered.

Theodosia turned down a ride from Riley. Instead, she wanted to walk home with Earl Grey and not face any more nattering questions. She needed time to think, to process what had happened. And riding with Riley, as dear as he was to her, would have meant an endless stream of questions along with the constant buzz and crackle of his police radio.

Besides, it was a lovely evening. Trees rustled softly in the breeze off the Atlantic and old-fashioned streetlamps gave off a golden glow. With all the trees and wrought-iron fences along the way, moon shadows danced everywhere, looking like some kind of elegant nighttime stencil. And it was still nice and warm, though summer's spell was beginning to fade and autumn was slowly coming on.

Just as Theodosia turned down Meeting Street, a black Mercedes emerged from the darkness, coasted to the curb just ahead of her, and stopped. She slowed her pace, nerves starting to prickle.

Will this night never end?

The driver's-side window slid down with a purr and a male voice called, "Hey, tea lady, mind if I have a word with you?"

Theodosia recognized the voice. Friendly, not dangerous. It was Ken Lotter from W-BAM TV.

"I heard about the murder at the Sea Witch," Lotter said. "Is there any sense in my getting a crew over there?"

Theodosia crossed the grass median, walked up to Lotter's car, and looked in. The console was super contemporary and glowed blue like the cockpit of a jetliner.

"I don't think so," Theodosia said. "The police have the place pretty well buttoned up."

"And there's nobody there wearing a sign around his neck that says 'I'm the Killer'?"

"Not that I noticed, anyway."

"How about a sign that says 'Kick Me'?"

Theodosia smiled. "How did you know I was at the Sea Witch?"

"A friendly tip from a friendly cop who heard the callout. One of my neighbors. In the TV business it helps to stay in good with the folks next door. You know, throw a few steaks on the barbie once in a while?"

"Sounds right."

"Hey, nice dog. What's his name?"

"Earl Grey."

Lotter grinned. "Why does that not surprise me?"

When Theodosia arrived home, she thought about calling Drayton, decided not to, then called him anyway. When he picked up, she could hear a series of squeaky little barks in the background—*arf, arf, arf.* It was Drayton's dog, Honey Bee.

"Will you quit that," Drayton was saying. "It's the phone, not the doorbell." Then, "Hello?"

"You know those weird calls you get when you don't expect them?" Theodosia said.

"Yes, I do. Fact is, I got one earlier tonight from *you*."

"This is another one," Theodosia said.

"What!"

"Do you have a few minutes?" Theodosia snapped the top off her bottle of Fiji water and took a quick sip.

"I'm all ears. What happened *now*?"

So Theodosia spilled her tale of woe to Drayton. Told him about seeing the Deveroux Electric truck repainted, going to Sea Witch and finding Helene dead, dealing with the police, and then having Quaid Barthel show up.

"Dear Lord," Drayton said. "You're telling me that Helene Deveroux was murdered in cold blood?"

"That's about the size of it."

"And that Quaid showed up because he'd been tasked to pick up some papers from Helene?" Drayton said.

"I don't know what that was all about. Quaid didn't even know. But it sure was strange having him show up like that."

"And you're thinking it wasn't a coincidence." Drayton stated it as a fact, not a question.

"I don't think Quaid murdered Helene, so I'm fairly sure somebody tried to set him up for it."

"But you arrived first and found the body."

"Lucky me," Theodosia said.

"Lucky for Quaid," Drayton said. "Otherwise the plan to make him a patsy or a suspect would have worked beautifully."

"But the question is—who set him up? Who's the master puppeteer pulling the strings?"

"And powering up the homemade electric chair last Monday and pulling the trigger tonight," Drayton said. "If, in fact, it's the same person."

"Oh, it's the same person," Theodosia said. "I just haven't figured out who it is yet."

"But you will," Drayton said. "Right? Because now it's an even bigger challenge."

Theodosia took another sip of water, considered Drayton's words, and said, "You're right. It *is* a challenge and I *will* keep working on it."

"Ah," Drayton said. "There's the Theodosia we know and love."

22

"You certainly got yourself stuck in the glue last night," Drayton said to Theodosia.

It was early Friday morning at the Indigo Tea Shop and Theodosia, Drayton, and Haley were sitting together at the little table by the fireplace sipping cups of Sweet Lady Grey, one of Drayton's house blends. Theodosia had just finished filling in the details about last night's wild escape from the attic, seeing the food truck, and then finding poor Helene Deveroux murdered at her shop. And when this morning's *Post & Courier* thunked against their front door, they were gobsmacked by the headline that blared: "SECOND MURDER-MYSTERY MOVIE DEATH!"

"Good grief," Drayton murmured. "Newspapers can be so tawdry." But it didn't stop him from reading the article in its entirety while Haley prodded Theodosia for a few more details about last night. Finally, Drayton folded up his newspaper, gazed at Theodosia, and said, "I still can't believe you stumbled onto Helene's murder."

"Neither can I," Theodosia said. "The whole thing is downright bizarre."

"Mmn, not really," Haley said. She was staring at Theodosia, a crooked half smile on her face.

Drayton peered at Haley over his tortoiseshell half-glasses. "Not really? What do you mean by that?"

"Theo found a clue on the back of that food truck," Haley said. "Which sort of pointed her in Helene's direction."

"Yes," Drayton said, drawing out the word.

"Which was good because Theodosia really has a knack for this stuff," Haley said.

"A knack?" Drayton looked as if he found Haley's words quite improbable.

Haley brushed back her stick-straight blond hair and reworded her statement. "Okay, maybe I should say that Theodosia being involved is more like providence, a kind of divine intervention."

"What?" Theodosia said. She didn't think there was anything divine about it.

"What on earth are you talking about?" Drayton said. "You're saying it's a *good* thing Theodosia found poor Helene?"

"In a way, yes," Haley said. "Look at it from this perspective— a crime was committed and Theodosia was first on the scene. That means she has a leg up when it comes to investigating."

Drayton peered at Theodosia with something akin to hope. "*Do* you have a leg up?"

"It doesn't feel that way," Theodosia said.

"But you were there," Haley insisted. "So you must have seen or intuited *something*."

"It was more like intense shock at finding Helene," Theodosia said.

Haley wiggled her fingers. "And what else?"

Theodosia closed her eyes, thought for a moment, then opened them.

"Well, there were the chairs," she said.

Drayton's brows pinched together. "What chairs?"

"Okay, I guess there is more to the story," Theodosia said. So she carefully explained about the metal folding chairs that had been leaning up against the bookcase in Helene's office. How they'd resembled the hotwired chair that had killed Josh Morro.

"You see!" Haley exclaimed. "That's something important right there."

"I thought so, too," Theodosia said. "But the police pretty much discounted any connection."

"Then they're dead wrong. I think those chairs have to mean something," Haley said.

"Maybe so," Theodosia said. "I know the Crime Scene guys were going to haul them back to the lab and analyze them." She stopped and thought for a moment. "But what if those chairs were placed there *after* Helene was murdered? What if they'd been left to intentionally throw off the police—to somehow cover the killer's trail?"

"You're talking about *planted evidence*," Haley said.

"I guess I am," Theodosia said.

"Another distraction," Drayton said. "Something to point the police in the wrong direction. I guess that could be it." He took a final sip of tea, stood up, and said, "All right, dear ones, these murder mysteries make for fascinating conversation, but we have a busy day ahead of us so we'd better hop to it."

"Agreed," Theodosia said. But that didn't mean she'd stop thinking about it.

It was *a* busy day. In fact, Fridays were always busy at the Indigo Tea Shop. Visitors who crowded into Charleston for a weekend jaunt were always drawn to the charming hotels, inns, and

B and Bs in the Historic District. And once they'd wandered the hidden alleys and lanes, once they'd marveled over Charleston Harbor, the amazing architecture, the Gibbes Museum of Art, and traveled Gateway Walk, they often found themselves ending up at the Indigo Tea Shop.

Today was one of those days.

By ten o'clock morning tea had hit a frantic pace. Every table was filled to capacity and at least eight people stood waiting eagerly inside the front door. Miss Dimple had called in at the last minute—some problem with her car, so she couldn't work today. But Beth Ann was there to help. Thank goodness.

Theodosia took orders, rushed them back to Haley, then picked up orders of caramel scones and apple tea bread to be delivered to guests. In between, she skittered to the front counter to grab steaming pots of silver needle, rose hips, and orange pekoe.

"You know," Drayton said as Theodosia grabbed a special order of black tea with peaches and ginger, "next time you stumble into a murder, you could wait until morning to inform me."

"Sorry to upset your sleep," Theodosia said. "But I thought you'd want to know."

Drayton ducked his head. "Truth be known, I was curious. Am curious. But finding Helene's body last night—it didn't worry you?"

"Did I say that? No, it didn't worry me, it scared the crap out of me. I barely slept a wink last night," Theodosia said as her cell phone chimed from inside her apron pocket. She pulled it out and said, "Hello?"

There was a moment of dead air, then a chuckle, then Riley said, "Boy, is Tidwell ever mad at you."

"He shouldn't be," Theodosia said. "If I hadn't gone to Helene's shop last night and found her, nobody would know the poor woman was dead until she didn't show up for . . . well, whatever. Then the trail would be even colder than it is now."

"You think the trail is cold?"

"I don't think your department is hot and heavy into the chase." Theodosia hesitated. "Or are you? Is there something I don't know?"

"Not really," Riley said.

"Did you turn up any forensics on those two metal folding chairs?"

"Just that they're two metal folding chairs."

"You know what I mean. Do they match the one that killed Josh Morro? Same model? Same make?"

"They're a close match, but not exact."

"What about DNA?" Theodosia asked.

"That takes time."

"Those chairs could be false clues, you know."

"We've considered that," Riley said.

"So you're not making brilliant headway on either case."

"Are you?"

"Not exactly." Theodosia gazed out across the floor of the tea shop. It looked warm and friendly, not a place to have such a cold discussion. "Tell me, did the Crime Scene guys discover anything worthwhile last night?"

"You mean besides a body? Nothing earth-shattering, I'm afraid. A shell casing that might be traceable, food crumbs on the carpet, some dust—which is no great surprise since there are so many antiques and artifacts in that shop."

"Anything else?"

"Some plant debris."

"What kind of plant?" Theodosia didn't remember seeing any plants in Helene's office.

"Actually, one of the lab guys put it under a microscope and surmised it might be some kind of algae."

"You mean from the ocean?" Theodosia asked

"Maybe the ocean. Or maybe from a creek, stream, swamp, estuary, or backyard puddle. To tell you the truth, Theo, we don't really know yet. Plus, whatever it is, it could have been there for some time," Riley said. "Maybe got ground into the carpet."

"Would it help if we got together and . . ."

"Hold that thought," Riley said. "I'm on my way to a meeting and am already ten minutes late."

"Call me later, okay?" Theodosia said.

But Riley had already hung up.

It was just as well, because now the clock was ticking down to their *Breakfast at Tiffany's* Tea. Theodosia grabbed a pot of vanilla chai and poured seconds and thirds, delivered checks to tables, and generally tried to gentle her guests along without seeming to actually hurry them. Time had become a key factor and she needed to start decorating.

But wait. There was still a major bump in the road.

"Theo!" Delaine screeched as she rushed into the tea shop. "Where's Theo?"

Heads turned, lips pursed, and patrons frowned at hearing such a bloodcurdling scream echo from the rafters. Which sent Theodosia running to head off Delaine, grab her, and forcibly sit her down at the table closest to the door.

"I can't believe it," Delaine wailed. She was practically hysterical. Her lipstick was smeared, her mascara had spackled under her eyes, and she shook like she was possessed by evil spirits. "Helene was my friend!" she bawled. "And now she's dead!"

"Shush," Theodosia said. She grabbed a hanky from her apron pocket and handed it to Delaine. "Try to pull yourself together. I know it's awful but you have to calm down."

"I'm trying," Delaine said, dabbing helplessly at her eyes. "But when something like this happens—a totally senseless murder—it rocks you to the core. Makes you come totally unglued."

As if to underscore her words, Delaine's right false eyelash came partially unglued and began to flap crazily with every blink.

"Drayton?" Theodosia turned to appeal to her tea sommelier. "Some strong tea, please?"

"Coming right up," Drayton said.

Theodosia reached over and rubbed Delaine's back for a few minutes until her friend finally got her crying jag under control. Then she said, "Feel any better?"

"Not really." Delaine sniffled loudly into her hanky. "I'm trying, but . . ." She blinked wildly, then said, "Theo, you have to *do* something."

Theodosia reached over and plucked off the offending eyelash, causing Delaine to let loose a tiny squeak and sit back in surprise. Then Theodosia said, as gently as she could, "It's not that I haven't been trying. You asked me to look into Josh Morro's murder and I have. Then, last night, well, that was me stumbling blindly into Helene's shop and finding her dead."

Delaine nodded. "I know. I heard it was you."

"How did you hear? My name wasn't mentioned in today's paper."

"Lewin Usher called me. You know, the producer who lives here in town?"

"Of course."

"News about Helene's death has spread like wildfire." Delaine turned sad puppy dog eyes on Theodosia. "You of all people should know how fast the rumor mill operates in Charleston."

"Unfortunately, I do," Theodosia said.

Delaine reached out and gripped Theodosia's hand. "I'm thankful it was you who found Helene. And not some unfeeling customer who might have just walked in to buy some random antique."

"Uh-huh." Theodosia wasn't happy about stumbling into yet another wrongful death.

"What if nobody had found poor Helene for *hours*? For *days*," Delaine blubbered. "Then her poor body . . ."

"But that's not what happened," Theodosia soothed. "Once I called the police they arrived at the scene almost immediately. And now they're working the case as hard as they can."

"I suppose."

Drayton brought a tray with a small pot of tea and two small Chinese cups to the table. "Here," he said to Delaine. "Try this. It should help you relax."

"Only if you dropped a Xanax in it," Delaine said. "But thank you anyway."

Drayton raised a single eyebrow and retreated while Theodosia poured two cups of tea and pushed one toward Delaine.

But Delaine was still fretting. "And Helene was definitely shot to death? Not electrocuted?"

"There was a bullet wound," Theodosia said. She didn't want to get any more graphic than she had to.

Delaine straightened up in her chair. "Do the police think I did it?"

"Did you?" Theodosia asked. She knew Delaine wouldn't hurt a fly, but it was typical of her to make Helene's murder all about herself.

"No!" Delaine screeched. "Of course not. How could you even *ask* such a thing?"

"Actually, you're the one asking all the questions."

"Okay, okay," Delaine mumbled, finally taking a sip of tea.

"Delaine, are you upset because Helene was your friend or because you think the police will view you as a suspect?"

Delaine pursed her lips. "Maybe a little of both?"

Theodosia nodded. Delaine's answer didn't surprise her. "I'm fairly positive you're not a suspect."

"That's good." Delaine took another sip of tea and said, "You know Helene had two cats, don't you? Butch and Sundance. Now what are those poor darlings supposed to do?"

"I don't know. Can you reach out to some of your animal rescue friends and maybe find them a new home?"

"I'll try, of course. But what I really want to know is . . . what are *you* going to do?"

"What do you mean?" Theodosia asked.

"You're the one who's been investigating Josh Morro's murder, you're the one who found Helene's body. I think . . . I think everyone involved is waiting to see what you'll do."

"Well, they shouldn't. Because I haven't figured anything out yet."

"But you will, right? You *have* to!"

"Detective Tidwell warned me to stay away."

"That blowhard," Delaine muttered. She rambled on for a few minutes, accepted a cinnamon scone when Beth Ann brought one to her, then suddenly gripped Theodosia's hand again and said, "You're still coming to my fashion show this afternoon, aren't you?"

"Are you still having it?"

"Why wouldn't I?" Delaine said. "And, truth be told, it's not a fashion show per se. More like a trunk show with informal modeling. A few models and close friends wearing some of the new dresses and sportswear that just arrived."

"That sounds nice."

Delaine suddenly brightened. "Doesn't it? Would *you* like to pinch-hit for one of the models who called in sick this morning? Can I count on you to help?"

"Delaine. No," Theodosia said. "I've got my hands full right here."

"And I'm juggling a dead ex-boyfriend and a dead friend and fellow board member!" Delaine pleaded as tears dribbled down her face again and she looked like she was on the verge of another ugly cry. "So I'm begging you . . . pleeease help!"

In the end Theodosia caved. It was just easier.

23

Time was relentlessly ticking away as Theodosia hurried into her office. She had to grab candles, favors for her guests, the Tiffany-blue ribbon, and . . .

"Oh, wow," she said when she spotted the gown draped on a peach-colored padded hanger and hanging from her brass coat-rack. The once-dowdy floor-length gown made of old lace now lit up the room with a golden, almost burnished glow.

Delighted, Theodosia ran a few steps down the back hallway and ducked into the kitchen.

"Haley, thank you! The gown looks absolutely fantastic. I'm thrilled you managed to resurrect it and give it a second life."

Haley looked up from where she was buttering a stack of English muffins. "Thanks. I thought it looked pretty cool my-self. That's the look you were going for, right? Kind of old-timey and elegant? A gold sepia tone?"

"It's perfect."

"I have to admit I did get a few words of wisdom from Dray-ton. A mixture of kibitzing and pep talk."

"Whatever you did, the gown is absolutely gorgeous. I'm sure the director and the wardrobe lady will be thrilled."

"Hope so," Haley said. Then, "Say, it's getting pretty late. Shouldn't you be hip-deep in decorating?"

"I'm on it," Theodosia said, flying out to the tea room. Where she got the surprise of her life.

The tables had all been cleared and Drayton and Beth Ann had dressed them up with Tiffany-blue tablecloths and were putting out the Noritake Evening Majesty china.

"You're one step ahead of me," Theodosia said, pleased.

"We thought we'd better take things in hand," Drayton said. "What do you think of the china Beth Ann selected?"

"White china with black and gold rims," Theodosia said. "Very upscale and classy."

"What else do you need for our *Breakfast at Tiffany's* Tea?" Beth Ann asked.

Theodosia put a hand to her head, thinking, then pushed back a hunk of auburn hair. "We need to put out our silver candelabras with white tapers, then drape them with strands of faux pearls. You'll find a bag full in my office. The bouquets of white tea roses should go in crystal vases and I'll arrange our Tiffany-blue swag bags at each place setting."

"And inside those bags is . . . what?" Drayton asked.

"Some blue soaps and tiny samples of Tiffany Wild Iris Parfum," Theodosia said.

"And then?" Drayton asked.

"And then we need to get changed."

Theodosia, Haley, and Beth Ann all slipped into black cocktail dresses, then added pearl earrings, matching necklaces, and high heels. Drayton, being Drayton, changed into one of his elegant tuxedos.

"Wow," Haley said to Drayton. "You look like the head waiter at a fancy restaurant."

"Excuse me, Haley, but this happens to be a Brioni tuxedo, not some purple velvet number straight out of a neon-lit cocktail lounge," Drayton said, which made them all explode with laughter.

"Do you think our guests will be wearing cocktail dresses and pearls, too?" Beth Ann asked.

"You never know," Theodosia said with a wink. Because she'd already asked several of her friends to do exactly that.

"And please remember," Drayton cautioned, "that Willis Conklin from *Tea Faire Magazine* will also be our guest for lunch. He'll be writing a review on the Indigo Tea Shop, hopefully a favorable one, so everything needs to be spot-on."

"It will be," Theodosia said. "And where will your Mr. Conklin be seated?"

"By himself. Small table by the window," Drayton said.

Ten minutes later it looked as if their guests had just stepped out of the pages of *Vogue* magazine, circa 1961, the year the movie *Breakfast at Tiffany's* was released.

Just as Theodosia had hinted, several guests came dressed in black cocktail dresses and pearls. And a few guests had taken it one step further and added vintage mink stoles. Brooke Carter Crocket upped the ante when she arrived wearing a glittering silver tiara in her short, gray hair, and Susan Monday wore a white suit, à la Truman Capote, the author who penned the book on which the movie was based.

There were even a few stylish women who wore what fashion

people called *le smoking*, which was a sleek tuxedo-style jacket with tailored slacks.

"This is amazing," Theodosia said, clapping her hands together. "Everyone really did go wild and embrace the theme."

But Theodosia was completely blown away when her aunt Libby and her aunt's cousin, Laura Lee Bouvier, showed up. She was never sure if Laura Lee was her second cousin once removed or her aunt-in-law. But whatever, it was grand to see them both.

"What a surprise!" Theodosia cried, embracing her tiny aunt, who was wearing a black boucle jacket and black silk slacks, then giving a hug to Laura Lee. "I had no idea you guys were coming!"

"We made secret reservations," Aunt Libby said with a grin. She cocked an index finger in Drayton's direction. "Thanks to your man, Drayton."

Theodosia turned to Drayton. "And you never gave me a hint!"

"What could I do?" Drayton said. "She swore me to secrecy."

More guests arrived, and then, last but not least, Willis Conklin from *Tea Faire Magazine* came in. He was a compact man, no taller than five foot six with a head of white hair, ruddy face, and cherubic smile.

"Thank you so much for having me," Conklin said, shaking hands with Theodosia and greeting her warmly.

"Thank you for coming," Theodosia said.

"It's an honor," Drayton added. "We're just hoping you . . ." He stopped, looking just this side of fluttery and unsure of how to proceed.

"You're hoping I write a favorable review?" Conklin said, favoring Drayton with a crooked grin.

"Well, yes." Drayton touched his bow tie nervously. "Needless to say, we would love that!"

* * *

When everyone was settled, when cups of tea had been poured and flutes of champagne delivered to the guests who wanted to imbibe, as "Moon River" played over the sound system, Theodosia walked to the middle of the room. Conscious of teetering on three-inch-high spike heels, she spread her arms wide (it helped with balance) and said, "Welcome to our first ever *Breakfast at Tiffany's* Tea." There was a nice round of applause and then she added, "I've never seen so many *chic*-looking women in my life." Which brought even more applause.

"Good style also extends to what we hope is a stylish menu. So for our first course today we'll be serving cream scones with Tiffany-blue icing as well as bejeweled scones, which are lemon scones embedded with multicolored bits of candied fruit. Our second course consists of Waldorf tea sandwiches, and our main entrée will be eggs Benedict topped with caviar. For dessert we'll be plying your sweet tooth with New York–style cheesecake and handmade petits fours." Theodosia paused. "Drayton, do you want to tell us about your special house-blend teas?"

"Nothing would please me more," Drayton said as he stepped forward. "For your sipping pleasure we've already filled your cups with a tea I call Two Drifters Off to See the World. It's my house blend of Ceylon black tea with pinches of cinnamon and ginger. And since we're all styling today . . ." He stuck his thumbs behind the lapels of his tuxedo and struck a pose. "I've created a second tea to specifically complement your eggs Benedict and caviar. It's called New York Minute and it's a blend of green tea, apple, and honey that takes barely a minute to steep."

From there they were off and running. Theodosia and Drayton poured more tea while Haley and Beth Ann served the two scone varieties along with bowls of poufy Devonshire cream and luscious four-fruit jam.

The Waldorf tea sandwiches also proved to be a huge hit.

"Theodosia." Brooke Carter Crockett reached an arm out to stop her. "What on earth is the magic recipe for the filling in these tea sandwiches? They're utterly delicious."

"Haley mixed apples, celery, and walnuts with mayo, then spread it on cinnamon-raisin bread," Theodosia said.

"And what kind of mayo?" another woman asked.

"That would be homemade, just like her bread."

"Please talk to us about baking scones," Elizabeth Armstrong said. She was the new president of the Broad Street Flower Club. "I want to hold a few organizational teas and I'm never sure if I should drop my scone dough into separate clumps on a baking sheet or pat the dough into a circle and use a cutter to score it into triangular segments."

"Either way is fine," Theodosia said. "The real trick is getting your scones to bake evenly and not get too dark on the bottom. And I always drizzle on my frosting or sprinkle on turbinado sugar while they're still hot."

When Theodosia stopped by the front counter to grab another pot of tea, she found Drayton on pins and needles.

"Take it easy," she said. "The tea is going beautifully."

"It's not the tea party I'm worried about," Drayton said. He glanced over to where Willis Conklin was seated. "The man is jotting notes. Copious notes, I might add."

"That's probably a good thing," Theodosia said.

"Or it could mean he's unhappy." Drayton stewed. "And is writing a scathing review. Oh dear, how I wish I could read upside down."

"Last time you poured a refill for Mr. Conklin, I'd say you did a masterful job of reading over his shoulder."

Drayton's face reddened. "Oh no, was it that obvious?"

Theodosia patted Drayton's shoulder. "Probably only to me."

The tea luncheon didn't so much end as reach a leisurely conclusion. Some of the customers shopped for tea gifts, others blew kisses at Drayton as they exited the front door, and Theodosia (finally!) found time to sit down with her aunt Libby and Laura Lee.

"You must come out and visit us soon," Aunt Libby said. She lived at Cane Ridge Plantation, a plantation house set on eighty sprawling acres, located on Rutledge Road just southwest of Charleston. Aunt Libby had inherited the plantation from Theodosia's grandparents and one day it would all belong to Theodosia.

"I know. I will!" Theodosia said.

"We don't see enough of you, dear," Aunt Libby said. "We have white-winged crossbills foraging in our tamarack and spruce and I've even sighted an occasional scarlet tanager." Aunt Libby was a bird lover of the first magnitude. Every day she put out oil seed, thistle, and cracklins for her winged friends.

"I need to grab some more grapevines, too," Theodosia said. She loved driving out into the woods to gather wild grapevines, then wind them around old wooden barrels to dry. Of course, decorating them with miniature teacups, spoons, ribbons, and honey sticks was fun, too. So was selling them.

"I mean it," Aunt Libby said as she stood up from the table, looking small and elegant. "I want you to call me next week, okay?"

"For sure," Theodosia said, kissing her aunt on the cheek, giving Laura Lee a hug, then walking them to the door.

Once everyone had said their final goodbyes and departed the tea shop, Theodosia, Drayton, Haley, and Beth Ann gathered together to eat the last of the scones and tea sandwiches.

"That was a very upscale menu you created," Drayton said to Haley.

"Do you think it made a good enough impression on your Mr. Conklin, the magazine guy?" Haley asked.

"I'd have to say that all our guests were impressed. Especially Mr. Conklin, which is quite a relief to me," Drayton said.

"That's great," Haley said. "Because the Indigo Tea Shop has a reputation to uphold. We're the high-end tea shop in Charleston. Ipso fatso."

"I think you mean ipso facto," Drayton said, a touch of amusement coloring his voice.

"If that's ipso, then it's a facto," Haley laughed.

As Beth Ann cleared tables and Drayton swept the floor, Theodosia and Haley put their heads together, planning for tomorrow.

"We'll prep everything early so when guests arrive for our morning prix fixe tea it'll be a no-brainer," Theodosia said.

"Like we're on autopilot," Haley agreed.

"That'll give us a jump start on making the desserts," Theodosia said.

Beth Ann walked over to where they were seated. "You're catering a party tomorrow?"

"Actually, it's a late-afternoon reception at the Library Society," Theodosia said.

Beth Ann looked interested. "So you'll be doing . . . ?"

"Peach puffs, turtle cheesecake, and walnut-coconut bars," Haley said.

"Do you need my help?" Beth Ann asked.

"Don't you want to take the weekend off?" Theodosia asked. "Have some fun?"

Beth Ann shrugged. "I'm having fun here."

"And at Brittlebank Manor?"

"That place . . ." Beth Ann pressed her lips together. "Truthfully it's starting to give me the creeps."

"You're not the only one," Theodosia agreed. "So maybe we'll get Miss Dimple to come over next week and spell you once in a while."

"That would be great," Beth Ann said.

Once they had their plans in place, Theodosia took a spin around the tea room to make sure everything was back in place.

"Everything good?" Drayton asked, leaning on his broom. "All spick-and-span?"

"Looks perfect."

"Except for . . . ?"

"Except for nothing," Theodosia said.

"Are you sure?" Drayton asked. "Because you're looking a bit thoughtful. More so than usual."

Theodosia reached up and scratched her head. "Probably because I just remembered something. When I was in Helene Deveroux's shop last night, it looked different."

"How so?"

"I'm not exactly sure," Theodosia said. "All I know is that it didn't have the same *feel* as the picture she showed me."

"What picture was that?"

"The one in Helene's magazine ad." Theodosia touched a finger to her temple and thought for a few moments. "Okay, it's this. In Helene's ad the shop was absolutely stuffed with antiques and art objects. But last night, I don't remember it looking that way. The shelves seemed a little less full."

"You're sure?" Drayton asked.

"No. Well, maybe."

"So you're surmising . . . what? That someone, presumably Helene's killer, made off with a good deal of her art objects?"

"I know that sounds weird, but that's exactly what I've been thinking," Theodosia said.

"So what do you want to do about it? See if there's an inventory list? Notify the police?" Drayton asked.

Theodosia pulled off her apron just as Haley and Beth Ann emerged from the kitchen. "I'll have to think about that," she said. "But right now I need to hotfoot it over to Delaine's boutique. I'm still not sure how she did it, but she conned me into being one of her models."

"Wow," Beth Ann said. "You're going to model in a real fashion show?"

"Cool," Haley said.

"Please don't be one bit impressed," Theodosia said. "First off, I'm only doing this as a favor to Delaine. And second, there's not going to be an actual runway with twirling lights and blaring music. It's just going to be what's called informal modeling."

"I'm not sure what that means," Beth Ann said.

Theodosia made a lemon face. "You know what? Neither do I."

24

∾❧∽

Theodosia found out soon enough what informal modeling was. Because the minute she walked into Cotton Duck, Delaine grabbed her by the hand and pulled her through a chattering, glittering crowd of women. They headed for the back of the shop, where a large makeshift dressing room had been set up behind a pair of billowing white curtains.

"I'm so glad you agreed to help out," Delaine hissed as, all around them, models pulled on clothes, sat for makeup artists, and talked on their phones as stylists braided extensions into their hair.

"Actually, you twisted my arm," Theodosia said as she looked at all the tall, skinny, young women. "And by the way, Delaine, all these women appear to be *professional* models. I seem to be the only civilian here."

"No, no," Delaine said hurriedly. "There are a couple of other women who are doing this just for fun."

"Where are they?"

Delaine's brows pinched together. "Good question." Then,

just as fast, she changed the subject and switched into business mode. "Here now, let's get you dressed up and looking glam." She lifted a hand and pointed to a rolling rack of clothes. "I set aside three options for you."

"And I'm supposed to pick one?" Theodosia asked.

"If you can manage a few quick changes, I'd love it if you could model *all three looks.* My guests always adore seeing what's new."

"Let's worry about one look for now," Theodosia said.

"All right, how about this silk evening gown?" Delaine pulled out a silver dress that was so sheer it looked as if it had been spun by starving silkworms.

"It's awfully sheer."

Delaine stuck out her lower lip. "That's a very hip look right now."

"But probably not for me," Theodosia said.

Delaine indicated a second outfit, a strapless, figure-hugging black cocktail dress. "How about this jazzy little number? Of course, you'd have to wear Spanx with it, to suck everything in. Maybe even two pairs."

"Skinny *and* strapless? I don't think so."

"Goodness, you do like to be covered up, don't you?"

"What's my third option?" Theodosia asked.

"How about this sundress?" Delaine said as she pulled it off the rack. "Spaghetti straps with a full, flouncy skirt, done in fuchsia and pink. Not too revealing, but very glam with a touch of fifties retro. You know, like Marilyn would have worn."

"Sure," Theodosia said. "As long as I don't have to stand over a subway grate." She didn't exactly love the dress, but it was the least revealing of the three.

"Now we're getting somewhere," Delaine said. She waited while Theodosia slipped into the dress, then said, "Fits you like a glove. Now we need to accessorize, kind of merchandise you up."

Delaine went to a table heaped with accessories and came back with a thick chain-link toggle necklace, charm bracelet, and a pair of hot pink sandals.

"Let's get this necklace on you," she said. Then, struggling with the clasp, said, "Doggone, I'm all fumble fingers today."

"Because you're still upset about Helene," Theodosia said.

"*Of course* I'm still upset." Delaine suddenly reared back, eyes snapping. "And I'm *frightened* as well."

Theodosia was genuinely surprised by Delaine's outburst. "What are you frightened about?"

Delaine favored Theodosia with her famous death stare, then said, "Because *I'm* on the Charleston Film Board as well. What if some demented killer decides to come after *me?* Or what if Josh Morro's fiancée, that crazy Carly person, killed him because she found out we were romantically involved?!"

"Then who killed Helene?" Theodosia asked.

Delaine thought for a moment. "Maybe Carly got all mixed up and thought Helene was me. I mean, we're both highly attractive women with impeccable taste in clothing. Maybe when Carly realizes she killed the wrong woman, I'll have a target on *my* back!"

"I'm not sure those murders are about you, Delaine."

"Oh, you think not? Won't you be surprised when you have to wear a dowdy black dress to my *funeral*!" Delaine shouted.

"What's going on?" Bettina asked as she came over to join them. "Aunt Delaine's planning her own funeral?"

Delaine shoved the toggle necklace into Bettina's hands and said, "Here, you put this on her. I've got more important things to worry about!" And with that she flounced off.

"What's eating her?" Bettina asked Theodosia as she snapped on the necklace.

"Delaine thinks she's the next target," Theodosia said. "She's afraid she'll end up murdered."

"Why on earth would she think that?" Then a slow grin spread across Bettina's face. "Oh wait, maybe because Delaine thinks absolutely everything is about her?"

Theodosia cocked a finger at Bettina. "Right on, sister."

A frizzy-haired woman with a tape measure draped around her neck gave Theodosia a little cardboard sign to carry. It indicated the style and price of the dress as well as the order number. In this case she was wearing FLIRTY SUNDRESS BY TRACY DEVIN for $189.99, number 6270.

"Do I have to carry this?" Theodosia asked the frizzy-haired woman.

She looked surprised. "Of course. It's informal modeling. How else will our customers know what to order?"

"Right," Theodosia said. And, "When do I start?"

"How about now?"

Theodosia walked out from behind the curtains into crazy land. The boutique was swarming with well-heeled bejeweled customers who were drinking champagne and zealously digging through racks of clothes as if they were excavating a pyramid at Giza.

Cotton Duck had always been known for its floaty dresses, lighter-than-air cashmere, sumptuous scarves, racks of silk blouses, and blingy jewelry. But today's spectacle was even more over the top. And Theodosia felt like the proverbial lab rat as she pushed her way through a maze of clothing racks packed with evening gowns, silk jackets, shimmery slacks, sporty blouses, teeny-tiny bikinis, designer jeans, and beach cover-ups.

"It's a lot to take in, isn't it?" Bettina was suddenly at Theodosia's elbow, giving her a sympathetic look.

"I don't know how I got roped into this," Theodosia said through a clenched-teeth smile.

"You're here because Delaine always gets her way. That's why I'm still here working for a pittance when I already have my degree in fashion merchandising."

"But now you've got an out," Theodosia said. "You're engaged."

"I know. Isn't it super?"

Theodosia reached out and squeezed Bettina's hand. "It sure is, honey."

"You know my fiancé, Jamie, is working here today, too."

"Why am I not surprised?"

"Come meet him." Bettina pulled Theodosia toward a make-shift bar lined with champagne bottles and glass flutes, and quickly introduced her to her fiancé, Jamie Wilkes.

"Oh my gosh," Theodosia said. "You're not even in the family yet and Delaine's put you to work."

Jamie cocked his head to one side. He was tall, broad-shouldered, with longish light brown hair and a sort of surfer-dude look. Theodosia figured most young women would consider him a serious hunk.

"Wouldn't you know it?" Jamie said with a wry smile. "The bartender who was scheduled to work here called in sick this morning so Delaine asked me to pinch-hit. Or so the story goes."

"There's a lot of pinch-hitting going on," Theodosia said. Like Jamie, she figured the "called in sick" excuse was Delaine's way of cheaping out and getting them both to work gratis.

"Anyway," Jamie said. "It is what it is. Say, would you like a glass of champagne? I'm getting rather skilled at pouring bubbly into tall glasses."

"Since I'm still on duty as a model I'd better not," Theodosia said. "Maybe later when I'm finished with this crazy gig."

Theodosia wandered off through the crowd, pausing every now and then for Delaine's guests to get a good look at her outfit. The informal modeling was probably a very smart marketing tactic for Delaine's boutique, but to Theodosia it was downright embarrassing. It was for sure no picnic being forced to smile, carry a little card with a number on it, and answer any questions that were asked about her outfit. And, strangely, there were quite a few.

"Is that dress made out of silk?" one woman asked.

"It's light and airy so I believe so," Theodosia responded with a friendly smile.

The woman pushed her glasses up on her nose, clearly not satisfied with the answer. "Well, is it silk or isn't it?"

"I'm sorry, I'm just the model here, the hired help. But you see that woman over there?" She pointed to Delaine. "That's right, the one who's probably on her second or third glass of champagne. She's the store owner and I'm sure she can answer all of your questions."

Another woman smiled at her and said, "It's refreshing to see a model who's not all skin and bones. Who doesn't have an eating disorder."

"Thank you," Theodosia said. "I think."

As Theodosia took a final spin around the boutique, deciding enough was enough, another woman tapped her on the shoulder. "Excuse me, but I have a daughter who's interested in becoming a model. Do you have any advice? Anything she should take under consideration?"

Theodosia nodded. "Tell her it helps to have thick skin."

Determined to escape while she could, Theodosia headed back to the dressing room and changed back into her own civilian clothes. A nice pair of jeans, loafers, and a silk blouse. Nothing froufrou, nothing transparent, thank goodness. She peeked around the end of the curtain, saw that Delaine was at the far end of the shop pitching two young women on the merits of a bustier teamed with a flouncy ballroom skirt.

Time to make my escape!

Theodosia dodged through the crowd, wove her way around two rolling racks, and was making a beeline for the front door when she skidded to a stop. There, checking out the silk scarves, was Carly Brandt.

Weird.

Of course Theodosia was curious as to why Carly was there. Was she really checking out scarves—or was she checking out Delaine?

By the time Theodosia got back to the Indigo Tea Shop, she was feeling exhausted, both mentally and physically.

"So now you're a model," Drayton called to her from behind the counter, where he was arranging tea tins. "How did it go?"

"Drayton, you don't want to know."

"Actually, I do."

"For one thing, Carly Brandt showed up."

Drayton looked surprised. "Morro's Hollywood girlfriend?"

"That's right."

"What was she doing there?"

"Not sure. I figure she was either shopping her little heart out or trying to get a bead on Delaine."

"You think Carly got wind that Delaine had been dating Josh Morrow?"

"Maybe. Or maybe the girl's just a shopaholic."

"But nothing actually happened between them," Drayton said. It was a statement, not a question.

"Not that I could see."

"Okay, other than Carly Brandt showing up, how was it?"

"Have you ever seen that old movie *Bedlam* with Boris Karloff? It was like that, only the inmates were all skinny women with money," Theodosia said. "Plus, I realized that I simply don't have the confidence to strut around a store showing off a frothy dress."

"Nonsense, you're one of the most superbly confident people I know."

"Maybe at running a tea shop. But interacting with fashion people? No way."

"How about interacting with movie people at Josh Morro's memorial service tonight?" Drayton asked.

"Oh no, do we have to?"

Drayton nodded. "I think we pretty much have to go and show the flag. Besides, you can always squeeze in a little more investigating."

Theodosia sighed. "There is that."

25

Josh Morro's memorial service wasn't churchy or religious or even one bit somber. Mostly it was a cocktail party with lots of movie people milling around, drinking wine and eating hors d'oeuvres as they rubbed shoulders with Charleston Film Board people and a few local actors and producers.

"Look at this," Theodosia said as she and Drayton walked in. "Most of our murder suspects are neatly rounded up in one room."

"Is that what you really believe?" Drayton asked.

"Whoever killed Josh Morro and Helene *has* to be part of this crew," she said. "I just don't see it as being an outsider."

"For a while you were laser focused on Craig Cole."

"Right," Theodosia said, looking around for him. "But I can't figure out Craig Cole's connection to Helene." She stood on tiptoes and finally saw the top of Cole's head bobbing among the crowd. "There's Cole now, stopping to talk with Carly Brandt."

"The ex-fiancée who may or may not be stalking Delaine."

Theodosia's eyes roved across the rest of the crowd. "I see Andrea Blair hanging out with her agent, Sidney Gorsk. And

Lewin Usher, our homegrown movie producer, just walked in. Ted Juniper just sidled up to what's probably an open bar."

"The one with the drinking problem," Drayton said.

"The one who's also the lighting expert."

"And deals in all things electrical and might know how to hotwire a metal chair?" Drayton asked.

"You got that right," Theodosia said. She tapped an index finger against her lower lip. "Who's missing? Oh, of course. Joe Adler, the director."

"Do you think he'll bother to show up?"

Theodosia shrugged. "Search me. Meanwhile, why don't we help ourselves to some munchies?"

"Sounds right."

But either someone had screwed up the order or the first wave of guests had devoured most of the hors d'oeuvres, because there were only a few cubes of cheese, a half-filled basket of crackers, and a sliver of pâté left when Theodosia and Drayton went to fill their plates. Still, they did the best they could, then sat down at one of the small tables to eat their appetizers.

"The food is scarce but the surroundings are nice," Drayton said. The memorial service was being held in the Madison Room, a gracious wood-paneled private room at the Lady Goodwood Inn.

"And look over there," Theodosia said.

Drayton craned his neck to see a small memorial set up in the far corner. There was a photo of Josh Morrow, a kind of standard Hollywood headshot, sitting on a small table with small floral bouquets on either side.

"Looks kind of meager," Drayton said. "Just like the food."

"You know, Helene was one of the people who helped plan this memorial, so maybe her murder last night screwed things up royally," Theodosia said.

Drayton nodded as he nibbled a sesame cracker. "Could be."

They were both down to their last cube of Gouda cheese, wondering if anyone was going to stand up and deliver a heartfelt testimonial about Josh Morro, when Delaine Dish came scurrying in. She'd changed clothes (for the third time that day!) and was now wearing a black sequin cocktail dress with a deep V in the front to show off her décolletage.

When Delaine spotted Theodosia and Drayton, she hurried over to their table and plunked herself down. "Did I miss anything?" she asked in a breathless whisper.

"Just the food," Theodosia said. No way was she going to tell Delaine about Carly showing up at her shop. That would send Delaine into a tailspin.

Delaine craned her neck in the direction of the buffet table. "Is it all gone?"

"I'm not sure there was much to begin with," Drayton said.

Delaine gave a sulky look. "And here I am, totally ravenous."

"You may have also noticed that this isn't exactly a true memorial," Drayton said. "Since people seem to be doing more drinking than memorializing the deceased."

"Maybe everybody's thrown for a loop because of Helene's murder," Delaine said, wiping away a tear.

"Maybe," Theodosia said. She'd just caught sight of Joe Adler as he strolled in. He looked confident and upbeat, as if he owned the place. Wearing a cream-colored jacket, purple T-shirt, and tight jeans, he cut through the crowd like an ocean liner gliding into port, glad-handing and backslapping everyone he saw.

Delaine narrowed her eyes as she watched him. "I've had my suspicions about that man."

"So have I," Theodosia said. "The fact that Adler was able to step in so quickly to direct the movie makes me wonder if . . ."

Theodosia's words were cut short as Carly Brandt rushed up

to Joe Adler, pressed both hands against his chest, and gave him a hard shove. Adler staggered backward, almost losing his footing, as Carly got in his face and shouted, "You jackhole! You killed Josh and everybody here knows it. The police are eventually going to prove it and then you'll be sorry!"

Carly's hurled accusation brought everything to a screeching halt. Heads turned, eyes widened, chairs were repositioned in order to get a better look at what seemed to be an explosive situation.

It was also readily apparent that Joe Adler wasn't about to take Carly's threats lightly. She'd ignited a flash point. With a disdainful curl to his lips, Adler shouted back at her, "You poor, deluded has-been. You're so angry about your own pathetic life that you're grasping at straws."

"I stand behind everything I say," Carly screamed as her face twisted into an ugly grimace. "You're a cold-blooded killer!"

"I happen to know *you're* the one who stands to inherit three million dollars in life insurance," Adler snarled back. "Which means I wouldn't be surprised if *you* killed Morro simply to get your grubby hands on that money!"

Theodosia turned to Drayton. "Are you hearing this?"

"Three million dollars in life insurance," Drayton said. "That's a serious motive in and of itself."

"Holy snickerdoodles," Theodosia said as their voices grew louder. "Do you think we've been looking in the wrong direction?"

Drayton shrugged. "Maybe."

"Now do you see what I've been talking about?" Delaine hissed. "I *told* you Carly was bonkers, that she could have murdered Josh. Now we have an actual motive!"

"Three million dollars," Theodosia said under her breath.

"That does add up to a lot of motives," Drayton said.

"Uh-oh," Delaine said as Lewin Usher, the producer, suddenly pushed his way through the captivated crowd. "Take a look at this happy crap."

Usher's mouth was set in a grim line as he fought to put himself directly between Adler and Carly.

"Enough!" Usher shouted, using both hands to physically pry them apart. "You two need to show some much-needed decorum. This is a *memorial*, for goodness' sake. It's neither the time nor place to hurl unfounded accusations or air petty grievances."

"There's nothing petty about three million dollars," Adler said, though he'd lowered his voice somewhat. "It's a motive, one of the oldest in the book."

"How dare you," Carly screeched back.

"Ah, you're not worth the expenditure of energy," Adler said as he backed away.

"Adler's very self-important, isn't he?" Drayton said.

"No kidding," Theodosia said.

But the moment had seemingly passed and Usher had successfully broken up the fight. Joe Adler retreated to the bar, where he ordered a double shot of Wild Turkey on the rocks, while Carly Brandt stormed out of the party looking shaken and angry.

"How do you like them apples?" Delaine snapped. "Here I was, dating Josh Morro, believing we were in a serious relationship, and it turns out he had a girlfriend. And not just any girlfriend, but a West Coast fiancée, a Hollywood hottie. And now she stands to inherit three million dollars!" Delaine's fingers closed in an angry fist as she slammed it down on the table, making everyone's drink glasses clatter and jump.

"Delaine," Theodosia said. "Take it easy." She wasn't sure if Delaine was more upset about Morro having a fiancée or missing out on the three million dollars in life insurance. Hard to tell what went on in Delaine's brain.

"I know, I know," Delaine said. "I shouldn't take this so . . ." Delaine's head suddenly swiveled like a periscope and she said, "Well, hello," to a small, dark-haired woman who'd broken from the crowd to come over and talk to her.

"People, people," Delaine said, waving her hands to shush Theodosia and Drayton and get their attention. "This dear soul is Molly. Molly Turner. She is—was—Helene's business partner."

"I'm so sorry for your loss," Theodosia said, as Molly took a seat next to Delaine.

"Thank you," Molly whispered. She offered a faint smile but was leaking tears at the same time.

"My condolences," Drayton said. "Helene and her philanthropic efforts will be greatly missed."

"I believe formal introductions are called for," Delaine said, interrupting again. "Molly, this is Theodosia Browning of Indigo Tea Shop fame."

"So nice to meet you," Molly said. "I've heard only good things about your tea shop."

"Thank you," Theodosia said.

"And this is Drayton Conelley, tea sommelier extraordinaire," Delaine said.

Molly nodded at Drayton. "Of course, I know Drayton from the Heritage Society."

Drayton smiled. "Miss Turner was kind enough to lend us some pieces from her private collection when we had that Sung Dynasty show last year. May I get you a refreshment? Cup of tea, glass of wine?"

"Nothing, thank you," Molly said.

Delaine grabbed Molly's hand and made a sad, downturned

face. "Such a terrible thing about our dear, dear Helene. You must be heartsick."

"I almost couldn't believe it when the police knocked on my door last night," Molly said in a strangled voice. "I'm still not clear if it was a robbery or something else."

"The something else being murder," Delaine said in a loud whisper. "I'm guessing the police think Helene's death is strongly connected to the murder of Josh Morrow, the film director?"

"The police do think it's connected," Molly said. "But the strange thing is, they questioned me about Helene's relationship with Josh Morro."

"What?" Delaine gasped.

"One of their theories being that Helene might have murdered him," Molly said.

Delaine clutched at her heart. "Oh my Lord. That can't be. Helene wouldn't, she couldn't . . ."

"That's what I told the police, but they didn't seem to take me all that seriously," Molly said. "Apparently they intend to tear into everything now—-background the two victims, talk to their friends and business colleagues, poke through personal papers. They're even going to investigate Helene's pro bono service with the Charleston Film Board."

"How will this affect your shop?" Delaine asked. "The Sea Witch."

"That's a problem," Molly said. "The shop will have to close for a while."

"Won't that adversely affect your income?" Theodosia asked. She was well aware that times were tough for small business owners.

"Actually, I was a minority partner," Molly said. "While Helene was, like, eighty percent owner. I just dabbled in antiques, never made a major commitment like Helene did. She was the one who did all the marketing, built a successful client base, and held the lease on the building. I was just kind of . . ." Molly shrugged. "Along for the ride."

"So most of the antiques in the shop belong to Helene?" Theodosia asked.

Molly nodded. "My pieces took up only one display window and two cases."

"Does Helene have heirs?" Delaine asked.

"I think there's a sister somewhere," Molly said. "But I couldn't tell you where she lives. Probably Helene's lawyer will have to figure all that out."

"So sad," Delaine said. "Sad, sad, sad. But if you need me as a character witness in case the police start coming after you, let me know. Or if you need help straightening out the business end of things."

"That's very kind of you," Molly said as her eyes sparkled with tears.

Drayton gave Theodosia a subtle kick under the table. Which prompted her to pipe up and say, "Drayton and I would be happy to help as well."

26

Since there hadn't been much food at the memorial—and not much memorializing, either—Drayton invited Theodosia to come home with him for a quick nosh.

Of course when they walked into Drayton's kitchen, Honey Bee ran up to him and did her girly-dog dance. Paws clicked against the slate floor as his Cavalier King Charles spaniel spun and twisted with excitement.

"Have you been a good girl?" Drayton asked as he cupped her furry muzzle. "Did Pepe come by and feed you?" Pepe was the neighbor kid who fed Honey Bee in a pinch and also helped Drayton trim his collection of backyard bonsai.

"Looks like a few pieces of kibble left in her dish," Theodosia remarked.

"Then Pepe was here. Good." Drayton straightened up. "Now we need something delicious for us." He gazed at Theodosia. "Can I tempt you with one of my cheese-stuffed egg clouds?"

"Is it like a soufflé? Does it have to bake for a while?"

"Not to worry. I've got a proprietary recipe that cuts the baking time down to around six minutes."

"Then I'm sold on your cheesy egg clouds."

"Excellent," Drayton said as he pulled two eggs and a wedge of cheddar cheese from his refrigerator and reached into a bin for an onion.

"Should I take Honey Bee out so she can stretch her legs?"

"Be my guest," Drayton said as he grabbed a knife and gave his onion a solid whack.

Theodosia was always delighted to hang out with Honey Bee, especially since Drayton had such a gorgeously curated backyard. Besides a brick patio and ribbon of lawn, the yard consisted of a curved fishpond surrounded by Chinese *taihu* rocks, thick groves of bamboo, winding paths, wooden pedestals where his prize Japanese bonsai were on display, and even a small three-sided Japanese pavilion with a peaked roof.

Once Theodosia had chased Honey Bee through the bamboo thickets and played hide-and-seek around the pond, it was full-on dark and time to go in. And when Theodosia and Honey Bee stepped inside, the kitchen was fragrant with cooking aromas.

Then again, Drayton's kitchen was designed for cooking. A six-burner Wolf gas range dominated one wall, the sink was custom-hammered copper, and the cupboards were Carolina pine faced with glass. The better to show off his collection of Chinese blue-and-white bowls and antique teapots.

Theodosia pointed to a blue teapot she'd not seen before. "Oh no, you did not."

"Oh yes, I'm afraid I did," Drayton replied.

"You bought the Nymphenburg Perl Blue teapot."

"Guilty as charged."

"I know that one of their luncheon plates is priced at well over two hundred dollars, so this teapot must have cost a fortune."

Drayton smiled serenely. "And then some."

The egg clouds came out looking poufy and delicious and Drayton fixed a side salad with sesame seed dressing to go along. Once everything was plated and placed on trays, they carried it into Drayton's formal dining room and sat down. Or more like reclined, since his French Louis XIV chairs were padded to the max and covered in whisper-soft silk.

"You have a new painting," Theodosia said. There was a painting of a horseman in a red jacket hanging on the wall where a painting of Charles, the second Earl Grey (former PM of the United Kingdom) had once been.

"No, I just moved things around. Put Lord Grey in the guest bedroom, brought this one down from upstairs so it could hang around for a while. I do that once in a while, mix things up."

"You are known for your wild spontaneity," Theodosia observed in a dry tone of voice.

"I know, I know, I can be a bit futsy and set in my ways. Some might even say a stick-in-the-mud. But it suits me."

"You'll get no argument from me," Theodosia said. "And by the way, these egg clouds are delicious."

"When I have a touch more time I often whip up a mornay sauce to go along."

"Please let me know when that would be," Theodosia said.

"Of course," Drayton said. Then, "What do you think about the police investigating Helene as Morro's killer?"

"I don't think Helene was even there when he was killed."

"But there is the electricity angle," Drayton said.

Theodosia nodded. "Which is worrisome."

"And what was your impression of Molly Turner?"

"Are you asking me if I think she could have killed Helene? Or Morro?"

"I suppose I'm veering in that direction. It's often the quiet ones you have to watch out for."

"I can't say I picked up any kind of murderous feelings from Molly. She seemed more lost than anything. Confused."

"It was nice of you to offer your help," Drayton said.

"Thanks to your prompting."

Drayton leaned forward. "Here's the thing. I thought if we talked to Molly, using business advice as a kind of clever ruse, she might relax and drop her guard. She might even tell us something about Helene that we don't know—that no one knows—without realizing it's an important clue."

Theodosia considered this. "Could happen I guess."

"So we talk to her?"

"I don't see why not. I'd also like to cozy up to Carly Brandt."

"You think she killed Morro?"

"No, but Carly was close enough to him that she might have insider information," Theodosia said. "She might think it's nothing but it could be important."

"Judging by tonight's fiasco, it seems to me Carly was focused squarely on Joe Adler as the main suspect."

"That could have been all bluster."

"You mean Carly was trying to flush out the real killer?" Drayton asked.

"For all I know, Carly's working with the police."

"If she is, do you think you can pry any details out of Riley?"

"All I can do is try."

When Theodosia arrived home, a piece of paper fluttered from her back door. Figuring it was a menu from some nearby takeout restaurant, she pulled it off and started to crumple it. But when she stepped inside where the light was better, she discovered it was something else entirely. It was a page torn from a book and Theodosia recognized it as the final stanza of Edgar Allan Poe's "The Lake."

Heart starting to blip uncomfortably, she read the words:

> Death was in that poisonous wave,
> And in its gulf a fitting grave
> For him who thence could solace bring
> To him lone imagining—
> Whose solitary soul could make
> An Eden of that dim lake.

What the heck?

Theodosia read it again. Was someone trying to scare her? Or send her a coded message? Or was it just plain nonsense?

I think I can rule out nonsense.

Okay then, what? Still pondering the who and the why, Theodosia clipped a leash to Earl Grey's collar and walked him outside. The moon was riding high in the night sky and a breeze had sprung up. It was tinged with just the faintest hint of salt from the Atlantic and the sweet scent of purple Chinese wisteria that hung freely over nearby fences. A heady combination.

As Theodosia and Earl Grey walked down the alley, her mind was doing its runaway thing. Worrying, wondering, thinking about the two murders, concerned over the strange poem, turning every last bit of information over and over as if polishing precious stones.

So fixated was Theodosia on her thought process, she wasn't even aware that someone had stepped directly in front of her, silent as a ghost.

"Whoa!" Theodosia cried when she finally glanced up and skidded to a stop. At the same time Earl Grey sounded his unease with a low growl.

"Hey," Quaid said, looking somewhat startled. Theodosia and Earl Grey had surprised him, too. "Your dog won't bite me, will he?"

"Probably not," Theodosia said. "As long as you remain on your best behavior."

Quaid looked taken aback and a little angry. "Excuse me, but are you making some sort of reference about last night?"

Theodosia shrugged. "At least you weren't arrested."

"Because I didn't *do* anything!" Quaid cried. He put up both palms, as if to deflect Theodosia's words. "I swear to you I did not touch a hair on that woman's head. I don't even *know* her. You saw me when I showed up last night—I'd been tricked. Someone impersonating a board member sent me to that shop under false pretenses. Whoever it was wanted to make me the patsy, the fall guy. Thank goodness the police let me go when they realized I was innocent."

"Good," Theodosia said. "Let's keep it that way."

"Are you always this hypercritical?"

Theodosia smiled. "Only when it's well-deserved."

Quaid frowned. "Seems more like—"

"You're living here, too?" Theodosia interrupted.

Quaid spun around to take in the expanse of the Granville Mansion. "It's a big house. Palatial, you might say. So, yeah, I'm bunking here for the time being."

"With Joe Adler."

"Yes, with Joe Adler. Because I work for him," Quaid said. "As a personal assistant."

"You didn't see anybody lurking around here tonight, did you?" Theodosia asked.

Quaid turned back to her. "Why? Did something happen?"

"Nope," Theodosia said. "I'm just being proactive. Keeping my guard up."

Quaid's gaze wandered back to the mansion again. "With two murders seemingly connected to the movie, I have to admit I'm a little nervous, too." He turned around, about to say more. But Theodosia had already melted into the night.

After a brisk three-block walk, Theodosia was back inside, re-reading the poem. Not liking the implication—plus the fact that someone had snuck into her backyard—she checked her doors and windows to make sure they were locked, pulled out her phone, and called Riley. When he answered on the first ring, her words tumbled out quickly, telling him all about the scary note she'd found tacked to her door.

"And you say it's a poem?" Riley said.

"One by Edgar Allan Poe."

"Ah, our former resident alcoholic poet. What's the poem about?"

She told him.

When he didn't respond immediately, Theodosia said, "I was thinking it might relate to the Poetry Tea we had this past Wednesday."

"Do you think the killer might have been one of your guests?"

"Maybe. I don't know. But it does creep me out."

"Do you want me to come over there?" Riley asked.

"No," Theodosia said. Then, "Yes."

"Okay, I'll come over and bring my service weapon. You know how it is with us duly sworn officers. We live to protect and serve."

"Happy to hear it. I'll open a bottle of wine."

Theodosia popped the cork on a bottle of California cabernet and set out two wineglasses. Decided cheese would be nice, too, so she sliced some Swiss and cheddar. She paced back and forth from her dining room to her living room, still wondering if one of her new neighbors—either Joe Adler or Quaid Barthel—had left the note in an attempt to frighten her.

Then lights flashed outside as Riley pulled up in front of her house, and Theodosia ran out to greet him.

27

"I have to show you something," Theodosia said to Drayton. She pulled the poem out of her apron pocket and handed it to Drayton. It was early Saturday morning and only a few guests had shown up so far. Haley was busy in the kitchen, whipping eggs and baking more scones, while Beth Ann poured tea and served strawberry scones with Devonshire cream.

"What's this?" Drayton asked as he accepted the crumpled paper.

"I found it tacked to my back door last night. When I got home from your place."

Drayton studied the poetry stanza. "This seems fairly ominous."

"You recognize it?"

"Absolutely. It's by Poe. One of his later works."

"You're good," Theodosia said. "Most people wouldn't be able to identify a partial poem so easily."

"Most people aren't on the board of the Heritage Society,"

Drayton said. "Most people don't spend their evenings reading Thackeray, Irving, Melville, Poe, Whitman, and Hemingway."

"You're so scholarly, Drayton."

"Would you rather have me thumbing a cell phone and watching Ticky Tocky videos?"

"That would be TikTok, and no I wouldn't."

"So what are you going to do about this?" Drayton asked.

Theodosia pursed her lips. "Worry?"

"What do you think this poem is supposed to mean?" Drayton asked.

"Besides a sort of warning? I have no clue."

"Actually," Drayton said, "It could be a clue."

"A clue that points to what exactly?"

"I'm not sure."

"Great. So we're back to square one?" Theodosia said.

"Oh no, I think we've hopscotched over square one and made a fair amount of progress. By the by, did you get a chance to ask Riley about Molly?"

"He said she's not a suspect in Helene's murder by virtue of her alibi."

"Which was?" Drayton asked.

"It turns out that Molly was attending a pottery class over at the Arts Alliance that night."

"Then what about the ex-fiancée, Carly? Is she working with the police as you suggested?"

"I asked Riley about that, too, and he said no. Actually, she's still sitting pretty on his roster of suspects."

"Then Carly should be on our roster, too. Now we just need to narrow it down."

"Easier said than done. We've been trying to narrow down our suspect list all week," Theodosia said as the front door opened and a half dozen people walked in, smiles and expectant looks on their faces.

"Then we have to try harder."

"I agree. I don't want justice to be an endangered species."

Drayton held up a finger. "I have an idea percolating. But first I have to make a call."

Theodosia seated their newly arrived guests and stopped by to chat with the ones who were already sipping tea and eating scones. Later on, when it was closer to lunchtime, they'd roll out Haley's Saturday prix fixe menu, which today consisted of two choices. The first was a lemon scone served with mushroom soup and duck terrine on toast, and the second was a cherry scone served with fruit salad and ham-and-sweet-potato casserole.

Just as Theodosia was digging out her Tea Totalers menu for a guest who'd asked about tisanes and herbal teas, the front door opened and Lois, the cheerful owner of Antiquarian Books, walked in. She was a retired librarian with a broad, friendly face, plumpish figure, and silver-gray hair worn in a braided plait down the middle of her back. Today Lois was wearing jeans and a pink T-shirt that said COMMIT TO LIT.

"Is it okay to bring Pumpkin in?" Lois looked expectantly at Theodosia as her adorable little long-haired dappled dachshund peered out from her plaid carry bag, her big puppy eyes shining like twin oil spots. "Drayton called and asked me to stop by. Said it was important. Something about a poem?"

"A poem, right," Theodosia said, casting a glance toward Drayton, who was busy brewing pots of dragonwell and Keemun tea. Then she turned back to Lois and said, "Lois, you carry books by Edgar Allan Poe, don't you?"

A smile crinkled across Lois's face. "Are you kidding? I have five shelves filled with volumes by Poe. He's one of my bestsellers. Why do you ask? Are you looking to buy one? If you're in the market for a rare Poe book I have one that dates from 1892 published by Thomas Crowell Company, and another printed in 1900 by Donohue. The rest of my Poe books are fairly run-of-the-mill and modern."

"Has anybody been in lately and bought a book of poetry by Poe?"

"Poetry." Lois closed her eyes, thinking. Then she opened them and said, "Now that you mention it, yes. Maybe a day or two ago someone came in asking for one."

"Do you remember—was your customer a man or a woman?"

"I'm fairly sure it was a man. Why? What's going on?" Then something akin to understanding dawned on Lois's face and she said, "Theo, does this have anything to do with those movie murders I've been reading about in the paper? I know you've catered food for the cast and crew over at Brittlebank Manor."

"It kind of does," Theodosia said. "It has to do with a poem and . . . um, I'm trying to track down as many clues as possible."

"To find the killer?" Lois looked horrified.

"Well, yes."

"But you wouldn't try to apprehend him all by yourself, would you?" Lois asked. She snuggled Pumpkin a little closer.

"Of course not. If I thought I'd actually caught a whiff of the killer I'd point the police at him."

"Wow," Lois said. "And poetry by Poe might be a clue?"

"Maybe. Do you have a record of who purchased the book? Like did they use a credit card?"

But Lois was already shaking her head. "They paid cash. And, as I recall, it wasn't a rare book at all, just something recent. A paperback in so-so condition."

"But the purchaser was a man," Theodosia said. She was thinking about Joe Adler, Craig Cole, Ted Juniper, and Sidney Gorsk, the agent.

"Pretty sure," Lois said. When she saw disappointment on Theodosia's face, she added, "I'm sorry I couldn't be of more help."

"No," Theodosia said, "you've actually been a big help."

"Lois," Drayton called from behind the counter. "Can you stay for lunch?"

"No time," Lois said. "Pumpkin and I are on our way to a book sale at a library over in Goose Creek. All the books you can cram into a shopping bag for five dollars." She glanced around. "But takeout would work, if it's not too much trouble."

"Not in the least," Drayton said. "How does a cherry scone and a cup of mushroom soup sound?"

"Delicious."

"That was plenty smart of you to ask Lois to pop in," Theodosia said to Drayton.

"Did she sell a book of Poe's poems recently?" His face wore a sly smile.

"She did, just as you suspected. A couple of days ago. To a male customer."

"Did she remember who it was?"

"No, she'd never seen him before. Plus, they paid cash," Theodosia said.

"Still, whoever bought that book could have been your unwelcome caller last night."

"Could have been," Theodosia said as she shivered inwardly. Though she thought of herself as independent, self-reliant, and not one who scares easily, this whole poem-on-the-door thing had spooked her. After all, there did seem to be an unusually high body count as of this week.

"There's something else I wanted to ask you about," Drayton said.

"What?"

"Something you said yesterday in passing," Drayton said.

"About?"

"Helene's shop. I believe you said the Sea Witch had a different *feel* to it. You know, different from the picture Helene had showed you."

"I did say that, didn't I?" Theodosia thought for a moment. "And I suppose I still feel that way."

"So?"

"So maybe we should go take a look-see?"

"Her shop's probably locked up tighter than a drum," Drayton said. "We'd for sure need a key."

"Let me think about that," Theodosia said.

During a slight lull, when Beth Ann seemed to have everything under control in the tea room, Theodosia slid into her office and called Delaine at Cotton Duck.

Delaine answered with a quick, "Hello?"

"Delaine," Theodosia said, "do you by any chance have a key to Helene's shop?"

"No, I don't. But . . . hold on a minute, will you?"

Theodosia held as Delaine said (to what must have been a customer), "Honey, that pale peach paired with the burnt sienna is to *die* for. It brings out the highlights in your hair."

"Delaine?" Theodosia said.

"Hmm?" There was more talking and faint music in the background.

"The key. Do you know where I can get one?"

Theodosia suddenly had Delaine's full attention. "Theo, what are you up to?"

"I'm not sure. With Helene's connection to her husband's electrical company, maybe . . . I'm trying to clear her name?"

The background noise cranked up for a few moments, then Delaine said, "Theo, that would be wonderful. I'll tell you what, let me give you Molly's number. She's the one you really need to talk to."

"Okay, great," Theodosia said. She dutifully scribbled down Molly's phone number, then called her.

When Molly answered, Theodosia introduced herself again and said, "This is going to sound strange, but I'd like to pay a visit to your shop."

There was a surprised noise from Molly and then she said, "Okay." Followed by, "Why?"

"Call me crazy but I'm trying to solve a murder. Actually, two murders."

"You really think you can do that?" Molly asked. "Because the police are . . ."

"Baffled. Yes, I realize they are. But I'm simply taking a shot in the dark here, not promising any actual results, I'm just . . . well, I guess I've mustered up a blend of curiosity and hopefulness, with a little righteous indignation thrown in for good measure."

"And you're working with the police on this?"

"Kind of," Theodosia hedged. "But mostly as an interested party. An *involved* party."

"Okay," Molly said. "But please remember, I'm only a twenty percent partner in Sea Witch. Mostly it was Helene's shop. I'm the one who was selling antique ceramics and locally made pots to a few collectors. You know, pots by Joy March and Tom Beamon and such. Helene, on the other hand, had a much larger inventory and tons of national and international clients."

"Helene must have been quite a skillful businesswoman,"

Theodosia said. As she was talking, she walked down the hall from her office and peeked into the main tea room.

"I had that feeling, yes, because Helene was always shipping marine artifacts to all sorts of customers," Molly said. "Though now that I think about it, many of them were dealers. At least those were the names I saw on the waybills." She fell silent for a few moments, then said, "You say you want to look around the shop. When would you do that?"

"Soon. Today if possible."

"So you'll need my key. If it's super important I can drop it by your tea shop. I live over on Legare, maybe six or seven blocks from you."

Theodosia glanced around, saw that most of her customers had been served and that Beth Ann wasn't terribly busy. "No, that's okay," she said. "I'll send someone over to pick it up. Just give me the address."

Theodosia thanked Molly, then hung up. And wondered if she might be setting herself up for a fool's errand. Maybe the look, the feel of the shop, had nothing to do with Helene's murder. And maybe Helene's murder had nothing to do with Josh Morro's murder. Then again . . . she could be wrong. And if there was a minute possibility of figuring out these two murders, then she was willing to give it a shot.

Twenty minutes later, just a small luncheon crowd lingered and Beth Ann had returned with the key for Theodosia. It was a small brass key with the words DO NOT COPY printed on it. The small key hung on a pink carabiner that was attached to an oversized key fob in the shape of a funky pink metal key.

"Molly said the key's for the front door," Beth Ann said. "And that the alarm system probably isn't turned on. But if it is, just punch six-two-five-one into the keypad."

"Okay, thanks."

Theodosia and Beth Ann cleared dishes, reset the tables, and served a few latecomers. In the kitchen, Haley put the finishing touches on their catering order for the Library Society. By three thirty the peach puffs, turtle cheesecake, and walnut-coconut bars were packed into airtight containers, then placed in large wicker baskets for easy transport.

That's when Drayton walked into the kitchen and said, "Theo, do you want me to start loading these baskets into your Jeep?"

"That'd be a great help," Theodosia said.

But before Drayton could hoist a single basket, Haley said, "That's okay, Beth Ann and I can take this stuff over to the Library Society. After all, we're the ones who are going to stay and help serve."

"But you'll need my Jeep," Theodosia said.

"Beth Ann drove her dad's SUV today," Haley said. "We can use that."

"For sure." Beth Ann nodded.

"I guess that's just about perfect," Theodosia said.

Drayton picked up a basket and said to Haley, "Show me the way and we'll get this party started."

As Drayton loaded the final basket into Beth Ann's SUV, as Theodosia was getting ready to lock up for the day, the phone rang. It was Riley.

"Apologies," Riley said, sounding somewhat breathless. "But tonight's dinner will have to be postponed. We're on our way to pick up Craig Cole!"

"You're kidding," Theodosia said. "Why Cole? What have you found?"

"It was a fluke, really. Crime Scene didn't expect to get any meaningful fingerprint evidence at the Sea Witch because it's a retail operation and so many people had been in and out. But

Cole's prints came up nice and clean on one of the glass cases and on the phone in Helene's office."

"Maybe Cole was shopping there. Maybe he and Helene were friends."

"Maybe. That's what we're about to find out."

"You're going to sweat him?" Theodosia said.

"We're going to try. I'm just not sure how sweatable the man is."

When Theodosia told Drayton about Craig Cole, he nodded sagely and said, "It's over, then. Time for us to let it go."

"It's *not* over," Theodosia said. "There's a big piece missing. A huge piece. I can buy the idea of Craig Cole murdering Josh Morro because Morro was always so nasty about his scriptwriting. But why would Cole turn around and murder Helene? What possible motive could he have had?"

"Don't know," Drayton said. "Maybe the murders are unrelated after all."

"We've tossed that idea around, but it still doesn't feel right."

"So you're telling me you want to go ahead and check out Helene's shop?"

"I need to take a quick look," Theodosia said. "To at least settle things in my own mind."

"A quick look and nothing else?" Drayton asked.

A thoughtful look stole across Theodosia's face. "I suppose it all depends on what we find there."

28

It was late afternoon by the time Theodosia and Drayton arrived at Helene's shop. They parked in front of the building, noting that no lights were on inside.

"Cute place," Drayton said. "Even though it looks deserted."

"Which is exactly what we expected," Theodosia said as they climbed out of her Jeep.

"So let's do it," Drayton said. "I want to be home in time to catch an episode of *Grantchester.*"

"You've already watched that series twice."

Drayton shrugged. "I want to see it again. Here, give me the key."

Theodosia handed over the key. Drayton bounced it in his hand and said, "Interesting." Then he slipped the key into the lock and pushed open the door. At which point an alarm began to beep loudly and incessantly.

"Nasty," Drayton said, covering his ears.

Theodosia hastily slipped past him and punched in the code, cutting off the annoying bray. Then there was only silence interrupted by a few ticks and tocks from the antique clocks on display.

"Now what?" Drayton asked as Theodosia snapped on the lights, causing the antiques, ceramics, and glass shelves to shimmer and sparkle. "What do you think you're going to find here that the police haven't already?"

"I've no idea. But something's been plucking at the back of my brain. I can't quite explain it . . . except I know I needed to come here." Theodosia walked between two cases that housed a collection of old coins. Shelves lining the walls held clocks, floral vases, antique portholes, and brass fittings. "Helene really did have some high-quality goods."

"Very impressive. And nothing looks out of order to you? Or out of the ordinary?"

"No, but I'd be interested in your first impression," Theodosia said to Drayton. "You're the one with a keen eye for art and antiques."

Drayton looked around. "I see some nice artwork, lovely old crystal, and . . ." He stopped in front of a case. "Well, what do we have here?"

Theodosia walked over and peered into the case with him. "What are those?" she asked.

"Looks to me like Roman coins. From the reign of Denarius Tiberius."

"Okay." Theodosia did another inspection of the shop, this time making a slow 360-degree turn. "Does this shop seem a little empty to you?"

"I can't say that it does. I always feel that when antiques are crowded too close together it looks a little junky."

"And this place looks . . ."

"Not junky," Drayton said.

Theodosia took a few more minutes to look around, then

wandered into Helene's office. She was dismayed to find the dark purplish stain still marring the carpet. Blood. A terrible reminder that a brutal murder had taken place in this very room.

Avoiding the stain, Theodosia studied what was left of Helene's office. Her desk was bare, as were most of the flat surfaces in the room. She decided that the police had taken all the papers and files that had been piled on Helene's desk and credenza as well as the ones that had toppled onto the floor when she was killed.

The only thing left in Helene's office was a five-foot-high statue of a Chinese scholar carved out of elm, and a bookcase filled with art books.

Theodosia wandered over to the bookcase as Drayton peered into the room. When his eyes fell on the carpet stain, his face twisted into an unhappy grimace.

"I know," Theodosia said. "Awful, isn't it?"

"Macabre." Then, "What are you doing in here? It would appear the police emptied most of this place out."

"They're probably digging through all of Helene's papers looking for clues. The only thing they left were her art books," Theodosia said, as she pulled out a book and hefted it. "Too heavy, I guess. Too much trouble."

"That's the thing about art books. They're always massive and difficult to hold, but they're still magnificent." Drayton took a step closer to her. "What have you got there?"

Theodosia glanced at the front cover. "This one's *Greek Vases from the Hellenistic Period.*"

"All in all a fine book collection," Drayton said, perusing the shelves. "I wonder what will happen to them now?"

"Don't know. Maybe they'll go to Helene's sister. Or get donated to a library somewhere." Theodosia tilted the book upright so she could slide it back into its slot.

The book wouldn't slide.

"Now what's the problem?" Theodosia muttered under her breath as she shoved the book harder. But it clearly wasn't going easily into its slot.

"There's something jamming it," Drayton said, reaching a hand in. "Looks like a piece of paper." He grasped it and pulled it out. "No, it's some kind of file folder."

"A folder on what?"

"Let's see," Drayton said as he opened the manila file folder. "Oh, nothing of much interest. Looks like some kind of contract or agreement."

"Let me see that."

Theodosia handed Drayton the book to hold while she took the folder.

"This is the rebate agreement between the Charleston Film Board and Peregrine Pictures," Theodosia said.

"Or at least a copy of the agreement," Drayton said. "It doesn't look like an original."

"Not an original, you're right," Theodosia said. But as she put it back in the folder, she noticed something else . . .

"But take a look at this, Drayton. It's the completion guaranty for *Dark Fortunes*."

"Completion what?"

"A completion guaranty is a kind of insurance policy," Theodosia explained as she skimmed the page. "In this particular case, if *Dark Fortunes* doesn't get made for whatever reason, the holder of the guaranty still walks away with . . . holy buckets . . . twenty-eight million dollars!" Theodosia looked up from the paper she'd been reading. "Wow."

"And who holds the right to this completion guaranty?" Drayton asked.

"It doesn't say here. Because this is a copy as well. One that hadn't been filled out and signed."

"Do you think the original's been filled out and signed?"

"I'm positive it has."

"It might be important to know who benefits. You know, who pockets the twenty-eight million dollars. Can you call one of the Film Board members to find out?"

Theodosia looked at her watch. "It's pretty late."

"Try anyway."

So Theodosia pulled out her phone, found the website for the Charleston Film Board, and dialed the number that was listed. It rang and rang until a voice mail came on telling her they were closed.

"Nada," she said to Drayton.

"Is there anyone else you can call?"

Theodosia thought for a moment, then said, "Maybe I could call Joe Adler? I think I've got his number in my contacts file."

"Do it."

So Theodosia called Adler's number. When he picked up, she said, "This is Theodosia, the tea lady. Can I ask you a question?"

"Make it quick," Adler said. "I'm on my way out."

"What do you know about a completion guaranty on your film?"

"Not a damn thing." Adler sounded bored and busy.

"But you know there is one."

"If there is it's not my concern. I intend to bring this film in on time and under budget so anything else is a moot point."

"Okay." Theodosia wasn't sure what her follow-up question should be.

"Anything else?" Adler asked.

"I guess, um . . ." Then just before Adler hung up, she said, "Wait a minute. Did you rent the Granville Mansion or did someone do it for you?"

"Lewin Usher arranged it."

"You're talking about the hedge fund guy?"

"Usher's also one of our executive producers. And let me just say that the man relishes his title. It totally trips him out and makes him feel like a Hollywood insider." Adler gave a low chuckle. "Though, from what I've seen so far, he's really more of a junkman."

Theodosia did a slow blink. "Excuse me, what do you mean by that?"

"You wouldn't believe all the crap he's got stored in the garage here. It's practically crowding out my Porsche."

"What kind of crap?"

"Crates full of stuff. Looks like most of it's off old ships or something. But what do I know? I'm from Hollywood by way of Albuquerque."

"Okay, thanks." Theodosia hung up. She looked at Drayton and said, "Joe Adler says there's all sorts of stuff from old ships in his garage. Why would that be?"

"I don't know. Who put it there?"

Theodosia shrugged. "No idea. Unless . . ."

"Unless what?"

"Lewin Usher arranged to rent the mansion for Joe Adler, so the stuff probably belongs to Usher." She frowned. "But why would Usher be storing stuff from old ships?"

Drayton stared at her as if he were working calculations in his brain. "Maybe because it's worth a fortune?"

"What are you talking about?" Theodosia asked.

"Marine artifacts command top dollar these days. Gone are the days when salvage operations could keep everything they found and dredged up. The South Carolina Underwater Antiquities Act of 1991 took care of that kind of wanton robbery and piracy. Now you need to obtain permission and do your exploring under the auspices of the South Carolina Institute for Archaeology and Anthropology. You probably even need to hire a licensed on-site marine archaeologist."

"You know this for a fact?"

"I know that a masthead from a seventeenth-century schooner sells for upward of a million dollars."

Theodosia digested this information for a few minutes as scattered bits of conversation zipped through her brain like chase lights on a theater marquee. She recalled her conversation with Delaine. It seemed like weeks ago but was only a few days. What had Delaine said? Oh yes, that one of Josh Morro's favorite hobbies was scuba diving.

Scuba diving.

Theodosia quickly told Drayton about the conversation she'd had with Delaine, then asked, "Do you think Josh Morrow's murder is somehow connected to those marine artifacts?"

"Don't know. Maybe you should call Delaine and press her a little harder."

So Theodosia did exactly that. And asked Delaine if Morrow was perhaps a collector of marine artifacts.

"Oh, gosh," Delaine said. "I do know that Josh was passionate about old shipwrecks."

"And diving for artifacts? And collecting them?"

"No," Delaine said. "Not at all. Josh was always battering on about how there were something like thirty-five shipwrecks in Charleston Harbor alone. Plus, another hundred and sixty in nearby waters. He thought they should all be carefully preserved. He hated the fact that some people—some divers—took up the sport just so they could freelance as treasure hunters and then sell the stuff for big bucks."

"Thanks, Delaine," Theodosia said. "You've been a big help."

Theodosia gazed at Drayton and there was almost an audible *click*, as if a piece of the puzzle had dropped into place for her.

"Do you remember Helene telling us how well she and Usher worked together?" Theodosia asked. "At the time I thought Helene was referring to the movie, to Helene helping with all that tax credit paperwork. But what if it was something more? Something different? Something to do with her shop?"

Drayton nodded. "Go on."

"When I snuck into Josh Morro's room . . ."

"What!"

"Hear me out. When I looked around his room there was a scuba diver's watch sitting on the dresser. And Riley told me there were bits of algae found on the carpet in Helene's office . . ."

"So what are you saying?" Drayton asked.

"What if Josh Morro had been out diving and seen something that was highly irregular? Some sort of illegal recovery operation?"

"And then he was killed?"

"Because Morro was a witness," Theodosia said. She held up a hand. "Okay, indulge me here. What if Helene got in over her head? What if she was unknowingly fencing marine artifacts for Usher? Let's face it, Helene was fairly trusting and a little bit ditzy."

"And when Helene realized she was being used, she got cold feet?" Drayton said.

"So maybe Usher had to get rid of Helene, too?"

"Who exactly is this Lewin Usher?" Drayton asked.

"He heads something called Dragon Capitol. I think it's a hedge fund."

"Call them."

"It's late. They won't be open."

"Give it a shot anyway."

Theodosia called Dragon Capitol and got a canned message. Blah, blah, blah, office is open weekdays from eight thirty to four thirty.

"What if you called Lewin Usher at home?" Drayton suggested.

"And do what?"

"Hint around that you know something? See what his reaction is?"

"I don't have his number," Theodosia said.

"Maybe try Information?"

Theodosia tried and, surprisingly, got the number. But when she called Usher's home, his housekeeper answered.

"I'm sorry, but Mr. Usher isn't home right now," the housekeeper said. "But if you'd care to leave a message I'll certainly relay it to him."

"It's urgent I get hold of him," Theodosia said. When she was still met with polite resistance, she added, "This has to do with the film that Mr. Usher is coproducing. It's pretty much an emergency."

"Oh," the housekeeper said. "A business emergency. In that case Mr. Usher is on his boat, has been for most of the day. I'm not sure he's reachable by cell phone but he should be coming in fairly soon."

"That's great. Thank you," Theodosia said. "By the way, do you happen to know the name of Mr. Usher's boat?"

"It's named after his company, Dragon Capitol. The boat's called *Dragon*."

Theodosia hung up. Her heart raced and she felt jittery, as if she'd finally found a hairline fracture that could lead to answers in these two mysterious murder cases.

"Well?" Drayton said.

"Here's how I see it adding up," Theodosia said. "Usher's out on his boat right now, which is named *Dragon*. He's storing what might be illegally obtained marine artifacts in the garage near me. And the Crime Scene techs found traces of algae on the rug in Helene's office. What do you think?"

"I think maybe we should head over to Charleston Harbor and take a look at that boat. What do you think?"

"I think . . . ditto."

29

"It's probably going to be a good-sized boat," Theodosia said as they coasted along East Bay Street, heading for Union Pier Terminal, where commercial boats were docked.

"How so?" Drayton asked.

"It might have some kind of crane for lifting and may even be disguised as a fishing boat."

"And you're sure Usher would keep it moored here instead of at the Charleston Yacht Club?"

"No, I'm not sure. But since it's more of a working vessel than a pleasure craft, I'm playing a hunch."

It was full-on dark as Theodosia hooked a right at Hasell Street, then right again on Pritchard. They were just north of Port of Charleston, where the large cruise and cargo ships came in, winding their way past warehouses, stacks of freight containers, construction shacks, and piles of metal that looked like gargantuan Pick-Up Sticks. Ahead of them loomed another series of large warehouses shrouded by a tall wire fence. The docks on the Cooper River were just beyond.

"Spooky," Drayton said. "Quiet."

"This whole area is supposedly going to be revitalized," Theodosia said. "There's a master plan floating around for new housing, parks, dog parks, and an entertainment venue."

"You think that's going to happen?"

"Maybe."

"But probably not in our lifetime," Drayton said. "There's always been a certain reticence when it comes to interfering with Charleston's DNA."

"We're an old city. I suppose many of us prefer to keep it that way," Theodosia said as she rolled to a stop. She'd come up against a padlocked gate posted with a sign that said STOP in large letters. And underneath that, NO TRESPASSING, NO OVERNIGHT PARKING.

"Looks like this is where the trail ends," Drayton said.

Theodosia popped open her door and climbed out. "Maybe there's another way for us to get down to those commercial docks."

Drayton climbed out reluctantly, looked around, and then peered at the tall metal fence that ran for several hundred yards. "There's no way we'll ever get over that."

"We have to." Theodosia looked up at the sky. No stars tonight, just low-hanging gray clouds and fog rolling in. The air was so heavy with moisture it felt like you could grab it and wring it out. The encroaching fog also put a damper on sounds and lent everything a hazy outline.

"Look at that monster fence," Drayton said, respect in his voice. "It's almost eight feet tall with curved pokey things at the top. If we try to go over the top it'll serve us up en brochette. And I don't fancy being a human shish kebab."

"Then we need to find another way."

"There isn't another way."

"Has to be."

Theodosia walked some twenty feet down the fence line, checking out the galvanized chain-link fence, looking for what she hoped might be a chink in the armor. She grasped the fence with her hands and rattled it. Drayton was right. It was a tough monster. She walked another fifteen feet where stringy weeds sprouted at the base of the fence, her eyes searching for what might be an answer to their problem. And just when she was about to give up, found what she'd been hoping for.

Next to one of the metal fence poles a small part of the fence had been cut and peeled back slightly. It was hidden behind the weeds like a rabbit hole, and Theodosia figured it had probably been made by marauding kids so they could worm their way closer to the Cooper River as well as the boat docks.

"There's a spot here, Drayton. A place where the fence has been ripped. I think we might be able to squirm through."

Drayton shuffled down to where Theodosia was kneeling, pushing away dry weeds, working at the hole, tugging the metal fence this way and that.

"That dinky hole?" he said. "There's no way we could ever squeeze through there."

"We have to try."

"You try. Just know that if you get stuck I'll have to grab your ankles and pull you out like a sack of flour."

"I'm going to give it a shot."

"Suit yourself."

Theodosia crouched down on her hands and knees and stuck her head through the hole.

"I think this might work."

After bending back more of the fence and figuring out a workable angle, Theodosia twisted one shoulder through the fence, then the other. From there it was a matter of twisting and turning and shimmying the rest of her body through.

Drayton peered at her through the wire. "Good grief, you did it. Then again, you are a rather small person."

"It wasn't so hard, Drayton, you try it."

Drayton bent forward in an awkward stance and grasped the torn fence with his hands.

"You have to get lower," Theodosia coached.

"I thought I was lower."

"Go ahead and scrunch all the way down."

Drayton dropped to his hands and knees. "Dirty down here. And grubby. It feels like I'm kneeling in an oil slick."

"I know. I'm sorry."

"Here goes nothing."

Drayton stuck his head through the hole in the fence, then followed that with one shoulder. He twisted slightly and got hopelessly stuck. He made a sound like a wounded crow as he backed out.

"Try approaching the hole from a slightly different angle," Theodosia suggested. "And think positive."

"I'm always positive," Drayton grumped. He dropped his right shoulder, rammed it through, fought some more, then somehow managed to jam his left shoulder through.

"You're halfway there," Theodosia whispered.

"But it's the wrong half."

"Now just wiggle."

"That sounds so ungainly. Couldn't I just . . ."

RRRRIP!

Drayton froze. "Drat. My slacks. Ripped on a sharp edge I guess and . . ."

"Don't worry about it."

"I *do* worry about it."

"But you're almost there. Here, give me your hand and I'll try to pull you through the rest of the way."

So Theodosia pulled as Drayton wriggled and rattled the fence. But, finally, after another few minutes of huffing, grunting, and ungainly contortions, Drayton got the rest of himself through.

"That was awful," he said as he stood up and dusted his hands together. He was filthy, exhausted, and his jacket was completely askew as he tried (unsuccessfully) to put himself back together.

"It's ripped," Theodosia said. She was staring at a pocket that hung by barely a few threads.

"I *know* it's ripped."

"I meant your jacket," Theodosia said. Drayton was wearing an ice-blue cashmere jacket that had basically been shredded.

Drayton looked down at himself. "Good heavens. My pants and jacket are in tatters and I've got grease stains all over me. I look like the proverbial hobo."

"But you're wearing a Sartorio jacket, so at least you look like a successful hobo," Theodosia pointed out.

"You're not helping."

"Sorry."

Drayton pulled out a hanky, swiped at the oil stains on the front of his jacket, then finally gave up when he made no visible progress. "What now?"

"Now we take a look at the boats."

They moved stealthily past dark warehouses, creeping along in the shadows like a couple of ninjas. Sometimes their feet crunched on gravel, sometimes it was broken blacktop. But, inch by inch, they crawled ever closer until they could hear the Cooper River slapping hard against the shoreline and the docks.

And there were boats bobbing there. Lots of boats. Most were moored to the old wooden docks that had been fixtures there forever.

"There's a boat coming in now," Drayton whispered. They were hunkered down behind a stack of giant wooden spools, hidden deep in the shadows.

"Fishing boat," Theodosia said. In the dark, with light reflected on the water, she could just make out a mast and rigging.

"What about that one?" Drayton asked as another boat cut its engine to a low sputter and bumped toward the dock.

"Same thing."

"Maybe we should get closer," Drayton said.

So they duckwalked another fifteen feet until they found an even better hidey spot behind a stack of old tires that were probably being held in reserve for use as dock bumpers.

"Can you make out the names of the boats that are already tied up there?" Drayton asked. "Do you see one with the name *Dragon* on it?"

Theodosia squinted into the darkness. "I see *Sea Lady* and *Narwhal*. Even one called *Jinx*, but nothing that says *Dragon*."

"So we wait?"

"Right. And if Usher really is running an illegal salvage operation, we watch for a boat that's coming in without running lights," Theodosia whispered.

"No lights. Right," Drayton said.

But there were no boats like that.

Drayton squirmed around, trying to get comfortable. "How long are we going to hang out here?"

"Until . . ."

"Until when?"

"Just until," Theodosia said.

They sat there for another twenty minutes, Drayton peering

at his watch every five minutes. Then, just as Drayton had finally settled down and closed his eyes, when his breathing had become deeper and more even, Theodosia saw it.

A boat slipping in without any running lights. A silhouette, really. And the only reason she noticed it was because it passed in front of a channel marker that had a glowing red light on it.

Could this be something? Is it worth investigating?

Theodosia jabbed an elbow in Drayton's ribs.

His eyes popped open. "What?"

Theodosia held a finger to her mouth, then pointed.

Drayton eased up from where he'd been hunkered and peered over the tires. He watched for a few moments, then nodded.

"Let's go," Theodosia whispered.

30

Hunched over, moving as quietly as possible, they approached the boat as it pulled up to the dock. They could make out two men on deck, talking in low voices, moving things about.

"That has to be it," Theodosia whispered.

"Catch them red-handed?" Drayton whispered back.

Theodosia nodded. Her breath caught in her throat. She was excited and knew they didn't dare bungle this. They'd have to sneak up to the boat, make sure it was Lewin Usher, and check to see if he was carrying contraband marine artifacts. Then they could creep off to a safe distance and call the police.

Okay, this is it.

The smell of river and dead fish heavy in their noses, Theodosia and Drayton snuck closer to the boat where the two men were talking to each other in low whispers. Carefully, tentatively, they stepped out onto the creaky dock, still moving slowly, hoping to catch the name of the boat, trying to see if they recognized who was on board.

And just as Theodosia stood up, just as Drayton followed her lead, a bright light popped on. Hung from the mast of the boat, it flooded the boat and nearby dock in cold white light.

"Hey there!" one of the men on the boat shouted as he caught sight of them. "What do you think you're doing?"

The other man on the boat rushed over to the railing and shook his fist. "It's those darn kids again, isn't it? You kids get out of here, this whole area's private property!"

Theodosia and Drayton turned and ran. They'd caught sight of the nets, of two large tubs that probably held their fresh catch of the day. It had been a fishing boat and they'd made a colossal mistake.

They retreated back to the pile of tires.

Drayton was shaking his head. "We messed up."

"Hard to tell what's what in the dark," Theodosia agreed.

They waited, hidden, watching as the two fishermen walked by them, got into a pickup truck, then backed their truck up to the dock. When they'd loaded their catch into the back, they drove off. Upon reaching the main gate, one man jumped out while the other drove the truck through. Then they locked the gate behind them.

"Looks like we're locked in," Drayton said. "I hope you don't intend to stay here all night. I think we've pretty much . . ."

Theodosia held up a hand to quiet Drayton. Another boat was coming in.

"No," Drayton whispered. "Not again."

But Theodosia watched carefully as the boat slipped to the dock. And from its shadowy outline, it didn't look like any fishing boat she'd ever seen before.

"Let's get closer," Theodosia whispered. Without waiting for Drayton to answer, she abandoned her hidey spot and sprinted for the dock again. Her head tucked low, she covered ten feet of ground, then hunkered down behind a rough wooden post. She could see a light shining on the deck of the boat and two figures moving around. One person was larger and bulkier and walked slightly bent forward just like Lewin Usher. The other man was taller and thinner and still wore his wet suit peeled down to his waist. They were talking, conferring about something. Their voices were pitched low, but Theodosia could detect a note of urgency and excitement.

Theodosia turned to wave at Drayton, wanting him to join her—and found he was already crouched directly behind her.

"Is it them?" he whispered.

Theodosia nodded. "I think so."

The men continued to move around on the boat, stowing lines, shutting down the engines, and tightening ropes. One of them walked to the front of the boat and looked out to where Theodosia and Drayton were hiding. Then he shook his head and went back to work.

Finally, they watched as one of the men—Theodosia was pretty sure it was Lewin Usher—backed his Lexus SUV as close as he could to the dock. Then he and the other man, who'd changed into jeans and a plaid shirt, hoisted a wooden crate into the back of the SUV.

When the back hatch was secured, the SUV pulled away. Nearby, the roar of a motorcycle pierced the air.

"I think Usher's driving the SUV," Theodosia said. "And the other guy's on a motorcycle." She hesitated. "We have to follow them."

Theodosia and Drayton watched as the two vehicles pulled up to the gate. Then, under cover of darkness, they quickly ran back to the hole in the fence. As they popped out, the SUV roared past, followed by the motorcycle. A trail of dust followed them.

"Hurry!" Theodosia shouted as she raced for her Jeep. She jumped in and cranked the engine just as Drayton jumped in a split second later. Eyes on the retreating SUV and motorcycle, Theodosia hurried to catch up.

"Don't get too close," Drayton cautioned as they wound their way along Pritchard Street and crossed over East Bay Street.

"Where do you think they're going?" Theodosia wondered. "To the Granville Mansion?"

But no, the SUV turned right on Cumberland, with the motorcycle following behind.

Theodosia tailed them down Earl Street, past Brett's Pub and Bobo's Lobster Shack. They passed a few more retail shops, closed now for the night, then followed them into a more industrial area. Theodosia slowed when she saw the SUV's brake lights flare and turn down an alley. She cut her lights and coasted to a stop at the mouth of the alley. A sign read RANDY'S SELF STORAGE. They watched as the motorcycle pulled up alongside the SUV and one of the garage doors rumbled open, casting a spill of bright light.

Yes, Theodosia thought with a blip of excitement. *That's for sure Lewin Usher.*

Usher and his coconspirator talked for a few minutes, then the motorcycle driver gave a wave and took off while Usher pulled his SUV into the garage.

"Usher's alone now," Theodosia said. "This is almost a perfect scenario."

"Shouldn't we call the police?" Drayton asked.

"Let's hold off for a couple of minutes. Maybe we can get a look at what's inside that crate."

"If I subscribe to your logic—and I think I do—it's going to be purloined marine artifacts," Drayton said.

"*Purloined* sounds so much nastier than *stolen,*" Theodosia said. She eased her car over to the side of the alley, close to a stand of scraggly palmettos. Then the two of them climbed out and tiptoed down the alley, sticking to the shadows, headed for the garage.

This is it, Theodosia thought to herself. *This is how to solve a murder. Probably two murders.*

She felt almost giddy as she stood just a few feet from the open garage door, ready to sneak in and see for herself what was in that mysterious crate.

And that's when Theodosia felt the business end of a pistol pressed coldly against the back of her neck.

31

"Don't make a sound or I will pull this trigger and blow your brains out through your ears," a voice hissed. "Then I'll do your partner."

"I won't. I'm not," Theodosia said. She tried to remain calm even though inside she was shrieking like a banshee. "But please let Drayton go, okay?"

"Not okay," said a second voice. Theodosia turned slightly to find Lewin Usher also pointing a small, ugly-looking gray pistol at them. He took a few steps forward, smiled crookedly, and said, "You really think I'd let him go?"

Theodosia didn't have an answer for that.

"Get inside," Lewin said, gesturing with his gun.

Not having much choice, Theodosia and Drayton marched into the garage.

"You two just love to meddle, don't you?" Usher said in a chiding tone. "Have to stick your noses where they don't belong." He let loose a deep sigh. "I'm guessing you've figured out most of the story?"

"We don't know anything," Theodosia lied.

"Bullwacky," Usher snorted. "Tony, move the old guy over here. In fact, put 'em both in the corner, and tie them up."

"Old guy?" Drayton muttered as he stumbled forward.

Tony, the motorcycle rider, herded Theodosia and Drayton into the corner of the garage. Then, as Usher pointed his gun at them, Tony sat them down on the cement floor and tied them up. First their hands, then their feet, then their hands to their feet, until they were trussed up like a couple of Thanksgiving turkeys.

"You don't have to do this," Theodosia said to Tony. He was young, maybe twenty-eight or twenty-nine, with dark curly hair and a chiseled face. "We'll tell the police you weren't involved."

"That we never even saw you," Drayton added.

Tony ignored them both.

"What are you gonna do with them?" Tony asked Usher. "Leave them here to starve?"

"Wouldn't work," Usher said. "What we need to do is get rid of them tonight. Take the boat out again and dump them ten miles offshore." His eyes darted back to Theodosia and Drayton. "Think you folks can swim that far? In a fast current in a cold ocean? Somehow I doubt it."

"This is gonna take all night," Tony said. There was a hint of peevishness in his voice.

"Don't worry, you'll get paid," Usher snapped. "What we gotta do first is get rid of today's haul."

"Take it to the same place?"

"No, I've got a storage locker in North Charleston that's safer. We'll stash everything there, then come back and pick up these two. Take them for a nice moonlight cruise."

"Ha," Tony chortled.

Usher walked over and nudged Theodosia's leg with the toe of his shoe. "You sit tight, okay? You and your nosy sidekick."

Theodosia lifted her chin and said, "Did you kill Josh Morro? Because he figured out what you were up to?"

Usher winked at her. "We might have had a hand in that. Tony here is a master electrician. All I had to do was set up the chair and jam the circuits. Clever, yes?"

"Not really," Theodosia said.

"Did you kill Helene as well?" Drayton asked.

Usher's smile turned cold. "She was a nice lady. Until she got a little too curious for her own good. Wanted to know where I was sourcing my marine artifacts. Yup, curiosity killed the cat, kind of like what's going to happen to the two of you." He turned to Tony and said, "Let's go. Make our drop and get back here."

"Wait a minute," Theodosia said. "So it wasn't about the completion guaranty?"

Usher smirked. "That's still my ace in the hole. In case things don't work out."

Usher and Tony left in the Lexus, leaving Theodosia and Drayton sitting in a dark corner of a garage that smelled like motor oil and mouse droppings.

"Do you think we should shout for help?" Drayton asked somewhat facetiously.

"It couldn't hurt," Theodosia said.

So they spent the next fifteen minutes shouting and screaming, pleading for someone to open the door and let them out.

Didn't happen.

"I don't think anybody can hear us through all this cinder block," Theodosia said. "Got a better idea?"

"Do you think we could kind of hump and bump our way over to the door and open it ourselves?"

"It's worth a try," Theodosia said.

But after twenty minutes of squirming and banging against the cement, rubbing their knuckles and elbows raw, they hadn't made much forward progress.

"I'm starting to get worried," Theodosia said.

"Wait a minute. Do you have your cell phone?"

"It's in the pocket of my slacks. I tried to reach it but . . . no luck."

"Let me try."

They squirmed and stretched as if they were playing a game of Twister, but that didn't work, either.

"We got nothin'," Drayton said, sounding dispirited.

"All I've got . . ." Theodosia wiggled around, tugging hard at her bindings and managing to slightly loosen one part. Which gave her hope. Sticking two fingers into her jacket pocket, she said, "The most I can probably manage is to reach that stupid key to the Sea Witch."

"Say what?" Drayton said.

"The key fob with . . ."

"Can you wiggle it out of your pocket?" he asked, a note of excitement coloring his voice.

"Maybe. But what good's it going to do us?"

"Indulge me."

So Theodosia struggled and strained some more until she was able to worm a hand all the way into her pocket. Finally, using her forefinger and middle finger, she was able to pluck out the key fob.

"You think we can saw our way out with this? It's just a big fake plastic key."

"Give it to me."

Theodosia passed the key fob to Drayton. He worked it around one-handedly, poking and prodding at one end. There was a soft *click*, then a small blade popped out one side of the key fob.

"Whoa, is that what I think it is?" Theodosia asked.

"It's a kind of penknife," Drayton said as he began sawing at his ropes. "And lucky for us, camouflaged as a key fob."

"Fantastic!" Theodosia was suddenly energized. Maybe they really could get out of here.

Drayton sawed the small knife back and forth, working at his ropes. He cut through one in a matter of a few minutes, untangled some of it, and continued sawing.

"How are you doing?" Theodosia asked, anxiety gnawing at her now.

"Still working at it."

"Maybe . . . work harder?"

Drayton did renew his efforts, and ten minutes later, they were both free from their bonds!

"We gotta book it and get out of here," Theodosia said. "Those goons are going to be back any minute."

She'd hardly uttered the words when they heard the crunch of gravel outside.

"Oh my Lord," Drayton said, clapping a hand to his chest. "They're here. Now what?"

Theodosia glanced around, looking for a weapon. A tire iron, a rake, anything they could use to fight their way out. All she saw was Tony's motorcycle.

Quick as a fox she jumped into the saddle. She held in the clutch, hit the start button on the right handlebar, then twisted the throttle to give it some gas. A split second later she was rewarded with a loud *whomp* followed by a nice throaty rumble.

"What are you doing?" Drayton shouted over the *vroom-boom* revving of the motorcycle's engine.

"Escaping," Theodosia said. "Hurry up and climb on behind me. And when that garage door goes up, be sure to hang on tight!"

It was like a scene out of a Tom Cruise movie. The garage door went up just as Theodosia and Drayton, crouched low on the bike, exploded out the door. Focused on making a quick and daring exit, Theodosia revved the engine so high they almost did a wheelie.

They were aboard a Honda Fireblade SP, a big mother of a bike with a 999 cc liquid-cooled engine. Theodosia had only ever ridden a Vespa before, so it was an extraordinary amount of horsepower for her to handle. She skidded wildly, almost tipping over as she hit loose gravel, then gave it a more judicious shot of gas. The bike straightened up immediately and shot down the alley like a bullet.

"Hang on!" Theodosia shouted as they came out on Bull Street and slewed left, the wind buffeting them like crazy.

"I am!" Drayton shouted. He was clinging to her for dear life. "But . . . dear me, I think they're following us!"

Theodosia risked a quick look back over her shoulder. Drayton was right. The SUV had roared down the alley, made the same speedy turn as they had, and was coming after them.

Would Usher try to shoot out the bike's tires? Theodosia figured he wouldn't hesitate.

As Theodosia tore down the street she racked her brain. What to do? Where to go? It had just started to rain, a nuisance sprinkle that glazed the pavement and turned the streetlights into colorful blurs.

She flew around a corner, barely missing a little blue Honda Civic, swerved dangerously, then gained control again. But the

SUV was still following them. In fact, it was right behind them and starting to gain some ground!

Pawing for her cell phone, Theodosia pulled it out of her pocket and passed it back to Drayton.

"Call Riley!" she cried. "Tell him what's going on, where we are!" The wind was stinging her eyes, causing tears to stream down her cheeks. There was a red traffic light up ahead. Muttering a silent prayer, Theodosia blasted right through it. Cars braked and angry drivers honked their horns at her.

The SUV still followed them!

"Drayton, call Riley," Theodosia shouted again. They shot past Banger's Pool Hall and Crowdy's Bar, where a few patrons were huddled out front on the sidewalk, smoking.

Drayton was hanging on with one hand, trying to punch in numbers with the other hand. Then they hit a bump—your basic manhole cover—and the phone flew out of his hand. It tumbled end over end, almost in slow motion, then hit the pavement with a sharp *crack* and skidded away.

"Oops," Drayton cried in Theodosia's ear. "I'm afraid I dropped your phone."

"Oops?" Theodosia said. "*Oops?* That phone was our only hope!"

They tore around a corner and headed down Meeting Street. They flew by the Old Market but there was no place to go there, nothing that would help them. All the boutiques and produce stalls were dark and closed for the night.

Theodosia turned on Chalmers Street, squeaked through another red light without getting them killed, then roared down Church Street. They passed Hearts Desire and the White Rabbit Children's Shop. Again, these shops were dark and deserted.

"I've got an idea," Drayton said, pounding a fist against Theodosia's shoulder.

"What's that?" They were going so fast, the bike's engine so loud, that Theodosia's voice barely carried back to him.

"Turn!" Drayton shouted.

Theodosia braked slightly. "Turn? Turn where?"

"Here, right here!" Drayton screeched. Do it *now*!"

Theodosia swerved hard and leaned into her turn, the bike heeling over at a good forty-degree angle as they plunged into the darkness of Stoll's Alley. The cobblestones beneath the tires were murder, causing their teeth to chatter and the bike to skitter and slew from side to side as they plowed along. Hanging vines swatted their faces, wrought iron and brass nameplates flashed by. Stoll's Alley was definitely one of the more picturesque of Charleston's many hidden lanes. And, thanks to Drayton's vast knowledge of historic Charleston, it was also the narrowest, ending at a mere five feet across. As Usher's SUV roared after them, the brick walls of the alley grew narrower and narrower, forming a delicious kind of bottleneck.

"I hope this works!" Drayton shouted as they shot down the alley. And then, right behind them, they were rewarded with a CRASH! And a CRUNCH! Metal scraped hard against cement in a harsh rasp that built into a caterwauling drawn-out SCREECH. And then, wouldn't you know it? Lewin Usher's SUV was jerked to a complete and shuddering stop as it caught firmly in the narrow, brick jaws of Stoll's Alley.

Feeling breathless, Theodosia rocked to a stop as they both turned around to look. And just like that, a harrowing chase with dangerous characters had suddenly turned into a Keystone Cops comedy bit. The SUV's horn bleated as if in agony, wheels spun uselessly, and Usher and Tony pounded frantically at the doors and windows, trying to escape. No dice. Stoll's Alley had them wedged in tight.

On hearing the terrible commotion, a man prepped out in

khakis and a pink golf shirt came flying out the back door of one of the alley's upscale townhouses. Spotting Theodosia and Drayton on the motorcycle, he cried, "I heard a crash! What happened? Is anybody hurt?"

Then he spun on the heels of his hand-tooled loafers and saw where the tightly wedged SUV had come to rest.

"Oh, holy Hannah," he cried. "You almost hit the devil!"

32

The devil was indeed a devil. A bronze statue of a devil playing a violin that had stood at the far end of Stoll's Alley for decades. He was not a frightening devil, more like a longtime guardian whose head had been buffed to a high gleam by the many tourists who'd walked past him, been fascinated by his presence, and given him a pat and a polish.

Explaining their situation to the police? Now that was a devil of a time for Theodosia. The surprised resident's 911 call brought two police cruisers screaming in. And once Theodosia related their peculiar circumstances to those officers, Detectives Tidwell and Riley were immediately called to the scene.

In his blue FBI T-shirt and baggy pants, Tidwell surveyed the stuck SUV and its captive inhabitants. Then he rocked back on his heels, turned to Theodosia, and said, "You did this?"

"Kind of," she said. "But mostly it was Drayton's idea."

Tidwell surveyed a bedraggled Drayton, who'd climbed off the motorcycle and was standing there, looking a bit winded, and said, "Nice suit." Both pockets on Drayton's jacket were missing.

"Say now," Drayton said, his brows puckering together.

Theodosia tried to defuse the situation by telling Detective Tidwell their saga of going to the Sea Witch, calling Usher, and making a tentative connection concerning stolen marine artifacts. And then she had to repeat a good part of it once Riley showed up.

"And how exactly did you end up here?" Tidwell asked as Riley stared at her with something akin to fascination.

So Theodosia related the second part of their story, starting with the search at the boat docks, then concluding with their capture, escape, and wild motorcycle chase.

"So you see," Theodosia explained, "it was Lewin Usher and his henchman who killed Josh Morro and Helene Deveroux. And it was all on account of valuable marine artifacts."

"And where are these so-called artifacts now?" Riley asked, looking a little shaken. He was still getting used to the fact that Theodosia and Drayton had led two dangerous felons on a life-and-death chase through Charleston's Historic District, then had the presence of mind to lure them into the narrow alley and mousetrap them.

"Some of the artifacts are being stored in the Granville Mansion right next to me, some are at Usher's storage locker in North Charleston," Theodosia said.

"You know where that storage locker might be?" Tidwell asked.

Theodosia glanced over at the SUV, where Lewin Usher, red-faced and angry, still battered at his windshield from inside, like a moth trapped in a jar. "No," she said. "But I bet Usher is about ready to make a deal with you."

Then a shiny red van with a satellite dish on top and the letters W-BAM painted on the side screeched to a halt. Ken Lotter jumped out, followed by his cameraman. The cameraman immediately switched on his light and began recording.

"What have we got? What happened?" Lotter cried. He was wild-eyed and excited as he stuck a microphone in Tidwell's face, where it was immediately swatted away. Lotter looked at the trapped SUV, then turned to Theodosia and said, "You did this?"

"You might say I'm partially responsible," Theodosia said.

"No," Tidwell said. "Go ahead, take all the credit."

"Say now," Lotter said. "That guy in the SUV—isn't he one of the producers for that movie, *Dark Fortunes?*" When nobody answered, he said, "This is about those two movie murders, isn't it?" He was jumping up and down with excitement.

"We'll be calling a press conference in the morning," Tidwell said.

"We gotta get some of this footage for the eleven o'clock," Lotter cried to his cameraman. "Keep shooting. Get as much as you can. Any video of this wedged car is golden. It's gonna send our ratings sky-high."

Tidwell watched as Lotter and his cameraman danced around the stuck SUV, trying to interview the two angry men inside. Then, bemused, he reached up and scratched his head. "We're definitely going to need a tow truck—if we can even get one in there."

"Going to be a tight squeeze," Theodosia said.

"Or we could call the fire department for one of their hydraulic tools that cuts and spreads metal," Tidwell said. "You know, the jaws of life."

"Such a shame to ruin a nice vehicle like that," Riley said as he stared at the hopelessly wedged Lexus.

"Has to be done," Tidwell said. "It's probably totaled anyway."

Riley sidled over to Theodosia and said, "What I want to know is—what made you decide to trap those two clowns in Stoll's Alley?"

"It was Drayton's quick thinking," Theodosia said.

Riley turned toward Drayton. "How'd you get the idea to turn in here like that?"

Drayton flashed an impish grin. "You might say the devil made me do it."

The Indigo Tea Shop

Killer Cinnamon Coffee Cake

CAKE

1 cup flour

3 tsp. baking powder

½ tsp. cinnamon

½ cup milk

½ cup sugar

½ tsp. salt

4 Tbsp. butter, melted

1 egg

TOPPING

¼ cup sugar

½ tsp. cinnamon

PREHEAT oven to 350 degrees. Combine flour, baking powder, cinnamon, milk, sugar, salt, butter, and egg in a mixing bowl. Stir until ingredients are thoroughly mixed. Pour batter into an 8-by-8-inch greased baking pan. Mix together sugar and cin-

namon for topping and spread evenly on top. Bake for 15 to
20 minutes. Serve warm. Yields about 9 servings.

Pineapple Crisp

2 (20 oz.) cans crushed pineapple (drained)

1 cup flour

1 cup brown sugar

1 tsp. baking powder

½ tsp. salt

1 egg

½ cup butter, melted

1 tsp. ground cinnamon

PREHEAT oven to 350 degrees. Spread drained pineapple into a
9-by-9-inch baking pan. In a medium bowl, mix together flour,
brown sugar, baking powder, salt, and egg until smooth. Spoon
mixture over pineapple. Pour melted butter over mixture and
then sprinkle with cinnamon. Bake for 40 to 45 minutes. Can
be served hot or cold. Yields about 6 servings.

Lemon Chicken

1 frying chicken (2½ to 3 lb.), cut into pieces

¼ cup olive oil

¼ cup fresh lemon juice

½ tsp. grated onion

½ tsp. salt

¼ tsp. thyme

Sprinkle of garlic powder

Butter

Chopped parsley and paprika for garnish

PREHEAT oven to 350 degrees. Blend together olive oil, lemon juice, onion, salt, and thyme. Arrange chicken pieces in a buttered casserole dish. Brush chicken thoroughly with lemon-oil mixture. Sprinkle lightly with garlic powder. Cover and bake for 50 to 60 minutes until tender, basting occasionally. Take cover off casserole for the last 20 minutes to allow chicken to brown. Garnish with parsley and paprika and serve with rice or a vegetable. Yields 4 servings.

Strawberry Tea Sandwiches

4 oz. cream cheese, softened

2 Tbsp. strawberry jam

5 slices thin white bread

5 fresh strawberries, sliced thin

COMBINE cream cheese and strawberry jam in bowl. Spread mixture on each of the 5 slices of bread. With a 1½-inch round cutter, cut out circles in the center of each slice of bread—you will get 3 or 4 circles per slice. Lay out half the circles and top with a strawberry slice. Top with remaining circles. Yields 15 to 18 tea sandwiches.

Double-Chocolate Scones

2¼ cups flour

¼ cup unsweetened cocoa powder

½ cup sugar

4 tsp. baking powder

¼ tsp. salt

1 stick cold butter, finely cubed

1 cup semi sweet chocolate chips

½ cup cream

½ cup milk

PREHEAT oven to 400 degrees and line a baking sheet with parchment. In a large bowl, whisk together flour, cocoa powder, sugar, baking powder, and salt. Using a pastry cutter, cut in cold butter until mixture resembles coarse breadcrumbs. Add chocolate chips, cream, and milk, stirring until a loose dough forms. Turn out dough onto a lightly floured surface and knead a few times until dough holds together. Pat dough into a 1-inch-thick circle. Cut dough into 8 wedges and place on pan. Bake for 25 to 30 minutes until scone tops are firm and sound slightly hollow when tapped. Let cool on pan for 10 minutes. Then remove from pan and cool on wire rack. Yields 8 scones. (Hint: Scones may be be topped with melted chocolate or caramel sauce.)

Waldorf Tea Sandwiches

1 cup apples, grated

½ cup minced celery

½ cup walnuts, finely chopped
½ cup mayonnaise
Butter
10 slices cinnamon-raisin bread

MIX together apples, celery, and walnuts. Add mayonnaise to make mixture spreadable. You can use a bit more mayonnaise if you want to. Butter 10 slices of bread, then spread mixture on 5 slices of bread. Top with remaining slices. Slice off crusts, then cut sandwiches into quarters. Yields 20 tea sandwiches.

Drayton's Egg Clouds

2 large eggs
Salt
¼ cup grated cheese, Gruyère or Swiss
2 Tbsp. finely chopped red onion (optional)

PREHEAT oven to 450 degrees. Separate the egg yolks from the whites. Eggs yolks should each go in separate small dishes, while egg whites go in a larger bowl together. Add a small pinch of salt to the egg whites, then beat them on low speed, increasing to a higher speed until stiff peaks form. Gently fold in grated cheese and onion bits, taking care not to deflate egg whites. Place 2 mounds of egg white mixture on a baking sheet covered with nonstick foil. Form the mounds so they look like nests, with indentations in the center. Bake for 3 minutes, then remove from oven and gently add an egg yolk to the center of each egg nest. Return to oven and cook for 3 more minutes. Serve immediately.

Ham and Sweet Potato Casserole

2 cups cooked ham, diced

2 Tbsp. butter

1 can (8 oz.) pineapple chunks, drained

3 Tbsp. brown sugar

1 can onion soup, condensed

Salt and pepper to taste

1 can (10 oz.) sweet potatoes, drained and sliced

½ cup pecans (or walnuts), chopped

PREHEAT oven to 400 degrees. Sauté ham and butter in oven-proof skillet until ham is slightly browned. Add pineapple chunks, 1 Tbsp. of brown sugar, and onion soup. Season with salt and pepper and bring to a boil. Remove from heat and layer sweet potatoes over ham-and-pineapple mixture. Combine pecans with remaining brown sugar and spread over sweet potatoes. Bake for 30 minutes. Yields 4 servings.

Haley's Super Easy Fudge

4 cups sugar

½ cup corn syrup

1½ cups water

4 squares (1 oz. each) unsweetened chocolate

1 tsp. vanilla

1 cup nuts

COOK all ingredients together, except nuts, in a saucepan until temperature reaches 238 degrees. Let cool to about 110 degrees. Beat until nice and creamy, then add nuts. Turn mixture out onto a cool surface and knead by hand, shaping fudge into a round roll. Slice off pieces and let chill in an airtight container for 24 hours. Yields 12 to 16 pieces.

No–Bake Chocolate–Oatmeal Cookies

2 cups sugar
½ cup cocoa
½ cup (1 stick) butter
½ cup milk
1 tsp. vanilla
3 cups quick-cooking oatmeal
½ cup peanut butter

COMBINE sugar, cocoa, butter, and milk in a saucepan. On medium-high heat, bring to a boil for 1 full minute. Remove from heat. Stir in vanilla, oatmeal, and peanut butter. Drop by spoonful onto waxed paper. Let cool for about 30 minutes. Yields 2 dozen cookies.

Seafood Bake

2 halibut fillets (4 oz. each)
6 scallops
6 shrimp, peeled and deveined

⅓ cup dry white wine

2 Tbsp. melted butter

1 Tbsp. lemon juice

½ tsp. Old Bay seasoning

Salt and pepper to taste

PREHEAT oven to 425 degrees. Arrange halibut, scallops, and shrimp in an oven-safe baking dish. Drizzle with wine, butter, and lemon juice. Sprinkle on Old Bay seasoning and salt and pepper. Bake until halibut has turned white and flaky, about 10 to 12 minutes. Yields 2 servings. (Hint: This could be served over rice.)

Peach Puffs

1 cup water

½ cup butter

1 cup all-purpose flour

3 eggs

1 can peaches in syrup

Whipped cream

PREHEAT oven to 450 degrees. Bring water to a boil and add butter, stirring until melted. Using a wooden spoon, gradually stir in flour until completely absorbed. Remove from heat and cool slightly. Beat in eggs, 1 at a time, beating well after each addition. Beat until mixture is no longer glossy. Drop mixture by large tablespoons onto a greased baking sheet. Place the puffs in the oven and bake for 5 minutes. Now turn your oven down to 350 degrees and bake for an additional 30 minutes until puffed and cooked thoroughly. Cool slowly so they won't fall. Using a sharp knife, make a slit in the side of each puff and spoon in sliced peaches with a little syrup. Top with whipped cream and serve. Yields 8 to 12 puffs.

Breakfast at Tiffany's *Tea*

Put "Moon River" on your sound system and glam up your table with white linen tablecloths, flickering tapers, and your finest china. If you can score some Tiffany-blue ribbon, throw on a few curls. Ask your guests to come dressed as *Breakfast at Tiffany's* Holly Golightly and give them strands of faux pearls to wear when they arrive. Start your luncheon with white chocolate chip scones and Formosan oolong tea. Segue into Waldorf salad tea sandwiches, then serve crepes stuffed with shrimp sauce for your entrée. For dessert, New York–style cheesecake and chocolate truffles would be perfect.

Craft Party Tea

This should be a casual tea built around scrapbooking, card making, or your favorite craft. Place craft materials, paper, glue sticks, stickers, etc. in the center of your table and then add your place settings. Kick things off right with chocolate scones, everybody's favorite, and serve Russian Caravan tea. (You can even use mugs since they're far less tippy!) Strawberry scones with clotted cream is a great first course. Then serve a medley of three different tea sandwiches such as bacon and goat cheese, honeyed chicken salad, and roast beef with thinly sliced cheddar cheese. Keep your desserts easy and bite-sized as well and serve fruit tartlets, lemon bars, and sugar cookies.

Yorkshire Tea

Hooray for our friends across the pond, because they literally invented tea time! Set your table with your best china, silver, and candles. Add a few small British flags from the craft store or give each guest a tiny tin of English tea as a favor. To eat royally, your first course might feature currant and almond scones with clotted cream or Devonshire cream. A delightful second course might be egg salad and watercress tea sandwiches. Cheddar cheese quiche would make for a perfect entrée. For dessert, choose strawberry tartlets or lemon shortbread cookies. And what tea to serve? English breakfast tea, of course.

Poetry Tea

Take your cue from Theodosia and Drayton for this event. Set an elegant table and add any elements that relate to poetry or writing—a stack of poetry books, old albums or notebooks, funky pens, even vintage eyeglasses. Start with a lovely Darjeeling tea served with orange scones and Devonshire cream. Your tea sandwiches could be cucumber and cream cheese on walnut bread and crab salad on sourdough bread. Chicken in puff pastry would make a delicious entrée. For dessert serve pineapple crisp or peach puffs. (You'll find both recipes in this book!)

Vintage Tea Party

Here's your chance to serve up a little kitsch with your tea. Set your table with a vintage tablecloth or make your own place mats by printing out old advertising that features vintage products. Add any vintage china and teacups that you have—and remember, it's more fun if they don't match! Now scour your cellar and attic for a few treasures, knickknacks, and funky little statues (cats or angels?) and scatter them across your table. Start your tea with apple-walnut scones with Devonshire cream, and serve a nice Assam tea. Savories could include curried chicken salad tea sandwiches or turkey and cranberry chutney tea sandwiches. For dessert, serve brownie bites or colorful macarons.

GET CREATIVE WITH SCONES

Theodosia and the Indigo Tea Shop gang aren't afraid to get creative with scones and neither should you be. To get you started, here are a few of Laura Childs's favorite "scone toppers."

- **Strawberry Jam and Devonshire Cream**—You can't go wrong with this classic combination.

- **Ricotta Cheese and Honey**—Spread on ricotta, drizzle on honey, and sprinkle with chopped pistachios.

- **Sun-Dried Tomatoes**—Spread on sun-dried-tomato paste, add a slice of fresh mozzarella, and top with fresh basil leaves.

- **Smoked Salmon with Cream Cheese**—Turn a basic scone into an updated bagel.

- **Brie Cheese and Chutney**—Spread on softened brie and top with your favorite chutney sauce.

- **Herbed Butter**—Softened butter mixed with rosemary, thyme, or your favorite herbs is delicious on scones.

- **Guacamole and Diced Tomatoes**—Create an elevated version of avocado toast.

- **Melted Gruyère**—Spread on Gruyère cheese and toast under the broiler.

- **Bacon and Egg**—This takes your scone into the realm of a hearty breakfast sandwich.

- **Blueberry and Maple Syrup**—Spread scone with cream cheese, top with blueberries and maple syrup.

- **Black Forest Scone**—Spread scone with black cherry jam, add a dollop of mascarpone, then top with chocolate bits and a maraschino cherry.

- **Fig and Blue Cheese**—Spread fig jam on your split scone and top with blue cheese crumbles. You can also add a shard of crispy fried prosciutto.

TEA RESOURCES

TEA MAGAZINES AND PUBLICATIONS

Tea Time—A luscious magazine profiling tea and tea lore. Filled with glossy photos and wonderful recipes. (www.teatimemagazine.com)

Southern Lady—From the publishers of *Tea Time*, with a focus on people and places in the South as well as wonderful tea time recipes. (www.southernladymagazine.com)

The Tea House Times—Go to www.theteahousetimes.com for subscription information and dozens of links to tea shops, purveyors of tea, gift shops, and tea events.

Victoria—Articles and pictorials on homes, home design, gardens, and tea. (www.victoriamag.com)

Fresh Cup Magazine—For tea and coffee professionals. (www.freshcup.com)

Tea & Coffee—Trade journal for the tea and coffee industry. (www.teaandcoffee.net)

Bruce Richardson—This author has written several definitive books on tea.

Jane Pettigrew—This author has written seventeen books on the varied aspects of tea and its history and culture. (www.janepettigrew.com/books)

A Tea Reader—By Katrina Avila Munichiello, an anthology of tea stories and reflections.

AMERICAN TEA PLANTATIONS

Charleston Tea Garden—The oldest and largest tea plantation in the United States. Order their fine black tea or schedule a visit at www.bigelowtea.com.

Table Rock Tea Company—This Pickens, South Carolina, plantation is growing premium whole-leaf tea. (www.tablerocktea.com)

The Great Mississippi Tea Company—Up-and-coming Mississippi tea farm now in production. (www.greatmsteacompany.com)

Big Island Tea—Organic artisan tea from Hawaii. (www.bigislandtea.com)

Mauna Kea Tea—Organic green and oolong tea from Hawaii's Big Island. (www.maunakeatea.com)

Ono Tea—Nine-acre tea estate near Hilo, Hawaii. (www.onotea.com)

Minto Island Tea Growers—Handpicked, small-batch crafted teas grown in Oregon. (www.mintoislandtea.com)

Virginia First Tea Farm—Matcha tea and natural tea soaps and cleansers. (www.virginiafirstteafarm.com)

Blue Dreams USA—Located near Frederick, Maryland, this farm grows tea, roses, and lavender. (www.bluedreamsusa.com)

Finger Lakes Tea Company—Tea producer located in Waterloo, New York. (fingerlakestea.com)

Camellia Forest Tea Gardens—This North Carolina company collects, grows, and sells tea plants. They also produce their own tea. (www.teaflowergardens.com)

TEA WEBSITES AND INTERESTING BLOGS

Destinationtea.com—State-by-state directory of afternoon tea venues.

Teamap.com—Directory of hundreds of tea shops in the U.S. and Canada.

Afternoontea.co.uk—Guide to tea rooms in the UK.

Seedrack.com—Order *Camellia sinensis* seeds and grow your own tea!

Cozyupwithkathy.blogspot.com—Cozy mystery reviews.

Thedailytea.com—Formerly *Tea Magazine*, this online publication is filled with tea news, recipes, inspiration, and tea travel.

Allteapots.com—Teapots from around the world.

Teasquared.blogspot.com—Fun, well-written blog about tea, tea shops, and tea musings.

Relevanttealeaf.blogspot.com—All about tea.

Stephcupoftea.blogspot.com—Blog on tea, food, and inspiration.

Teawithfriends.blogspot.com—Lovely blog on tea, friendship, and tea accoutrements.

Bellaonline.com/site/tea—Features and forums on tea.

Napkinfoldingguide.com—Photo illustrations of twenty-seven different (and sometimes elaborate) napkin folds.

Worldteaexpo.com—This premier business-to-business trade show features more than three hundred tea suppliers, vendors, and tea innovators.

Fatcatscones.com—Frozen, ready-to-bake scones.

Kingarthurflour.com—One of the best flours for baking. This is what many professional pastry chefs use.

Californiateahouse.com—Order Machu's Blend, a special herbal tea for dogs that promotes healthy skin, lowers stress, and aids digestion.

Vintageteaworks.com—This company offers six unique wine-flavored tea blends that celebrate wine and respect the tea.

Downtonabbeycooks.com—A *Downton Abbey* blog with news and recipes.

Auntannie.com—Crafting site that will teach you how to make your own petal envelopes, pillow boxes, gift bags, etc.

Victorianhousescones.com—Scone, biscuit, and cookie mixes for both retail and wholesale orders. Plus baking and scone-making tips.

Englishteastore.com—Buy a jar of English Double Devon Cream here as well as British foods and candies.

Stickyfingersbakeries.com—Delicious just-add-water scone mixes.

TeaSippersSociety.com—Join this international tea community of tea sippers, growers, and educators. A terrific newsletter!

Melhadtea.com—Adventures of a traveling tea sommelier.

Bullsbaysaltworks.com—Local South Carolina sea salt crafted by hand.

PURVEYORS OF FINE TEA

Plumdeluxe.com
Adagio.com
Elmwoodinn.com
Capitalteas.com
Newbyteas.com/us
Harney.com
Stashtea.com
Serendipitea.com
Marktwendell.com
Republicoftea.com
Teazaanti.com
Bigelowtea.com
Celestialseasonings.com
Goldenmoontea.com

Uptontea.com
Svtea.com (Simpson & Vail)
Gracetea.com
Davidstea.com

VISITING CHARLESTON

Charleston.com—Travel and hotel guide.

Charlestoncvb.com—The official Charleston convention and visitor bureau.

Charlestontour.wordpress.com—Private tours of homes and gardens, some including lunch or tea.

Charlestonplace.com—Charleston Place Hotel serves an excellent afternoon tea, Thursday through Saturday, 1:00 PM to 3:00 PM.

Poogansporch.com—This restored Victorian house serves traditional lowcountry cuisine. Be sure to ask about Poogan!

Preservationsociety.org—Hosts Charleston's annual Fall Candlelight Tour.

Palmettocarriage.com—Horse-drawn carriage rides.

Charlestonharbortours.com—Boat tours and harbor cruises.

Ghostwalk.net—Stroll into Charleston's haunted history. Ask them about the "original" Theodosia!

Charlestontours.net—Ghost tours plus tours of plantations and historic homes.

Follybeach.com—Official guide to Folly Beach activities, hotels, rentals, restaurants, and events.

Gibbesmuseum.org—Art exhibits, programs, and events.

Boonehallplantation.com—Visit one of America's oldest working plantations.

Charlestonlibrarysociety.org—A rich collection of books, historic manuscripts, maps, and correspondence. Music and guest speaker events.

Earlybirddiner.com—Visit this local gem at 1644 Savannah Highway for zesty fried chicken, corn cakes, waffles, and more.

Highcottoncharleston.com—Low-country cuisine that includes she-crab soup, buttermilk fried oysters, Geechie Boy grits, and much more.

ACKNOWLEDGMENTS

An abundance of thank-yous to Sam, Tom, Elisha, Yazmine, Dru, Terrie, Lori, M.J., Dustin, Devin, Bob, Jennie, Dan, and all the wonderful people at Berkley Prime Crime and Penguin Random House who handle editing, design (such fabulous covers!), publicity (amazing!), copywriting, social media, bookstore sales, gift sales, production, and shipping. Heartfelt thanks as well to all the tea lovers, tea shop owners, book clubs, tea clubs, bookshop folks, librarians, reviewers, magazine editors and writers, websites, social media sites, broadcasters, and bloggers who have enjoyed the Tea Shop Mysteries and helped spread the word. You are all so kind to help make this possible!

And I am filled with gratitude for all the special readers and tea lovers who've embraced Theodosia, Drayton, Haley, Earl Grey, and the rest of the tea shop gang as friends and family. Thank you so much and I promise many more Tea Shop Mysteries to come!

KEEP READING FOR AN EXCERPT
FROM LAURA CHILDS'S NEXT
TEA SHOP MYSTERY . . .

Peach Tea Smash

Masked figures slipped down twisty paths as a neon orange Cheshire Cat peered down from its perch high atop a crumbling stone wall. The Red Queen cackled as she held court on a candlelit patio overflowing with guests dressed in tuxedos and cocktail dresses. Over on a patch of manicured lawn, excited shrieks rose up as bets were placed on a do-or-die croquet match.

It was the Mad Hatter Masquerade, an autumn fundraiser for the Charleston Opera Society, and what Theodosia Browning decided was a voyage into crazy-town. As the owner of the Indigo Tea Shop on Charleston's famed Church Street, Theodosia was used to staging exciting events. A Firefly Tea at an old plantation, a Murder Mystery Tea in a haunted house, even a Honeybee Tea in Petigru Park. But the Opera Society's masquerade party at the old Pendleton Grist Mill near the City Marina was the most unconventional venue she'd ever seen. The grist mill's twisty walkways, jagged walls, and flaming torches brought to mind the ancient battlements of a ruined Scottish castle. But sprinkle in strolling musicians, fire-eaters, dancing fairies, a dozen or so *Alice in Wonderland* characters, two bars, and three hors d'oeuvres stations and you had yourself a first-class high society soiree.

Gathering up her ankle-skimming black silk skirt, Theodosia turned to Drayton Conneley, her tea sommelier, peered through the eye slits of her peacock-feathered mask, and said, "Can you believe this party?" She was practically agog at the revelers and entertainers streaming past them.

Drayton, who was decked out in a tuxedo and white half mask reminiscent of *The Phantom of the Opera*, said, "It's really quite magnificent. The Friends of the Opera have truly outdone themselves this time." He took a sip of his peach tea smash and nodded to himself as if to punctuate his words.

"Aren't you glad we helped with the appetizers?"

"I'm just tickled we got invited."

Theodosia laughed a rich, tinkling laugh that crinkled her startling blue eyes and caused her mass of auburn hair to shimmer in the candlelight. She'd never consider herself Charleston high society, but that didn't mean she couldn't party her head off. After all, she was still mid-thirties, unmarried . . . well, okay, she *was* in a relationship . . . but did love a big-time gala. A girl had to slip into her dancing shoes once in a while, right?

Drayton, on the other hand, was sixty-something, well-heeled, and an old hand at rubbing elbows with Charleston money. He served on the board of directors at the Heritage Society, had done stints on the boards of the Dock Street Theatre and Carstead Museum, and, at last count, owned three tuxedos. While Theodosia came from a hustle-bustle marketing background, Drayton had cut his teeth at the tea auctions in Amsterdam and taught culinary classes at the prestigious Johnson & Wales University. Theodosia may be the clever entrepreneur bubbling with new ideas, but Drayton had been *around*.

A White Rabbit dressed in tie and tails skittered past them followed by a fairy dancer in a long, diaphanous gown. As the fairy ran by, she thrust a crown of flowers and trailing pink ribbons into Theodosia's hands.

"Tea roses and freesia," Drayton said, as Theodosia placed the floral crown atop her head and scrunched it down over curly locks that were suddenly reacting adversely to the evening's high-test humidity. "With all those flowers in your hair and your long dress, you look as if you just stepped out of a Renaissance tapestry."

He'd barely uttered his words when a short fellow wearing a floppy blue suit and enormous mouse head ran up to them.

"It's the Dormouse," Theodosia exclaimed. "Which means Alice must be dancing around this Wonderland as well."

The Dormouse shoved a silver scepter into Drayton's hands and then scampered away.

"I'll say this," Drayton said, giving the scepter a playful twirl. "This certainly is an immersive experience. I mean, look at this place. Who'd have thought you could turn a historic old grist mill into such a magical, slightly secretive setting?"

"I know," Theodosia said. "The twisty paths, the crumbling walls with curls of ivy, the fact that every time you step around an old stone pillar or column another weird tableau presents itself."

"Speaking of which, shall we help ourselves to another peach tea smash?"

"I'm so glad you allowed them to use your signature recipe," Theodosia said.

"White tea, peach slices, and fine old bourbon," Drayton said. "You can't go wrong with that."

They walked down a cobblestone path and entered one of the grist mill's open sheds, where a crowd of masked partygoers was dancing to a jazz trio playing an up-tempo rendition of Dave Brubeck's "Take Five."

"It's hard to recognize your friends when everyone's wearing masks," Theodosia said. "But I think I see Delaine. The one in the black lace dress dancing with the fellow in a Chinese mask?" Theodosia turned to study another group of guests. "And maybe, over there, the man behind the silver bird mask is Timothy Neville?"

"I'm sure they're both here tonight, along with half the inhabitants of Charleston's Historic District," Drayton said. "After all, this is one of the major events of the fall season."

"On second thought, I think *that* might be Delaine," Theodosia said as she eyed a woman in a red sequin dress with strappy black leather stilettos. "You see when she kicks up her heels there's a hint of red on the soles of her shoes?"

Drayton touched a hand to his bow tie. "What's that mean?"

"Louboutins," Theodosia said in a knowing tone.

"Ah, shoes. Expensive, are they?"

"You have no idea."

But the woman in the spendy shoes saw them watching, and suddenly spun away from her partner and danced over to Theodosia and Drayton. She lifted her red-and-gold Venetian mask and gave a wink. "Right shoes, wrong name."

"Cricket!" Theodosia exclaimed. Cricket Sadler was the executive chairperson in charge of the Mad Hatter Masquerade. She'd single-handedly come up with the theme and roped in Theodosia and Drayton to help with hors d'oeuvres.

"Dear lady," Drayton said, taking Cricket's hand. "Your party is exquisite. So much merriment and exotic entertainment going on around us."

"Believe me when I say I had *beaucoup* help," Cricket said, fairly bubbling with excitement. "Entire committees, if you must know, tasked with decorations, performers, costumes, entertainment, and even lighting." She rolled her eyes expressively. "Then there was the food and liquor—well, *you* know about all that because you catered it. And I have to say our guests are love-love-loving it!"

Theodosia was pleased by Cricket's words. She, Drayton, and Haley, their young chef at the Indigo Tea Shop, had kicked around lots of ideas, but finally settled on steak bites, miniature shrimp kebab, duck pâté on crostini, and a selection of local cheeses. They'd spent the entire afternoon prepping, cooking, assembling, and then, finally, schlepping everything over here. But that had been earlier in the day, before all the candles and twinkle lights were lit, before the musicians and performers had arrived to spin their magic.

"We were just on our way to grab another drink," Drayton said to Cricket. "May I get you one as well?"

"A tasty offer," Cricket said. She was petite, had short brown hair with chunks of honey blond, and was draped in real-deal gold earrings and necklaces. She hitched up her shoulders, leaned forward, and said, "But right now I need to make the rounds and see if I can hustle up a few more donations from our invitees. Then I for sure have to find my husband. Last I saw of Harlan, he'd wandered off with the Red Queen."

"And probably having a merry time of it," Drayton said. He turned back to Theodosia and said, "The bar is which way?"

"I think maybe over this way," Theodosia said. They crunched their way down a dimly lit gravel path past a giant papier-mâché mushroom, turned a corner, and—whoops, this wasn't the right way to the bar at all. They'd suddenly found themselves smack-dab in the heart of the grist mill.

"Looks like we took a wrong turn," Theodosia said, then stopped dead in her tracks to gaze at the hulking pieces of machinery that stood in the center of the room. There were interconnecting wheels and some kind of old motor attached to pulleys, chains, and leather paddles. Overhead was a honeycomb of low wooden beams and a ragged hole in the ancient roof that let in a small spill of moonlight. A faint rustle of wings filled the air as birds flitted from beam to beam.

"Amazing," Drayton said as he walked a few steps closer to the apparatus. "This old grist mill is really something."

"It's also a little scary," Theodosia said. In the semidarkness the wood beams and stone walls seemed to press in on them as well as tamp down the sounds of outside revelry. In fact, she could barely hear any music at all.

But Drayton remained fascinated. "Early grist mills were water-run, powered by sluiceways. But this particular mill was automated in the late eighteenth century. You see that large wheel?"

Theodosia nodded. From her perspective it looked like something from a torture chamber.

"Throw the bevel gears and that wheel drives the whole shebang. See, there's the giant millstone where grain was ground, then carried up by those leather paddles."

Theodosia walked a little closer and peered at the central workings of the old grist mill. "This is some place. And I'm amazed at how well-versed you are about its operation."

"Because it's interesting, a piece of Charleston's history. And you know how much I like history."

"Oh, I do," Theodosia said. Drayton was known to go on for hours about Charleston's old churches, mansions, single houses, plantations, and hidden lanes and alleys.

"But imagine how noisy and inhospitable this place must have been a century ago when grain was milled here practically day and night," Drayton said.

"It's not that hospitable now." The mill was dark and Theo-dosia felt as if shadows were flitting all around them. Maybe it was the flicker of torches from outside? Or just her imagination?

"All that chaff filling the air, making it difficult to see and breathe," Drayton continued. "And the noise and clatter of clank-ing machinery."

As if to punctuate Drayton's words, a low hum rose up from the nearby machinery. Then a leather belt started to vibrate.

Drayton took a cautious step back. "What just happened here?"

"Maybe someone threw a switch?" Theodosia said. She'd caught a faint scrape of footsteps behind her. "For a demonstra-tion of some kind?" But when she turned and looked over her shoulder, she didn't see a soul. "Huh, this is weird."

The noise increased in pitch, building from a low hum to a loud, repetitive *clickety-clack-clack* as chains and leather belts began to move. It was as if the machinery, untouched for de-cades, had suddenly been sparked to life. Now, with everything thumping and thrumming, Theodosia could barely hear any-thing at all.

"I don't think we should be in here," Theodosia shouted in Drayton's ear, feeling foolish even as she said it. Of course they shouldn't be here. These old mill contraptions were dangerous. As if they could grab somebody and . . . the phrase *grind his bones* suddenly popped into her head. She spun hastily, ready to grab Drayton's sleeve and pull him away from this strange, shadowy place. But Drayton was rooted to where he stood, mouth open, seemingly dumbstruck. Then he slowly lifted a hand and pointed.

"What?" Theodosia shouted. When Drayton didn't answer, she said, "What?" a second time. Then she lifted her eyes, blinked hard, and did a kind of double take. Because something, Lord knows what, was caught in the giant heavy chains that pulled the leather paddles up toward the ceiling.

"What do you think that is?" Drayton asked her. "Rags? A bunch of old gunny sacks?"

Theodosia shook his head. "I don't know."

But the strange thing was, she *did* know. Because whatever was caught between those giant paddles had a definite shape to it. Two arms, a leg . . . maybe a head?

"Help!" Drayton shouted as he suddenly arrived at the same conclusion. He turned and sprinted for the doorway. "Help!" he called out. "There's been an accident, we need help in here!"

His plaintive cries brought a half dozen curious people.

A man in a white dinner jacket yelled, "What's wrong?" while behind him Theodosia's friend Delaine Dish shouted, "Oh no, that's a man dangling up there!"

The chains and leather paddles had pulled the body even higher. Now the onlookers' screams blended with the noise of the machines and rose to a fever pitch. Their screams drew even more people, who lifted their collective voices in a dreadful cacophony that seemed to billow through the ancient grist mill, matching the enormous clouds of dust being spun up by clanking machinery.

"Someone's caught in the gears," a man shouted.

"Somebody do something," a woman in a bright yellow gown cried.

Even Cricket Sadler ran in and started screaming for help.

But everyone just stood there, taking in the abject horror of the situation, too paralyzed to do anything at all.

Theodosia didn't know *what* to do, but she knew she had to do *something.* She waved a hand in front of her face, trying to see through the swirl of dust and chaff, then edged over to what Drayton had pointed out earlier as bevel gears.

Reaching a hand out, Theodosia pushed one of the wooden levers, hoping to stop the machinery. Nothing. The clanking grew louder and the screams from the crowd increased in volume. She touched a hand to a second lever, pushed hard, felt it start to give, *want* to give. Blowing out a stream of air, trying not to choke as she cleared the terrible dust from her nose and mouth, she leaned hard into her task. Pushing with all her might, she managed to throw the lever hard left. There was a deep shudder, a terrible screeching noise, and then the machinery finally, mercifully, ground to a halt.

"Get him down! Help him!" came countless cries. Now a dozen hands reached up to try and free the trapped man. But no one could reach him. Seconds dragged by, then a full minute while a ladder was found and lifted up. A young man in a green-and-yellow Caterpillar costume scrambled up the ladder and worked feverishly to untangle the man from the chains. After two minutes of twisting and turning, he was finally able to free the injured man. Balancing precariously now, he bent forward to lower the victim into waiting arms. But at the last second, he fumbled and lost his grip. The victim cartwheeled away from him, plunged fifteen feet down, and hit the cobblestone floor like a sack of flour.

More screams of horror reverberated throughout the old mill as Theodosia stumbled her way through the crowd, pushing past a couple of the entertainers in their White Rabbit and Mad Hatter costumes. Her heart was in her throat and she was hoping against hope that the man had somehow survived.

But wait. He'd been chewed up by those chains and paddles, then fallen and landed badly. Now he was curled up like a bug in a cocoon, breathing shallowly and not moving a single muscle. His suit was ripped; his hands and feet were battered and bloodied. Worst of all, his head oozed copious amounts of blood that streamed down over his black mask and soaked into his tartan plaid bow tie.

"Who is it?" a woman asked in a shaking voice as the bleeding man's right foot seemed to tremble on its own.

Ever so gently, Drayton reached down and removed the man's mask.

Coughing, shuffling their feet, the crowd pressed in closer. To see if they could identify this poor soul.

And that's when Cricket Sadler took one look, moaned softly, and fainted dead away.

WATCH FOR THE NEXT NEW ORLEANS
SCRAPBOOKING MYSTERY FROM LAURA CHILDS

Cadmium Red Dead

An excavation in the French Quarter reveals a bizarre crime that
pulls Carmela and Ava deep into a dark and deadly mystery.

Find out more about the author and read excerpts
from her mysteries at laurachilds.com or become
a Facebook friend at Laura Childs Author.